T0278811

THE
Perfect Guy
DOESN'T EXIST

THE
Perfect Guy
DOESN'T EXIST

SOPHIE GONZALES

WEDNESDAY BOOKS

NEW YORK

First published in the United States by Wednesday Books, an imprint of St. Martin's Publishing Group

THE PERFECT GUY DOESN'T EXIST. Copyright © 2024 by Sophie Gonzales. All rights reserved. Printed in the United States of America. For information, address St. Martin's Publishing Group, 120 Broadway, New York, NY 10271.

Designed by Jen Edwards

www.wednesdaybooks.com

Library of Congress Cataloging-in-Publication Data

Names: Gonzales, S., 1992– author.
Title: The perfect guy doesn't exist / Sophie Gonzales.
Other titles: Perfect guy does not exist
Description: First edition. | New York : Wednesday Books, 2024. | Audience: Ages 13–18.
Identifiers: LCCN 2023045088 | ISBN 9781250819185 (hardcover) | ISBN 9781250819192 (ebook)
Subjects: CYAC: Friendship—Fiction. | Fan fiction—Fiction. | Interpersonal relations—Fiction. | LCGFT: Novels.
Classification: LCC PZ7.1.G6532 Pc 2024 | DDC [Fic]—dc23
LC record available at https://lccn.loc.gov/2023045088

Our books may be purchased in bulk for promotional, educational, or business use. Please contact your local bookseller or the Macmillan Corporate and Premium Sales Department at 1-800-221-7945, extension 5442, or by email at MacmillanSpecialMarkets@macmillan.com.

First Edition: 2024

10 9 8 7 6 5 4 3 2 1

To the fandom kids, past and present.
You keep the magic alive long after the story is over.

THE
Perfect Guy
DOESN'T EXIST

Chapter One

PAST

I think my pacing is alarming Mack.

She's sitting on my bed with her hands pressed together in a praying pose on her lap and one eyebrow quirked as she watches me go around and around my bedroom. I've been doing it for a while now. It's not that I've backed out of telling her or anything. More that, now the moment is finally here, I can't seem to remember a single word in the English language.

She tucks her hands in the pockets of her oversized Nike hoodie—a men's one she found in her favorite shade of teal last year—then takes one hand straight back out and sweeps her long braids back over her shoulder. She's stressed, I'm stressed, this is *stressful,* and I wish I didn't decide to do it today, but I did. I'm committed now, and I'm going to.

Eventually.

"You could write it down?" she suggests finally, and I give my head a vigorous shake. "No problem," she says, half to herself, as I resume my pacing.

"Okay," I say, stopping in the middle of the room. I'm facing my wardrobe, which means I can only see Mack out of my peripherals, but right now I like it that way. "It's actually not a big deal. I know it's not, because it's you, and I already know it can't go badly."

"Great."

"It's just . . . I need a second to . . ."

"There's no rush."

I know what I want to say. Or, rather, what I should say. It's not a complicated point to get across. I'm bi. It should be easy to spit out. It's only two syllables. And it's Mack, so it's not like I need to explain the concept like I probably will when I tell my parents, which is a huge plus. It's not even one of those facts I think I want to keep to myself forever, like the fact that I'm almost definitely in love with Mack. I *want* people to know I'm bi. I'm ready.

But I can't say the words. For some reason, they feel huge, and intimidating. Like jumping into an ice bath all at once.

So, I decide to wade.

"You know how, last year, everything Alice Kennedy did annoyed me?" I ask.

Mack nods. "I noticed, yeah."

Her eyes are locked on me. I've always been fascinated by the color of her eyes. They're brown—but such a dark, rich shade of it that if you take a few steps back, you can't tell where her pupils end and her irises begin. *They're like spilled ink,* I told her once, staring at her in a sort of stupor. She hated that. I meant it as a compliment, but it probably would've landed better if I'd just stuck to telling her they're beautiful. Which they are.

Back to Alice Kennedy. "She did annoy me, but she also didn't. I didn't hate her at all. I just . . . have you ever thought about someone all the time, and all you wanna do is talk about them?"

"Avery."

"Right. Like Avery." Also known as Mack's summer camp crush from last year. "Um. But I couldn't really talk about Alice the way I wanted to talk about her, because I didn't want you to know the things I thought about her. So, I thought, hey, if I only bring her up to complain about her, no one could think that's weird. And it doesn't really make sense saying it out loud, but it made sense at the time, and it felt safe. Safe-*er*."

Mack won't tear those eyes away from me, so I focus on the wall to get the rest out. "Because I didn't want her, or anyone, to know that I actually thought she was perfect. I mean, god, everything about her was flawless, you know? So I pretended she drove me up the wall whenever I spoke to you about her. Just so you didn't realize."

Mack is giving me a funny look, but she's cautious in her answer. "So I didn't realize . . . you didn't hate Alice?"

"So you didn't realize I had a crush on Alice."

I'm fairly sure Mack suspected what I was getting at before I spelled it out. But she waits until I say the words to react. "Oh my god," she says. "Oh my god, Ivy, you like girls?"

"I do," I say, like it's truly no big deal at all. Like this isn't the most momentous thing I've ever told anyone.

Mack shrieks and jumps to her feet. "No. No, no way, con-gratulations!" And before I know it, she's wrapped me in a bear hug, and we're jumping on the spot in the middle of my bed-room floor. "This is amazing, this is amazing," she chants, and I'm laughing with her, and I'm utterly weightless.

For one naive second, I even let myself wonder if she'll say something about us. It's not that I expect her to or anything. It's that, for just a second, everything is so perfectly wonderful I can almost believe something like that could happen to me.

But, instead of confessing her undying love for me, she just lets go of me and flops back down on the bed. "Oh, man," she says. "This is huge. I'm so glad you told me this. Oh!"

I rub my upper arms right where she was hugging me a second ago and sit beside her gingerly. "I was worried you might think I'm copying you," I admit, and she blows a raspberry at that.

"Not for a second. Anyway, you like guys, too, right? Or do you?"

"No, I do," I say, and she nods eagerly.

"So, what are you thinking? Pan? Bi? Questioning?"

I grin. "I'm thinking probably bi? If I don't have to lock that answer in permanently."

She shakes her head, and I shuffle back on the bed and relax against the wall. "Nothing's permanent," she tells me.

I clasp a hand to my chest and pretend to be offended. "*Oof.* I hope some things are."

Drawing her knees to her chest, Mack tips her head back and looks sideways at me. "Okay, you're right. Some things are. But only the things you want to be permanent."

Before I say something wildly, recklessly romantic, like *I want you to be permanent,* I take a deep breath and try to clear my head. "Okay. Phew. One down."

"I'm the first person you told?"

"Of course. Who else am I gonna tell?"

"Your parents? They know everything else about your damn life," she says, giggling, and I groan.

"Yeah, no. I'll tell them later, but not today."

Mack folds her arms. "You know they'll make having a queer daughter their whole personalities once you tell them, right?"

"Oh, I know. But there are worse reactions to get from your parents."

"True." She nods thoughtfully, then wiggles in place, like she can't hold her happiness in. "Ah, I can't believe you like girls, too. We have so much to discuss. There's a forum I want to add you to and, oh, there's a book I know you'll love, and—"

"I'm so glad you're not weirded out by this." I don't mean to cut her off, but I'm so tightly wound. Somehow, I'd convinced myself that she would think I was just too scared to do anything alone. Heterosexuality included. It *is* true I'm the kind of person who loves to do things in pairs. For example, I joined the volleyball team when Mack joined it. Also, Mack introduced me to seventies rock, which is now my most-listened-to genre. Plus, after she went to summer camp in sixth grade, in seventh grade I begged my parents to enroll me, too. But just because Mack did all those things first, it doesn't mean I only pretended to enjoy all of it.

And I knew I liked girls way before Mack came out as a lesbian a few months ago. It's only that I wasn't brave enough to say it out loud until I saw Mack do it.

"Not only am I not weirded out by it," Mack assures me, "it's the best news I think I've ever had. Now I'm not alone."

Even though I obviously didn't do this for Mack, I feel like I'm sinking into a cloud hearing her say that.

I'm so glad she feels that way. Because I never want her to be alone.

PRESENT

I have spent endless hours wishing my parents would give me space, but now that they're finally doing it, I have reservations. In my defense, almost three thousand miles is quite a lot more space than I pictured.

"I'm just not sure I'm trustworthy without supervision," I protest, following Mom down the hall as she lugs a plastic wheeled suitcase behind her. "What if I make bad choices?"

"You seemed pretty sure you were trustworthy when we were booking the tickets," Mom grunts, pausing in place as the suitcase tips on its side. I kneel to help her straighten it, then silently curse myself for aiding and abetting child abandonment.

"Yeah, but, Mom, I was, like, fifteen then. I thought I'd be more mature by now, but I'm not. Being sixteen didn't change anything, it just gave me acne!"

That, and I'd been too focused on the many pluses of having the house to myself to consider the fact that I'd be totally alone. Pros: I can stay up late, walk around the house in my underwear, eat as much junk food as I want, and hang out with Henry for hours without anyone asking us to give the TV back. It's a substantial list. In contrast, the cons list only has one point, but now that D day is here, it's starting to feel like one *huge* point.

And that point is, I am going to be solely responsible for keeping myself alive if an emergency happens for five solid days.

These are not the kinds of stakes you take lightly. If I don't keep myself alive, I could *die*.

Mom approaches the doorway and, together, we lift the suitcase over the frame. At the bottom of the driveway, Dad stands examining the inside of the car trunk.

I discovered the other day my parents were planning to drive to the airport, to my great surprise. As far as I'm concerned, only exorbitantly rich people use the long-term parking lot at the airport, and my family is, to the very best of my knowledge, not exorbitantly rich. We're a proud tap-water-drinking, coupon-cutting, "you'll grow into it" sort of family. Always have been. This trip Mom and Dad are taking, a business trip to LA for Mom that Dad's tagging along on, is the bougiest thing I've ever seen them do.

But, still, taking the car to the airport seems like a step too far. They insisted it was for convenience, but I'm pretty sure it's because they don't trust me not to drive it in their absence. Because, apparently, leaving me at home to fend for myself against house fires, and tornadoes, and Jehovah's Witnesses is all well and good, but if I were to *very briefly* borrow their car to visit Henry, suddenly they'd have concerns about my safety.

"You've got the Gleasons right across the road," Mom says as she loads the suitcase into the trunk. "We've left you a fridge full of food, we'll call you every day, you've got our number, you've got the Gleasons' number. . . ."

Oh, joy, the Gleasons. Can't wait to never take them up on that.

"What if there's an earthquake?" I ask before I can stop myself. I *know* bringing it up is just going to panic them, but I can't *not* blurt out anxious thoughts when they pop into my head.

"Get under the desk," Mom says at the same time Dad says, "Stand under a doorframe."

My parents give each other a look that I don't like one bit.

"Standing under doorways isn't recommended anymore," Mom says with great confidence. Personally, I feel like it's misplaced confidence, given that, as far as I know, Mom is not the foremost expert on recommended earthquake procedures any more than Dad is.

"Yes, it is," Dad insists. "Load-bearing ones."

"Ivy's not going to know which doorways are load-bearing, David, she can barely turn on the oven." Mom's confidence is faltering. Great. Now they're either going to call me every hour on the hour to check if there's been an earthquake, or cancel the trip altogether. *What if there's an earthquake,* come on, Ivy, really?

"I can so turn on the oven," I protest with dignity. "It's the grill that confuses me."

"What if she's not in her room when the earthquake hits?" Dad asks. "No desk."

"She'll have to use her common sense and find an equivalent," Mom replies.

"Does that seem wise?" Dad asks.

Ouch. But not unwarranted. I don't have a lot of common sense. In my defense, though, it's one of those skills that's hard to develop when someone else is making your decisions for you all day every day. Ask me how I know.

"We'll take her through the house and point out all the load-bearing doors," Mom says with a brisk nod.

"Do we have time?" Dad asks.

"You're already late," I point out, and Mom looks stricken. "Besides, when do we ever get huge earthquakes? We don't."

"That's true," Dad says.

"Well, Pompeii had never had a devastating volcanic eruption before," Mom reminds us. "The dinosaurs had never had a planet-destroying meteor before. Since when is that an excuse not to be prepared?"

"Look at it this way, Mom," I say as she closes the trunk. "If something that catastrophic hits, my death will be so sudden, all the preparation in the world couldn't have saved me. *You* couldn't have saved me. If it's my time to go, that's just how it'll be."

I realize too late it doesn't come out quite as comforting as I meant it. Mom drops her hands to her sides and takes a deep, slow breath. Now I've done it.

Dad steps around the car and wraps his arms over Mom's shoulders from behind. "Everything is going to be fine," he says in a soothing voice. "We trust Ivy. She's responsible, and smart, and she can keep herself alive for a week."

"She can," Mom repeats, closing her eyes.

"She has plenty of food in the refrigerator."

"Lots in the freezer, too."

"Right. She has contact numbers, she has a support system, and we're only a plane flight away."

"Or a really long drive if there's an apocalypse and you can't get a plane," I add unhelpfully.

Mom, wisely, ignores me.

After one last sweep of the house, it's time for my parents to leave, and I find myself with an inconvenient lump in my throat.

"You're sure you'll be all right by yourself?" Mom asks.

"Do you remember the emergency number?" Dad asks.

I blink. "You mean nine-one-one?"

"Thank god. See, Nadia, she knows the one."

Dad grins, pleased with himself, while Mom shoots him an exasperated look.

"We'll message you when we land," Mom assures me, pulling me in for one last hug. Now that, I can be sure of. With them, it'll be less a matter of a message, and more a matter of waking up to ten messages and two missed calls. But for the first time I can remember, the thought doesn't bother me. At least, not as much as it usually does. "And if you need *anything* and you can't reach us—"

"The Gleasons."

"Honestly, sweetie, I'd call them in an emergency before the police," Dad says. "Much quicker reaction time, and more competent to boot."

Some of them, anyway. I agree when it comes to the three older Gleasons. The youngest, however, leaves much to be desired.

"I had a thought," says Mom. "We should do a quick demonstration of the fire extinguisher."

"Absolutely not; we still have to get through security," Dad says in a conversation-ending sort of tone. "If there's a fire, throw a blanket on it. Or run."

"But try to save the photo albums, if you have time," Mom says anxiously.

"I'll be sure to only save myself if absolutely necessary," I joke, and she looks horrified.

"No, Ivy, that's not what I meant, don't you *da*—"

"There's not going to be any disasters," Dad says over her. "You will be absolutely fine. The week will fly by. You'll hardly notice we're gone."

Finally, *finally*, they climb into the SUV. I'm almost shocked when they do. I think a part of me truly expected them to back out after all. But just like that, they're rolling down the driveway and onto the street, and, with one last honk, they drive off into the sunset.

I stare after them for a second, not sure how I feel.

Then, all at once, it hits me. I can do whatever the hell I want—as long as I can cover up the evidence—for the rest of the week.

This is a freedom I've never known.

My trepidation forgotten, I trot to the pantry, grab an un-opened pack of chocolate chip cookies, and start demolishing them while I message Henry to come by whenever he wants. The new episode of *Hot, Magical & Deadly* is out, and we have a long-standing tradition of watching it together at my house. Plus, we have a presentation to give in class tomorrow, and we're mostly done but we should probably go through it and give it any finishing touches it needs. While I wait for him, I open a new carton of milk and take a swig straight from it, kick off my shoes in the middle of the kitchen, and take my laptop into the living room. Usually there's no point using it out here, because if my parents can see me, they want to be talking to me, even if I tell them I'm trying to work on my latest fanfic or that I'm messaging someone.

What was I worried about? This is *awesome*.

Ten minutes later, there's a knock on the door, and I jump up to answer it, licking crumbs off my fingers. To my delight, Henry Paramar is waiting on the doorstep with a shopping bag full of junk food. One of the many reasons he's my best friend now, and someone else, who isn't worth mentioning the name of, *isn't*.

"Holy shit, your hair," he says as soon as he sees me.

"Is that a good 'holy shit'?" I ask, touching the velvety-soft side of my head. Of course, he's seen photos since I chopped most of my hair off yesterday morning, and he said he loved it, but maybe in person he feels differently. Not that I'd regret it if he does. My new hairstyle, which consists of shaved sides and tousled, longer waves at the top, is much more up my alley.

"Duh," he says as he dumps the bag of junk food on the couch. "I think, in the least-weird way possible, you're hot now."

"Oh my god, thank you! Wait, 'now'?"

Henry cocks his head in a half shrug. "You were pretty before. But I'm pretty sure you're objectively what a lot of people would call 'hot' now. *Really* good call to chop it off."

"I think that's the nicest thing you've ever said to me."

Henry hesitates. I think he might be replaying his words back in his head. "Not that I need to clarify, but I'm obviously not attracted to you."

"Obviously." I think someone would have to pretty much propose to me for me to consider they might be into me like that, so he'd be in the clear even if I didn't know he's aroace. Still, it's nice to think that someone who's not Henry could potentially find me attractive. I'm not sure if that's ever happened before, and if it has, the person never looped me in. Maybe if this possibly imaginary, possibly real admirer *did* fill me in, I'd be more likely to accuse people of being into me. But as it stands . . .

"Whoa," Henry says, circling the living room, bringing me back to the present. "It already feels emptier without your parents."

He kicks off his sneakers and climbs onto the sofa in his socks. As usual, he's wearing one of his eye-catching outfits. Dad calls them "a phase he'll be embarrassed of one day"; Mom calls them "peacock looks"; I call them "damn, my best friend has taste." There's always something unusual about his outfits, from bright red pants, to floral-shirt-and-shorts combos—often on a crisp white background to provide contrast with his brown skin—to oversized jackets layered on top of shirts layered on top of other shirts. It's the kind of stuff you need to have a really good eye to put together. Henry does. I have the eye to tell it looks great, but not the eye to attempt anything like it myself.

Today, for example, he's wearing a matching sweatshirt-and-sweatpants set covered in patches that range from dark gray to black, broken up by the hem of a white shirt peeking beneath the sweatshirt. That, plus his handsome face, makes him look kind of like a fuckboy, but in the nicest way possible. Like, you wouldn't be surprised to find out he's the rich son of a famous, asshole music producer, and not the middle-class son of a nursery-school teacher and an office worker.

It's not a surprise half the grade's had a crush on him at one point or another since middle school.

"It's nice, right?" I say as I sort through the shopping bag. Potato chips and corn chips on the far end of the coffee table, candy in the center, soda on the end. It's like the superior version of charcuterie. I am nailing this whole host thing.

"You know, at first, I wasn't sure what the weird sound was," Henry says, ripping open a bag of chips. "Then I realized it's the sound of *sweet silence*. No one's asking how our day was, what we're doing, what we're watching, what we're eating, if we need anything, what our deepest fears are. . . ."

I snort. "Don't get too used to it, they're back in five days."

"Eh. See how the flight goes."

"*Henry!*"

"I'm just saying, a lot of things can go wrong when you're that high up."

I throw a potato chip at his head, and he deftly ducks to dodge it.

"So," I say, dragging the syllable out. "Guess who got left enough money to buy us both pizza tonight?"

Henry lights up. "Garlic bread, too?"

"Duh."

"Scratch everything I just said about your parents. I love them, they're the best, I hope they never change."

As I put in Henry's order on the app—I double-check with him, but, as I figured, I got his order right on the first try—he gathers bowls and glasses from the kitchen. Finally, we're ready to start the new episode, and I'm practically vibrating out of my skin with excitement. This has been the longest week of my life, because last episode, like every episode, ended on a huge cliffhanger.

Hot, Magical & Deadly follows a group of teenagers from the same modeling agency (catalogue, not high fashion) who accidentally receive elemental powers when a photo shoot held near a portal to a parallel universe goes wrong. For four seasons now, I've watched them grow from awkward, outcast teen models to confident, charming teen superheroes, expertly fighting the silhouette demons that entered our world through the same portal.

Without Weston Razorbrook and the others, the demons would've taken over the world by now, because their plan is sort of ingenious: shapeshifting into, and stealing the identities of, America's biggest influencers. I mean, think about it. If all the influencers in the world simultaneously decided it was cool to jump off a cliff, we'd have barely anyone left. The demons could practically stroll into power after that.

I watch, absentmindedly gnawing on a fingernail, as Henry sets the episode up on the TV. When Henry glances at me, he makes a face. "Chew a bit harder, Ivy. If you put your mind to it, you can eat the whole nail. I believe in you."

"I'm *stressed,* okay? I saw an article today that basically confirmed they're going to get rid of a huge character this season."

"They're not gonna kill someone off in a random episode halfway through the season. If someone dies, it'll be in the finale, and anyway, my money's on Jacques."

"Yeah, you and everyone else," I say. "But if I were one of the writers and I wanted to make an impact, I'd kill someone no one expects, when they don't expect it. *That's* good television."

"Oh yeah, kill off a fan favorite with zero warning or buildup. That's always a famously great choice for ratings moving forward." Still, he folds his arms across his chest as he settles into the couch, his brow shifting into a concerned furrow.

Last week's episode ended with Weston Razorbrook tied to a pier during a rising tide after he discovered famous movie reviewer Edmund Marquis was possessed by a silhouette demon. The pier thing was devious, because Weston's air powers can only work if his hands aren't submerged or covered. And for the life of me, I cannot *think* how he's going to get rescued, because he told no one where he was going, and the waves were drowning out his screams.

It was all very distressing. I have been in a state of constant suffering all week.

It wouldn't even be the first time *H-MAD* killed off someone important. Last year, one of the models who had real runway potential was eaten by flying pigs with no warning after they broke through the portal. And I didn't even know pigs are vicious carnivores before that, until Henry looked it up and we found out that real-life pigs actually love a good murder. The wings just made the slaughter easier for the fictional *H-MAD* ones. Anyway, the whole fandom went into meltdown that week, and we can't go through that again, we just can't. Especially not with Weston.

I would almost rather die myself than see Weston drown tonight.

"Whatever happens," Henry says gravely as the theme music begins, "we'll get through it together."

It's a rare moment of seriousness from him. Now I'm even more nervous.

I stuff a fistful of potato chips into my mouth.

The episode starts with Vanessa's storyline, which is just teasing. Vanessa is the girl everyone's convinced is bound to end up with Weston. Everyone being the majority of the fandom, that is. The thing is, I'm is pretty sure the showrunners picked her as the love interest on account of her being a fire element, pretty, and blond, and for no other reason. Now, there is nothing wrong with being any of those things—or even all three of those things at once—but it isn't enough to throw two pretty people together and call it love. There has to be chemistry, and passion, and complementary traits. *Bonding,* for goodness' sake!

I'm also pretty sure the writers of *H-MAD* have never read a romance novel in their lives. Like, take right now. Vanessa is off dealing with the B plot, which is about finding a lost elemental child someone discovered in a boarding school, who may have been present at the fated photo shoot. While Weston is being *actively murdered.* Why isn't she there, desperately hunting for him? God, the opportunities for tropes are endless. They could have Vanessa using Weston's first name in a panic, instead of calling him "Razorbrook." She could almost lose her own life in the process of saving him, causing him to panic and realize his love for her. They could squeeze a solid two or three episodes out of Vanessa caring for Weston in the aftermath of his near death if they really went for it! But no. Yet again, Vanessa is swanning around on the other side of the state, being of no help to anyone important. It's anti-feminist, is what it is.

Finally, the camera cuts to Weston, and we both sit up straighter. Weston's perfect, icy-blue hair (it turned that color as the elemental magic flowed through his veins) is stuck to his face, and his hands are still bound tightly beneath the water. The ocean laps higher and higher, high enough now that he has to lift his chin with each wave. There's not much time.

Suddenly, his eyes narrow. "Wait," he whispers to himself. "Of course."

Of course?! So, there is a solution? He's not dying after all? Of course *what*?

Three loud bangs follow. It takes me a second to realize they're real-life bangs. Someone with the worst timing *ever* is at the door, and I am going to kill them.

"Pause it, pause it, pause it," I screech, and Henry fumbles with the remote. Weston freezes mid-sentence, and I get to my feet with a scowl.

"That's the fastest pizza delivery I've ever seen," Henry says. "Is the oven in your front yard or something?"

I don't think it's the pizza, though.

In fact, I have a sinking feeling I know exactly who's on the other side of that door. And I am not going to like it.

I open it, and find my worst fears confirmed.

Chapter Two

PAST

At the end of volleyball practice, I collapse on the gym bleachers with my water bottle while Mack hangs back to talk with the other girls on the court. Mack's always fit in with the team much better than me. They're not mean to me or anything, they just don't seem to notice I exist when we're not playing. I guess we just don't have all that much in common, and the few times I've made small talk with them, I've gotten the distinct impression we've all been bored out of our minds. Which is funny to say, when Mack and I get along so well, but it is what it is. I'd rather sit in silence than force awkward chatter any day. *Any* day.

Mack's talking to Brianna Wells, an auburn-haired senior who Mack's had a crush on since . . . well, since her last crush, Avery. Mack can be a bit of a serial romantic. At least, in an unrequited sort of way. She hasn't ever had a girlfriend before, which is tough news for her, but good news for me. Sort of. It's not that it makes me happy to see Mack unhappy, it's just that I'm extremely relieved I don't have to watch her dating someone else while pretending I'm thrilled about the whole affair. I just don't think I'd be a good enough actor to pull that off.

Even watching Mack flirting with Brianna right now, shifting from foot to foot and touching her fingertips to her collarbone and laughing just a little too loudly, makes me grit my teeth. I take a big enough sip of water to half drown myself, just so I have something else to focus on for a few seconds. When I put the bottle down, I see Mack making her way over to me, and the world brightens in an instant.

"Hey," she says, stopping in front of me. "Amazing block at the end there."

I crane my neck up at her. "Thank you!"

"You're getting so good," she says, and I beam at the rare sports-related compliment. I get none from the coach—for good reason, to be fair—so I appreciate the acknowledgment. Especially if it means Mack was watching me. That she was proud of me.

Mack looks back at the girls, who have scattered to change. "Everyone's going to grab some sushi for dinner. Wanna come?"

A part of me wants to say yes, of course. But if we go to dinner, either I'll be sitting in awkward silence while everyone talks around me—which has happened before, more than once—or Mack will have to entertain me the whole night instead of talking to everyone else—something that's also happened before. I don't want to ruin her night by forcing her to babysit me.

"Nah," I say as offhandedly as I can, scrunching my nose. "Thank you! But the new episode of *H-MAD* actually comes out tonight, so I wanna get home to watch that."

"You sure?"

"Yeah, totally." Before I can stop myself, the words tumble out. "Besides, I don't wanna distract you from *Brianna*."

At least it comes out playfully, without a hint of a bite to it.

Maybe I'll be better at acting than I thought when Mack does eventually get a girlfriend. Mack just grins and rolls her eyes. "Shut up. I'm over Brianna, anyway."

"Since when?"

"Since I found out she kissed Shaun Pierce."

I gape and slam my water bottle onto the bleachers in protest, like I'm not secretly thrilled to hear Mack's over her. "What? You didn't tell me that."

"I didn't tell you," Mack says, "because I don't care."

"Right. You're totally unaffected."

"None of my business what straight people get up to."

"Well," I say, "we don't know she's straight, just because she kissed a guy."

"You're right," she says, pointing right at me. I'm the evidence, I guess. "True. She's just got bad taste, then."

"That," I say, "I'm not gonna argue with."

Mack bursts into giggles, and holds out a hand to help me to my feet.

PRESENT

A familiar girl is standing on the porch with a casserole dish in her hands and an awkward grimace on her usually smug face. Her thick, tight black curls are speckled with raindrops because she's left the hood of her Nike sweatshirt down, like she's forgotten the whole point of it. She smells like vanilla and judgment, so strong it overpowers the rain. And rain is notoriously strong smelling, so that's saying a lot.

My stomach plunges as soon as I take her in. It often does when I see Mack. I think it's the rage.

"Mack," I say, letting my irritation come through my tone. In my peripherals, I spot Henry making a face at the door.

Why couldn't it have just been the pizza?

"Ivy," Mackenzie Gleason says, copying my tone. I cannot believe the audacity. "My dad wanted me to bring around something for you to eat. Considering you're alone now."

"Thank you," I say stiffly, accepting the dish. It weighs about ten pounds. "That's very thoughtful of your dad." The statement removes Mack from the "thank you," and I meant it to. But, even as I say it, I feel suddenly ashamed. Neither of us like each other, obviously, but there's icy, and then there's bitchy. We're bigger than bitchy. "And . . . thanks for bringing it over."

"Well, he made me."

Never mind, shame gone, bitch back. "Then I withdraw my 'thank you.'"

"Always a pleasure, Ivy," she says. "So glad you're not going to starve."

"I *can* cook, you know," I say. Why does everyone think I can't use an oven? "I'm not gonna starve either way."

"Toast doesn't count."

"More than toast," I snap. Mack's eyes narrow, and for just a moment I lose my train of thought. They're so intense that you feel like you're being tugged into their center if you get too close. Like they've got their own gravitational pull. Even now, looking at them makes me feel a tugging in my gut. I yank myself out of her orbit as quickly as I entered it, huffing as I do. "In fact, tonight Henry and I were going to have beef Wellington."

It's the first meal that comes to mind, one I came across in a fanfic last week, and it isn't until the words leave my mouth that I realize I don't actually know what a beef Wellington is. I'm pretty sure one of the ingredients is beef, but beyond that, it's anyone's guess. Caviar, maybe? Hopefully Mack won't ask for details.

"Hi, Henry," Mack bellows. Somehow, she manages to make the words sound like an insult.

Henry leans over the back of the couch and directs several extraordinarily rude gestures toward the door with both of his hands. I do my best not to glance at him. "He's in the bathroom," I say. "Anyway, we don't have to bother cooking anymore, because we have food now, which is convenient."

"'Convenient' is the word that came to mind for me, too," Mack says drily, her eyes flickering to the casserole in my hands.

"So, if that's all, we're in the middle of *H-MAD*."

Historically, there's been no easier way to get Mack to check out of the conversation than to mention *H-MAD*. It used to be our friendship's fatal flaw, but now it's an easy way to get her out of my hair without resorting to drastic measures like faking an emergency, or using simple, clear communication. As I suspected, it works like a charm.

"I'll leave you to it, then," Mack says. "Bye, Henry."

"Bye," Henry snaps, before clapping a hand over his mouth when he remembers he's meant to be in the bathroom. Mack shoots me a triumphant look, which she's still wearing when I shut the door in her face.

As annoyed as I am by having to interact with Mack, it does fill me with the warm and fuzzies that Mr. Gleason thought of me when he was cooking. When Mack and I commenced our war, her parents were among my biggest casualties. They were basically my surrogate parents for most of my life. It's not fair I had to lose them just because their daughter turned out to be one of the worst people I've ever met. In hindsight, we should've figured out some sort of custody arrangement, where I got to hang out with them for a couple of afternoons a month, just talking about our days, or baking, or whatever normal shit teenagers do with their parents when they're not trying to micromanage their lives. Preferably while Mack's at volleyball practice. Now that she's captain she gets there early and finishes late, so it could work. We'd have plenty of time.

"What sort of casserole is that?" Henry asks hopefully, hanging over the side of the couch to watch me as I bring it to the kitchen.

"Henry, the pizza is, like, five minutes away."

"Where's the hospitality? I'm starving, Ivy, I might not make it."

But he does make it. And, thankfully, so does Weston.

Weston's just being pulled from the icy grip of the ocean waves by Jacques, his old modeling agent and current superhero mentor, when my app tells me to make my way to the front door. The delivery driver is on the porch for twenty seconds—thirty at *most*—but just as I take the food from her, I notice a flash of movement in the house directly across the street. It's Mack, peeking through her living room window, a gloating grin on her face. Spying on me. As soon as our eyes lock, she vanishes in a swish of curtains.

"I SEE YOU, MACK!" I screech, causing the driver, who's only halfway down the driveway, to jump clean out of her skin. "COME OUT HERE AND SAY IT TO MY FACE!"

Mack does not. Yeah, that's what I *thought*. Scowling, I squirrel the pizza inside and onto the coffee table, where Henry's cleared a space.

"What's with the possessed screaming?" Henry asks.

"I'm just having a *day*," I say, opening one of the pizza boxes in a swirl of steam. I swear, the moment I finish school, I am moving somewhere far away from Mackenzie Gleason. Hopefully to Wesleyan, but I'm not picky. If I don't get in there, I'll go to Iowa, or Australia, or Mars. The farther, the better, as long as Henry can come. The last day I ever have to see Mack's face will be one of the best days of my life. I can feel it.

"Want to talk about it?" Henry asks warily.

"Nope," I say through a sweet-and-salty mouthful of pizza. "Put Weston back on, please."

Henry, being much more respectful of my privacy than I'd probably be in his position, obliges.

After *H-MAD* is over—nobody dies, by the way—Henry and I pore through our presentation as quickly as we can, then spend an hour playing video games. They've always been Henry's thing, mostly first-person-shooter deals. Personally, if I'm going to play a game by myself, it's going to be a sweet farming simulator where I get to help the local townsfolk. But it's what Henry likes to do, and when you're friends with someone, you make an effort to get involved with their interests. I believe that to my core. So, while that doesn't extend to gaming with Henry while he's not at my house—he does all his online gaming with some of the other guys from our school—it did extend to me begging my parents for a PlayStation and two controllers for my birthday last year.

By the time Henry's mom comes to collect him, the drizzle has turned into a full-blown, howling hurricane.

Or, at least, that's what it sounds like to me. I *knew* some sort of natural disaster would hit the moment my parents left me alone. I warned them, didn't I? And now look at the state of things. The wind is whistling with a frankly alarming ferocity, the way a tornado probably sounds when it's just about to swallow you up. On top of that, peals of thunder keep exploding, loud enough to shake the walls. I'm pretty sure no house has ever collapsed from thunder, but I'm nervous all the same.

I hope my parents' plane didn't get caught in this weather.

I also wish—for a brief, desperate second that I intend to vehemently deny if anyone asks—that I agreed to stay at the Gleasons'. Mack or no Mack.

Another ear-splitting clap of thunder shocks me out of my reverie with a jump. It suddenly occurs to me to double-check all the locks. Not that I think I'm at risk of the thunderstorm breaking and entering. That would be ludicrous. It's just that, if someone *were* to break and enter, my neighbors wouldn't be able to hear my screams for mercy over all this rain, so I'd better make it as hard on my would-be attackers as possible.

Luckily, all the windows and doors are as steadfast as they're ever going to be. It doesn't quite satisfy me, but it's the best I can do. On second thought, I drag one of the heavy wooden dining chairs to push it against the front door, figuring that if someone *does* manage to pick the lock, the scrape of wood on wood will alert me and give me time to grab a weapon. Not that there are any useful weapons in the house for me to use. None of us even play baseball.

My parents truly have left me completely defenseless here. Imagine leaving your child unsupervised with zero access to deadly force weapons. What kind of parents *are they*?

With the hatches battened down to my satisfaction, I take myself to my bedroom and set up at my laptop to work on my next chapter.

I've been writing *H-MAD* fanfiction for over a year now, since around the time I met Henry. On bad days, and good days, and everything in between, writing and reading fanfiction is guaranteed to make everything feel at least 20 percent more bearable. I'm not exactly famous in the *H-MAD* fandom. I get a few dozen reviews at best, and usually from the same few strangers with great taste who follow everything I upload, or the odd random reader who's just here to critique my (admittedly shaky) spelling and grammar. It's not really about the readers for me, though. The readers are a plus, sure, and it always makes my night to get a surprise message from someone begging me to upload the next chapter. But, mostly, fanfiction is a chance for me to leave the real world and live somewhere better for a couple of hours a day.

The *H-MAD* fandom is honestly the one thing in my life that makes me feel free. Where I can read stories by people who like exactly what I like instead of making me feel boring and one-track. Where I can escape into a world where kids are in control and have the power to change their own lives and the lives around them, instead of being totally micromanaged by their parents. Where I can scroll through pages and pages of content curated by kids who feel like me, and think like me, and share my struggles and hopes.

H-MAD fanfics let me imagine a world where I could be strong, and interesting, and desirable, all at once. The fandom gives me a community of people I can follow, and videos to comment on, and threads I can join in on, knowing for a fact the others involved won't find what I have to say irritating, or boring, or too intense.

They get me before I even say a word.

At the moment, I'm working on a coffee shop AU—or "alternate universe"—between an original character, Yvette, and Weston Razorbrook. It's not as popular as my Y/N hate-to-love fic, but I love it anyway. My Y/N fics—short for "your name"—tend to get the most hits. People like reading about themselves having magical, sweeping romance adventures more than almost anything else, apparently. I can relate. I, too, think that any story starring me becomes at least 50 percent more interesting. And they're 100 percent more interesting than any story starring *Vanessa*. Even though some especially talented authors are able to turn the TV version of Vanessa into a character with an actual personality and story arc, it still isn't enough to convince me to read anything starring her.

Nope, if I read *H-MAD* fics, it's either Y/N or original character romances, just like what I write. Every now and then, if I'm feeling adventurous, I might dabble in romances between Weston and some other side characters. Once, I even read a surprisingly popular romance between Weston and water. Like, *water* water. Not water as represented by a sprite or spirit or something, just . . . the element of water. It was, admittedly, a little bit of a strange read, but it was still a better love story than Westessa.

Tonight, though, no matter how many times I try to start the next chapter, I can't seem to focus. My earlier angst-driven motivation is gone. All I feel at the moment is . . . sort of lonely.

The rain is coming down even harder now, if that's even possible, slamming against the roof like it wants to break it in. My parents would be well across the country by now, at least. Just in case, I do a quick search for "plane crash," but nothing's been reported on, so that's probably a good sign.

I stare at my document for another ten minutes before sighing and slamming my hands on the keyboard, bringing the word count up to one. It's not happening tonight. For the first time in a long time, my stories aren't providing me any comfort. And I owe my readers more than a rushed chapter I forced myself to write just to get something out there.

So, instead, I decide to write something new. Something only for me.

Something specifically for me.

The emptiness of the vast, vacant house echoed like a never-ending train tunnel without a train in it. Ivy had never felt so very alone before. Everyone had abandoned her. Her parents. Mack. Even Henry had gone home, which was totally fine because it was a school night, but even if it was fine, it didn't make Ivy any less lonely or alone.

"Ivy?"

The voice is warm and familiar, and it made the pit of Ivy's stomach swoop in anticipation. Ivy turned slowly, hardly daring to believe it. But it was him! She let out a breathe she didn't know she was holding as her eyes drank him in.

He was so hot! His windswept, ice-blue waves were messy, like they'd been styled by the wind. His beautiful glowing orbs were extraordinarily wide and soulful. His biceps were visible through the thin cotton of his shirt.

"Weston!" Ivy cried, her heart coming to a shuddering halt. "Is it really you?"

Weston cupped Ivy's face in his warm hands. He smelled of pine and oak. "Of course it is?! Who else would I be? You'll never be alone now, Ivy. Never again! I won't let you go to conferences alone, or go to sleep alone, or sit in your room alone. I think your the most interesting, lovable, important person I've ever met, and that means there's nowhere else I'd rather be, ever. I will be wherever you are now."

"But how?" Ivy asked wonderingly? "I thought you weren't real."

"Ivy," Weston murmured romantically. His expression is unreadable. "Do these hands feel real? Does my voice repeating your name, in this eternal litany of 'Ivy, Ivy, Ivy' sound real? Does my love feel real?"

"Yes." Ivy whispers in awe. "It feels real. But I—"

Weston scooped her up into a hug, and it was easy for him, like she was a doll he could toss around. But of course, Weston wouldn't do that, because he knew she was a human who needed to be cherished. But he could toss her if he wanted to. But he didn't want to.

Ivy felt so vulnerable and safe in his strong arms.

"How is it that you can believe in me, in Vanessa—who recently had to move country's, by the way—and in Jacques, and yet doubt the existence of magic? Ivy: we are magic. All of us."

"Not me, though!" Ivy said sadly.

"Especially, you. Mostly you even. I might have the power to control the very fabric of the earth, but you know what you have? Love. Magic is love. And you love as strongly as anyone. How can you say there's not no magic in you?"

"I want there to be. But—"

"Then there is," Weston whispered quietly. "There is."

"I love you Weston," Ivy quietly whispered.

Weston gave her a crooked smile, and a deep dimple appeared. "Look at that," he said.

Ivy looked around, but couldn't see anything. "What? Where?"

"Everywhere," Weston murmured. "Your love just made it stronger."

Then he kisses her.

And that's where I'd end the chapter, if I was going to upload it. Which I am most definitely *not* going to do. I would sooner throw my laptop down the storm drain to be swallowed by rainwater and murderous clowns than let anyone see this. I know it's not exactly poetry, but it's soothing to write. Like I can erase all the things I hate about real life with a few keystrokes.

Feeling calmer at last, I lean back in my desk chair, tipping my head over the top of the backrest. It still feels weirdly weightless to do so. The phantom swish of my once long blond hair isn't gone just yet.

I check my phone. They still wouldn't have landed, so, unsurprisingly, there's nothing from them. Just a message from Henry, who's sent me a video to watch. I turn it on and walk with it, watching it on full volume while I do one more round of the house to check I'm definitely locked in.

When I climb into bed, the storm is still going in what I consider to be an attention-seeking display at this point. Honestly, any self-respecting storm knows to either progress to a hurricane, or wrap up after a couple of hours. It's just getting embarrassing.

Henry messages me.

You okay alone?

Totally! See you tomorrow.

Okay! Night.

Night x

Then, I message my mom, in one of the first cases in history where I've even had the *chance* to be the first one to check in.

Going to bed. Let me know when you get their safe. Love you!

In the morning, I'll have a reply, hopefully, and I can tell my anxiety to calm down for a day. Or an hour, at the very least.

I close my eyes and snuggle into bed. My thoughts go to Mack, which they often do as soon as it gets dark and I stop policing them. It's a lot like back when I had a crush on her, except then it was always hopeful sorts of thoughts, but now my gut just twists with sadness and something that almost feels like regret.

I wonder what she's doing right now. If she's asleep already. If she's been judging my new haircut the way she always judges everything about me. Or if, maybe, she even liked it a little.

Those impossibly pretty eyes had flickered to my hair for a second, I'm sure of it. And she hadn't looked disgusted or anything. At least, not with my appearance. So, it's possible, right?

Right.

I'm just starting to drift off to sleep when the room is filled with a blinding flash of light, followed almost immediately by the loudest thunderclap I've ever heard. It's so loud the sound is distorted, like a speaker that can't handle the volume it's been set to. For a wild moment, I think lightning has just struck inside my room. Then I realize it was probably just my house, or the yard or something. Of course. Of *course* my property has to get personally attacked by Mother Nature the second I'm left alone. Heart pounding, I sit up in bed, overcome with a sudden, completely irrational anger. "*I get it!*" I shout to the ceiling. "*It's raining! You've made your point!*"

Another flash, this one a little less intense, lights up in response. The ensuing thunder is also a little less intense. It feels almost like I've scared the storm into submission. Or, at least, into backing off a little bit.

"That's what I thought," I mutter, lying back down.

Ha. This must be how Weston feels all the time. One of the perks of being an air elemental is, obviously, control of the weather.

"If I had air powers," I say to the ceiling, kind of aimed at the storm, kind of aimed at no one, because storms can't realistically hold much of a conversation, "I'd shut you up so I could go to sleep."

The last part of my sentence is drowned out by a roar of thunder.

"It's rude to interrupt!" I snap, and the storm doesn't reply.

If Weston were actually here, like in tonight's fanfic, he wouldn't only stop the storm. He'd guard the house, so I wouldn't have to worry about something happening during the night, while I slept. He'd promise me nothing happened to my parents on their flight, and that I'm definitely not an orphan, because he could feel the plane's engine pulsing through the vibrations of the wind. He'd make me forget Mack—and the fact that Mack hates me now, which I don't even care about because I hate Mack even more—altogether.

He'd make me feel light, and safe, and happy, the way watching him on-screen does. The way reading about him does. The way writing about him does.

He'd climb into bed behind me, and stroke my hair, and promise that he'd never leave me. And I would believe him, because he's never let anyone down as long as I've known him.

"Good night, Weston," I mumble to myself, the words muffled by my pillow. If I concentrate hard enough, I can almost feel the weight of him in the bed. I can almost hear the soft sound of him breathing in the darkness. I can almost smell his cologne, which I'm sure would probably smell of pine needles.

And, for a beat, it's like I'm not alone at all.

Just as I feel sleep pulling at the edges of my mind, the storm outside comes to a sudden, shuddering end.

Chapter Three

PAST

"So, what's everyone's plans for the week?" Mack's mom, Keisha, asks over dinner.

Keisha used to be in competitive aerobics—there are trophies all over the Gleasons' living room to prove it—and it left her with a habit of saying everything with an extra level of pep. Everything with her comes with a huge smile, expressive hands, and a ton of energy. So, when she asks you a question, you're left feeling like she's really interested in your answers.

Unlike my mom, who always seems to be waiting to offer her much more competent take.

It's one of the many reasons I'm always eager to accept an invitation to Sunday roast dinners at the Gleasons'.

Mack's brother, Zeke, helps himself to another crispy roast potato from the piled-up tray in the table's center as he answers. "Liam and I think we'll be done with the coding on our game soon," he says. "Then we'll be able to show you, finally."

Mack's dad, Victor—quieter than Keisha but no less warm—

makes an impressed face. "You'll have to walk us through it," he says. "But I can't wait to see what you've put together. I don't know where you get it from. I can't even type with more than two fingers."

"Might have something to do with the generation he was born into," Mack points out from her place on my left.

"And what about you, sweetheart?" Keisha turns to Mack.

"Well," Mack says. "Layla asked me to hang back after training tomorrow for some one-on-one training."

Keisha raises her eyebrows. "What does that involve?"

Mack shrugs. "Not really sure."

"Layla told her last week she can see her being made captain next year," I say, and the Gleasons break out into exclamations.

Mack shoots me a chiding look. I should've known she was too superstitious to tell her family about that before she knew more. "Nothing's earned until it's earned" is Mack's philosophy.

"That's so exciting," Keisha says, hands waving.

"We'll see how it goes," Mack says. "It's not like they're deciding this week or anything."

"And what about you, Ivy?" Keisha asks when everyone's done wishing Mack luck. She's always careful to include me. "Anything fun happening this week?"

"Same old," I say, suddenly self-conscious. "I've finally saved up enough to get tickets for this conference for my favorite TV show, but that's not really news."

"That's excellent," Keisha says. "Is Mack going with you?"

"Yeah," Mack says, pouring herself another glass of water. She tops mine off when she's done. "It should be good."

I end up lost in thought as Keisha and Victor start talking about their upcoming week. The thing is, there is something that's happening this week. I've decided to quit the volleyball team. At least, I'm pretty sure I'm going to. I really want to pull out right away, but there's not too much longer left in the season, so I might not re-enroll next year. I'm undecided. But what I do know is I am quitting. It just doesn't make me happy, other than as a way to spend more time with Mack, and I'm pretty sure your extracurriculars aren't meant to be the low point of your week, right?

But, even though I'd love Keisha's and Victor's wisdom here, I can't tell them before I break it to Mack, and I'm planning on doing that tonight after dinner. She's going to be disappointed in me, so I've been putting it off.

She'll definitely get it, though. She knows I'm not exactly psyched about volleyball. Besides, if she does get captain, she'll be too busy to hang with me much during practice anyway. The only reason I really do it is to spend time with her. And if I can't do that at volleyball, we'll just have to make more plans on the nights we're both free.

It'll be fine.

PRESENT

The next morning, I awaken to the shrill trumpeting of my phone alarm, and many, *many* texts from Mom. She landed safe, she wants me to remember my presentation, she wants to know how hanging out with Henry went, she wants to know how much the pizza cost and if I starved, and why I haven't woken up yet, because I haven't read her texts and I'd better not be sleeping in to avoid breakfast because breakfast is the most important meal, and—

Something just touched my leg.

There's something warm in my bed.

I catch my breath and go completely stiff. Is it a bear? Why is there a bear in my bed? How did it get in?

That's when I realize. Whatever it is *got in*. It managed to break into a house that was locked down like a prison, and, as a first port of call, decided to silently climb into bed with the only human it could find in the house.

Yeah. There's a person in my bed.

My first thought is Henry, but the person lets out a small, sleepy sort of noise, and, mother of Christ, it is not Henry's voice. It's a stranger, a stranger has broken into my house, and is right behind me. In, and I cannot stress this enough, *my freaking bed.*

Now, I have spent a lot of time picturing my own murder. Maybe more time than the average sixteen-year-old, although I don't really know for sure, I've never done a survey. Anyway, murder by intruder-in-the-night is definitely something I've considered more than once. In those considerations, the first thing I always do is scream. It seems like the logical thing to do in such circumstances. But now I'm living it, I don't scream. In fact, for a long time, I wait, breathing as quietly as I can. I don't dare look behind me, because somehow it feels like I can pretend this isn't happening as long as I can't see the intruder's eyes.

Then, all at once, my instincts decide that's ridiculous. Something primal kicks in, and I launch myself out of the bed and through the bedroom door. "Holy fuck," I squeak as I run. "Holy shit. *What the fuck?*"

I listen for footsteps as I run, but the only ones I can hear are mine. For now, at least, I'm not being pursued. But what do I have? Minutes? Seconds? Seconds seems likely.

A weapon. I need a weapon. We still have no baseball bat in the house, which clearly needs to be fixed as a matter of urgency. A knife could work, but it seems pretty short-range. I stop in the kitchen and turn in a desperate circle, scanning my options. Boiling water? It could actually work, but waiting for the water to boil might put me at a battle disadvantage. Suddenly, an idea pops into my mind. I grab a large, family-size can of soup from the pantry, dart to grab a pillowcase from the linen closet, and shove the can inside. There. If I get enough momentum on this baby, I can knock the murderer out. Maybe.

Or, maybe I should just run and seek refuge at the Gleasons'.

Yeah, now that I think about it, that's a much smarter idea than confrontation. My fight-or-flight instinct might need some fine-tuning.

I'm just about to make a run for it, pillowcase in hand, when a strangely familiar voice calls out, "Ivy?"

For the life of me, I still can't place the voice. It's not Zeke. Not Dad—obviously. Someone from school? Wait, am I being attacked by someone I know? I did read somewhere most people are murdered by a friend or acquaintance. Did I piss someone off that badly? What have I ever done to deserve murder? I don't even have a bully; how have I jumped straight into having a mortal enemy?

I prepare to swing the pillowcase, and pray I'm coordinated enough to pull this off. "I'm armed," I call out. "I'm warning you! If you leave now, no one has to get hurt."

In response to this, footsteps thump down the hall at top speed, and my heart jumps into my throat. Before I can even get a full swing going with the pillowcase, my attacker bursts into the kitchen. Shrieking at the top of my lungs, I fling myself under the kitchen table, hard enough to bruise my knees. The soup flies out of the bag and skids along the floor, only stopping when the intruder steps on it with a pair of heavy, black lace-up boots. Whoever it is has paired those boots with black jeans.

Exactly what a murderer would wear.

"Ivy?" asks the intruder. "Are you okay? Who's getting hurt?"

Step by step, the feet come closer. I shuffle backward, but there's nowhere to go but the wall. My instincts really do suck. They're doing a terrible job at keeping me alive.

Then the murderer crouches down to peek under the table, and my instincts leave the party altogether. No fighting, or flee-ing, or anything. Just a strange, floating sort of sensation, while

I try to figure out what on earth has happened to my grasp on reality. Because the intruder has very familiar windswept, ice-blue waves and glowing blue eyes.

"You're Chase Mancini," I force out. My voice is croaky and weak, which is not the impression I planned on making on Chase Mancini when I finally met him one day, but it's been a hell of a morning so I forgive myself.

But it can't be Chase Mancini. If only because there's no reason on the planet that a B-list celebrity would head on over to small-town USA, break into the house of someone who happens to be a mega-fan of the show he stars in, and climb into bed to practically spoon said mega-fan.

But I have spent hours upon hours upon hours staring at this very face, and it has to be Chase. He even has tiny little moles where Chase has tiny little moles, and a bump in the nose where Chase has a bump, and Chase's widow's peak hairline.

"Who's Chase Mancini?" he asks, and, okay, I was right the first time, apparently. Although that doesn't really fit, either, because if Chase Mancini's doppelgänger has broken into my house, it seems unlikely he's never been told he looks like Chase Mancini before.

"Um . . . who are you, then?" I ask.

He gives me a funny look, like I've asked him the most obvious question in the world, and he isn't sure if he's missing the joke. Then, eyebrows raised, he replies, "Weston?"

I'm not following. "Are you asking me a question, or answering me?"

"I'm answering you. It's me, babe. Weston."

Oh.

Suddenly, the idea that Chase Mancini has come to my hometown, broken into my house, and is suffering some sort of delusion seems like the most likely option here.

"Let's get you out from there, huh?" he says cheerfully, grabbing my hand and tugging me forward. I'm too stunned to resist, so I just let myself be dragged across the tiles, slumping. Somehow, I end up on my feet, and then in a blink I'm being led down the hall and helped onto my bed by the intruder while I desperately try to make sense of reality. He then proceeds to sit on the edge of the mattress and takes one of my hands in his, staring at me with concern knitting his brow.

Okay. I'm starting to put this all together. In a weird way, it makes a lot of sense. A B-list celebrity, tired of being universally adored and obscenely wealthy, runs away from it all and ends up in a small town. Gets spotted by an obsessive fan, or the paparazzi or something, runs away, acquires a brain injury, and very briefly believes he's the character he plays. Seeks shelter in a house he thinks is abandoned, only to discover he's unwittingly stumbled across the path of the love of his life. It's the premise of, like, at least a hundred rom-coms, and stories are always based on real life if you go far back enough. I could write it in my sleep.

It *does* make sense, right? It has to, because if it doesn't, then none of this has any logic to it at all, and I'm stumped on what to do next if that's the case.

"Hey, Chase?" I ask. He doesn't flinch. I take a deep breath, and adopt a gentle, understanding tone, so he knows he can trust me not to run to the media, or the police, or his fan clubs or anything like that. I want him to know I'm one of his rational, loyal, thoughtful fans, not an obsessive, impulsive, fame-hungry one. "I know it's you. It's okay. You're safe here. I won't tell anyone. And no one will find you accidentally, either. Honestly, my parents aren't in the state, and I have, like, one friend, and I can keep him out of the house for a while. He's really easy to keep track of, too, he's not quiet at all. The chances of this getting out are minuscule."

He blinks, clearly confused. I guess I was rambling a little. In my defense, my brain feels like it's been through a blender. Okay. I'm talking to him like he's Chase. But he said his name was Weston. Am I sure he actually thinks he's Weston? Or was it some sort of weird joke?

"Do you know who you are?" I ask, to be totally certain.

"Yes," he says without pausing. "I'm Weston Razorbrook."

God, the poor thing. He's really confused. Thank goodness it's my house he ended up in, because who knows what sort of mess he could've gotten himself into if he broke into a place where no one recognized him.

His management team must be worried sick about him. I just have to figure out how to contact them, and then we'll whisk him to safety, and—oh my god, now I know Chase Mancini. This is *great*. Maybe once he's recovered, he'll reach out to thank me, and we'll become best friends. And then, who knows, maybe we'll click, and he'll fly me to the set on his private jet, and then afterward we'll go grab a coffee, and I'll drink it even though it probably won't be sweet enough for me, because it'll make me look sophisticated, and then we'll go for a walk by the ocean, and—

And I'm getting ahead of myself.

"Okay, Weston," I say carefully. "Can you tell me how you got here?"

Chase smiles blankly. "I woke up here, silly."

Weird. He's speaking in an American accent, just like Weston, but Chase was born in Australia to Italian immigrant parents. There's no non-concerning reason he should be speaking in an American accent. Is that part of the injury? Maybe that's how these things work. I wouldn't know.

And another thing. Chase has dark brown eyes, but right now, he's wearing the glowing contacts his character wears on the show. Did he have to film something recently? I don't understand how, considering filming wrapped up a while ago and isn't due to start again for ages.

"Right. But how did you get into my bed?" I press. "Do you remember?"

He thinks about it for a long moment, then sticks out his bottom lip. "Huh. Uh, not really. Does it matter?"

I choose not to go into the details on why it might matter very much. Instead, I grab my phone and navigate to Chase's social media. Obviously I can't just up and contact Chase's management team on there. But, if nothing else, it might give me a jumping-off point as to how to contact them.

"Do you have your phone with you?" I ask as I type.

"No, I don't. Sorry."

Figures. He probably lost it during the accident.

Chase looks around. "Hey, Ivy? Is there anything to eat?"

"Oh, sure. Help yourself to whatever's in the kitchen."

As I pick up my own phone, it starts buzzing with a call from Mom. Figuring now isn't the best time to take a call from my very observant, always-listening-for-changes-in-my-tone parents, I let it ring out before scrolling to Chase's profile page. Then I freeze. According to the screen, Chase had a live that ended about two minutes ago. Was he . . . filming me?

With a burst of panic, I open the video. Going by the time stamp, it started streaming about seven minutes ago.

On the screen is Chase Mancini. Only, he's not wearing a leather jacket and jeans. He's dressed in a sleeveless shirt and shorts, streaming in front of what looks to be a private plunge pool illuminated by string lights. Even in the dark, his skin is obviously more tanned than usual. He looks relaxed, and cheerful, and, most damning of all, apparently quite clear about who he is. "Hey, *MAD* fans," he says, referring to us by the moniker the *H-MAD* fandom gave ourselves years ago. "I'm coming to you from the *future*—it's already tonight here in Australia—to tell you I'm sharing some *amazing* news soon! Make sure you watch this space for the next week, because you'll hear it here first."

For the first time in my life, I can't bring myself to care what the *H-MAD* news is. My mind is completely blank. Because the intruder has walked back in the room, munching on an apple, and it appears he is . . . most definitely not Chase Mancini.

Which means a Chase Mancini lookalike has broken into my house.

"What are you watching, my love?" the intruder asks, leaning over the bed, and I lock my phone in response. Okay. This is fine. I am going to be *fine*. I will simply not do anything to upset the intruder, while I figure out an excuse to get him out of the room so I can call for help. And if that fails, Zeke and Mack will be by to pick me up for school pretty soon. I can totally keep a possible murderer calm for fifteen minutes, right? Who couldn't?

The thing is, I'm so busy thinking about how I've got this that I forget to reply with something soothing and wise in order to calm the intruder down. Noticing my sudden lapse into silence, the intruder narrows his eyes and pats my calf. "Is something wrong, darling?"

"No," I squeak. "I'm fine, I'm not upset or worried or anything. This is fine. Don't even worry about me being worried, because I'm not."

There, that'll buy some time.

The intruder, amazingly, doesn't seem convinced by this. "You don't look very well," he says, and I'm relieved to note he sounds genuinely concerned. Not, like, "I'm pretending to care for you and I'm going to get you some medicine, but the medicine is actually cyanide" vibes. I'm at least partially sure I'd be able to tell if that were the case. Before I can let my guard down, though, the intruder grabs my feet and shoves them under the blankets. I instinctively shoot up into a sitting position, but he forces my shoulders down until my head hits the pillow, all the while shushing me. Okay, this is bad. This is a definite emergency situation. I am not safe with this guy.

"I'll be right back, beautiful," he says, before ducking out of the room.

This is my chance. Gingerly, I pull out my phone, with every intention of dialing 911. But before I can even unlock the screen, the intruder reappears as quickly as he vanished, holding a tray laden with various items. I make out a steaming cup of tea, some cough syrup, Band-Aids, a wet washcloth, and, alarmingly, some unidentified pills. I grit my teeth as he sets the tray on the foot of the bed.

A sluggish, confused part of my brain points out that he must have either prepared this tray earlier, or pulled these items out of thin air, given he was gone all of four seconds, but I don't have the energy to try to sort through that logic hole right now.

"What are those pills?" I ask.

"Tylenol," the intruder says casually. "You were groaning a lot last night. It sounded like you might be in pain. I know you don't like to complain, but you don't need to be brave with me."

"Last night when I was . . . sleeping?" I ask.

"Yeah."

"How . . . long were you in my bed?"

I don't really want to know the answer. I shouldn't have asked at all. And do I believe him about the Tylenol? I'm not sure, but I do know I'm not taking those pills for anything in this world.

"Are you cold?" the intruder asks instead of addressing the question. "You're shivering."

"Shaking" is the more accurate word, but it's possibly unwise to correct him. So, without replying, I pull the covers to my chin while the intruder lays his jacket over me, on top of the blanket. Under the blankets, I dig my nails into my thigh, just in case I'm dreaming. The pain that follows is pretty sharp, and I don't wake up, so I have to conclude that I am, unfortunately, very much awake.

"How many sugars in your tea?" he asks, turning his back to me. Can I knock him out if I throw something at his head? It doesn't seem smart to try. If I miss, I'll probably just anger him.

How far away can Mack and Zeke be? Surely they'll come by any minute now.

"I don't mind," I force out. Then, something feels different. My bewildered mind is struggling to process the entire situation, and, therefore, it can't quite figure out what that something is, until I take a closer look at the intruder. He's wearing the jacket again. The one he just laid across me. I check, and, sure enough, the jacket is not on top of me anymore. The "something different" I'd felt was the weight of it vanishing.

Maybe I'm the one who hit my head.

"Um, excuse me, sir," I say. "I'm still cold. Would you mind putting your jacket on me?"

He turns around, holding the tea. "Please," he says, as he places the cup on my bedside table. "Just Weston is fine."

Once the jacket is back on top of my legs, I stare at it fiercely. While I do, the guy stands above me, scanning my head with a concerned expression. "You really don't look good," he murmurs. "Would you allow me to do a full-body examination?"

"No, thank you," I reply automatically.

"Okay. But you need to check yourself thoroughly when I leave the room, because if you have an infection, things could get bad, fast."

I don't reply, because my attention is elsewhere. Namely, on the empty spot on my blanket where the intruder's jacket sat seconds ago.

It disappeared *right in front of me*. Right in front of me. Like a glitch in reality. And now it's back on the intruder's body.

None of it makes sense. Life, the world, the universe. It's all meaningless. Reality itself doesn't exist. Possibly never existed. Or perhaps it's simply me that doesn't exist.

I don't think I'm okay.

"You remind me of an old friend," the intruder says as he sits on the edge of the bed, gazing down at me. "Her name was Vanessa."

"I'm *nothing like Vanessa*," I snap automatically. I can't help it, it's a reflex.

"I suppose not," the intruder says. "I can tell you're much more interesting."

At this, reality starts to piece itself back together. It no longer looks anything like the reality that I'm used to, but at least it's starting to seem a little less like the random gibberish rapidly firing neurons might produce. Because—if I look at the evidence—in a way that makes absolutely no sense, it makes sense. Last night, I was thinking about how great it'd be to have Weston here with me. This morning, someone who looks exactly like Weston, but isn't Chase, somehow appeared inside my locked house. Someone who has a magic jacket, and who can conjure up tea and medical supplies out of thin air, and who knows the sorts of things Weston would know.

The closest rational explanation would be that this is a Chase Mancini impersonator, or an *H-MAD* fan, but neither of those scenarios can account for the apparent magical abilities at play here.

So, under these circumstances, the only *rational* rational explanation—even if it seems to challenge the very meaning of the word "rational"—is that the guy standing before me, who calls himself Weston, is, somehow . . .

"Weston?" I whisper.

"I'm right here, Ivy," he replies, brushing a lock of hair from my forehead. "I'm not leaving you."

Downstairs, there's a knock on the door.

Chapter Four

PAST

Mom turns up to speak to Ms. Gomez right as we're wrapping up practice. I notice her hovering by the gym doors right away—her neon pink blouse makes her hard to miss—and she gives me a little wave. I smile at her in return, and Mack comes to my side. "This is it, then?" she asks, bumping her shoulder against mine.

"Mm-hmm." I stare at the spot on my arm she touched as she pulls back.

"You could've told Ms. Gomez yourself, you know," she says gently. "She'd understand."

"Mom insisted," I say. "I hesitated in our script rehearsal and she got all concerned I'm gonna back out halfway through if I do it myself."

"Maybe, but isn't that a 'you' lesson?"

I don't reply.

We wrap up practice, and Mom heads straight over to Ms. Gomez. I hurry to join them, as the rest of the girls on the team watch curiously from the stands.

"What's going on?" Brianna asks Mack, loudly enough for me to hear, but Mack just shakes her head.

I expect Mom to take Ms. Gomez somewhere private, but to my horror, they only take a few steps away from the team before Mom launches into things. "So," she says, once the greetings are over. "I just wanted to come in and let you know Ivy's decided to take a bit of a break from volleyball."

"Oh," Ms. Gomez says, startled. She glances at me, and I promptly disappear into a puddle of shame. Everyone can hear them. And now the whole team knows my mom does my dirty work for me. Not that I care what they think about me, because it's not like any of them are even my friends aside from Mack, but at the same time, I care a *lot*. It's a paradox. I don't know, maybe it's normal to want people to think you're at least a little cool, even if you have no intention of becoming besties with them. I make a mental note to google that later.

"Yes," Mom says. Well, no, she doesn't say it. She *projects* it. She *bellows* it. She might as well add an interpretive dance to it, just to make sure everyone in the vicinity hears *exactly* what's going on. "Nothing's happened, there's nothing to be concerned about. I just think it's time for Ivy to explore some new options with her after-school activities. . . ."

Ms. Gomez starts walking now, directly away from the team, in an effort to give me some privacy. Mom matches her step, oblivious. Obviously, Mom's got this, just like she always does. There's no need for me to be there for this conversation. Pretty much from the moment I told Mom I was thinking about quitting, this was my fate.

I hang behind, hugging my arms to my chest, not even daring to check how much of the team is staring at me right now. Or worse, whispering about me.

Still, I should probably be grateful. Plenty of kids have parents who won't let them quit sports, or won't let them join sports. My mom lets me do whatever I want. She just doesn't trust me to do it correctly without her involvement.

I'm lucky she's always there for me, right?

Then why do I feel like running out of the school and finding a new family to take me in somewhere? Somewhere less embarrassing. Like the circus. I hear they're always on the lookout for tortured teens with decent flexibility. Tick and tick.

"Did she seriously get her mommy to come and help her quit the team?" Ruby Moretz stage-whispers to Brianna, loud enough to make me crack and finally turn around.

Mack, who's started making her way toward me, has stopped in place to glare at Ruby. "What was that, Ruby?" she asks in a cool tone.

Ruby shrugs and averts her eyes instantly.

"It's okay," I say in a hushed voice as I reach Mack's side. "They're just mad I'm leaving you a person short."

"That doesn't give them free rein to be awful."

She touches my arm to steer me in the opposite direction of the rest of the team. We end up standing near the gym doors, where no one can hear us. "I can't believe you're really going," Mack says, crossing her arms over her chest.

When she says it like that, small and sad, it's almost enough to convince me to sprint in there and tell my mom not to worry about it. Almost. "It's not like I'm any good at it," I say. "And I don't really like it. So, what's the point?"

Mack scans my face, and something flashes across her eyes. Something that looks a lot like hurt. I'm not sure what I said that hurt her, though. If I knew, I'd take it straight back.

"I get it," she says. "But it's going to suck not having you around."

"Only at volleyball," I say quickly. "It's not like I'm moving or anything."

"No, I know."

"It's a few hours less a week." I smile. "Nothing else is gonna change. We can just make an effort to spend time together doing other stuff. You can come over my house whenever."

Mack nods, but there's something distant and uncertain about it. "Yeah," she says. "I guess so."

PRESENT

"I need you to stay here and be quiet," I say urgently. Until I figure out what is going on, I no longer need Mack and Zeke to rescue me. In fact, the less they—or anyone—know about this, the better right now. All I know is the most logical answer is also the most illogical answer, and if I ask someone else to believe that what I think is happening is, in fact, happening, *someone* is going to call my parents on me. And *that* sounds like an extra layer of mess I truly can't handle right now. I have hit my complication limit in one fell swoop.

Weston—god, I can't believe I'm calling him that—draws his eyebrows together and nods, the picture of seriousness. "I'll listen nearby in case you need backup," he says as I climb off the bed.

I pause, halfway to the door already. "No, really, you need to stay hidden."

"Ivy, I'm not letting you face danger alone."

"I'm not facing danger," I say, "I'm facing a knock at the door."

"You don't know what's on the other side of that door. It could be your archenemy."

"That's where you're wrong," I mutter. "I already know it's my archenemy."

Weston splays his hands to the sides, and I realize too late I'm not helping my case.

"The only way I can be in trouble is if she finds out you're here," I say, desperation tingeing my tone. "I'm begging you, *please*, stay here."

Weston folds his arms. "I'll stay out of sight, and I will only intervene if absolutely necessary. Are those terms acceptable, Ivy?"

I don't think he needed to add *quite* as much sass as he did in the last part there, but otherwise, I figure it's about as good an offer as I'm gonna get. With a sigh, I beckon him to follow me downstairs, where I deposit him in the hallway while I continue on.

Mack's standing on the porch with her hands on her hips, waiting for me with pursed lips. When she sees me—or, more accurately, when she sees my outfit—her expression changes from impatient to baffled in one fluid motion. I'm still wearing my patchwork pajama shorts and the oversized NUTELLA LIFE T-shirt my grocery store gave out in a promotion last year. As a sleeping outfit, it's passable, as long as no one I want to impress is around. As a school outfit, it's pretty lacking. Guess it's a good thing I'm not going to school today.

"What, did your alarm not go off?" Mack asks.

On the street behind her, Zeke has already climbed into his beat-up Ford. I can't hear anything from over here, but I can make out Zeke dancing in his seat to whatever music he's put on, totally oblivious to me in my pajamas. Thank goodness. It's bad enough that Mack has to see me like this, and she's seen me in much more embarrassing outfits over the years.

"I . . . was just about to text you," I lie. "I'm actually not feeling well."

Honestly, I expect Mack to raise her eyebrows at me, given how convenient the timing is. But to my surprise, she looks concerned. "Oh. Are you okay?"

"Mmm, yup," I say, stealing a glance at the hallway. If Weston's listening nearby, he is, thankfully, doing a good job of concealing himself. "I'll be fine. Go on without me."

"Are you sure?" Mack asks, brows knitted. "Mom's working from home today if you want to go over there?"

I remember what Keisha is like when someone's sick. She's all chicken soup and thick knitted blankets and full control of the TV remote. Thinking about it, something pulls at my chest. I wish I really were sick, and I could head on over there and be coddled like a little kid. Having a cold or a headache is a fixable problem. Or, at least, a problem with a pretty clear end date. I don't know if I can say the same about my current predicament.

"That's okay," I say, before putting on the world's fakest yawn. "I'm probably just gonna head back to bed."

Before Mack can reply, Zeke toots the horn twice and shrugs through the driver's window at us.

"You can *wait, Ezekiel*!" Mack shouts at him, and Zeke lowers his window.

"I've got a meeting with Mr. Stefanson before first period, *Mackenzie*. Vamanos!"

"Vamanos? Really? Like he didn't spend *forty minutes* in the bathroom this morning," Mack mutters, catching my eye with a conspiratorial smile, and for a stolen moment it's like we're sophomores again. My mind races, sifting through possible responses that will make her laugh, or spark her interest, or earn her forgiveness. Something I can say to keep this moment in place forever, before we have to go back to barely tolerating each other. Of course, my mind simply shrugs at me. It might as well have a BACK IN FIVE MINUTES sign hung up. To be fair, minds are wont to do that when they're presented with evidence that the laws of physics don't apply anymore. Asking my mind to accept that I might have the physical form of a fictional character waiting feet away from me *and* to suggest a charismatic quip is simply too much. When I do nothing but give her an awkward, silent smile, she seems to remember herself. "Okay, well, you're good?"

Those words, brisk and clipped, snip the invisible thread that linked us seconds ago. "I'm great," I lie. *Now* her eyebrows are raised. I scramble to correct myself. "Situationally, I'm great. Physically, I'm a five at best."

"Great."

"Yeah."

"So . . . okay. Later."

"Have a good . . . bye," I say, full of wit and charm, as always.

Weston pokes his head around the hallway entrance the moment the coast is clear. "I didn't stab anyone," he informs me, which concerns me more than I think he intends it to.

"Stab?" I repeat. With a nod, he brings his hand out from behind his back to show me the carving knife he apparently grabbed from the kitchen the moment he was unsupervised.

"Woah, okay. Weston," I say, trying my best to keep my voice steady. "I'm going to need you to promise not to stab anyone. Ever."

Weston shrugs and turns the knife over between his fingers. "I won't make that promise. I will stab anyone necessary if your life is in danger."

"As we discussed, my life was *not in danger.*"

"Yes, and *nobody got stabbed,* which is my point." He slips the knife into the belt of his jeans. "I think we're arguing the same thing here, Ivy."

My head is swimming so much I can't form a coherent enough thought to argue further. Instead, I wander to the couch and flop down in a daze. Weston sits next to me, and the weight of him jolts the couch cushion. Somehow, it surprises me. I almost expected him to be weightless. A figment of my imagination.

"That girl is your nemesis, you said?" Weston asks. "Or were you referring to the boy in the car?"

Who knows, maybe I *am* sick. Maybe I have a fever that's so off the charts I skipped the "feeling bad" part and went straight to auditory and visual hallucinations.

"Ivy?" Weston prompts, and I try to focus back in on what's passing for reality right now.

"Uh, yeah, I meant her," I say. "Her name's Mack, and we do *not* get along."

"And what did this Mack do to earn your vitriol?"

I'm discussing my problems with a fictional character. This makes sense. I shift in place, then bring my feet onto the couch and lean in to the madness. "It's a long story. We were friends, now we aren't, that's all you need to know."

Weston has a look of concentration on his face. "But I would like to know. I want to know everything about you, Ivy. Even if the story is long and complex. Even if the recounting of it cuts into our mealtime. Even if the tangents are myriad, and the morals murky."

Well, the story isn't as complicated as all that. But, if he really wants to know . . .

So, I tell him. About the growing tension between us. The two huge fights we had last year, and why the second one was impossible to come back from. What Mack said to me. What she said about *Henry*. Everything.

Weston is silent for a long time, long enough that I wonder if he's about to tell me I'm actually in the wrong. I brace myself for him to point out all the ways that I was actually a bad friend, or dramatic, or demanding—all the things I've told myself a million times whenever I think of Mack. But instead, he places a hand gently on my knee. "It sounds to me like she didn't value you at all."

I stare at him. I've never heard Mack's behavior described that way, but yes, *yes,* exactly. *That's* why our friendship ended. Because I never meant as much to her as she did to me.

"You deserved so much better than that," he continues, watching me intensely.

The validation of those words shocks me so much that, for a moment, I can't find the words to reply. Finally, I manage to squeak out a small "*Thank* you."

He gives me a soft smile, and lightly touches my knee with his fingertips. So gentle it's as though he expects me to flinch away. When I don't, he rests his palm on it. His hand is warm and weighted. Just like a human's.

"I would never do that to you," he whispers. "I'd never leave you."

And suddenly, it doesn't matter that none of this makes sense. It doesn't matter that Weston shouldn't exist, or whether he does at all. All I know is I'm looking at him, and touching him, and he's real to me.

And however he got here, I'm not mad that he's here.

Not mad at all.

Chapter Five

PAST

We're halfway through the *H-MAD* pilot, and Mack looks bored out of her mind.

When she told me she couldn't really watch *H-MAD* with me because she couldn't follow the plotline, it made perfect sense. So, I offered to watch it from the start with her, to get her on the hype train. She was totally down, or, at least, she said she was. Maybe she was expecting something different, I don't know. What I do know is I feel irrationally panicky at the thought of her being bored with my stuff, and when I get panicky, I get chatty.

"Okay, so that's Vanessa," I say, when she makes her on-screen appearance—storming down a crowded New York street in a boho skirt so long it drags along the filthy sidewalk. "We hate her."

"Yeah?" Mack asks. She's on her phone, scrolling mindlessly. "Why?"

"She's the most useless of the group. She's got these awesome fire elemental powers and she barely ever uses them because she's, like, afraid of conflict, so she mostly just hangs around wringing her hands while her loved ones are tortured right in front of her. Like, there's conflict, it's happening, and all you're doing is refusing to put an end to it. You know?"

Mack doesn't reply. I stare at her until she notices my look, then she quickly locks her phone and turns back to the screen.

"This job is going to change your career trajectory," Vanessa's agent is saying to her over the phone.

"A catalogue placement?" Vanessa says skeptically, like she's too good for that. "Really, Icarus?"

"Really. Plus, Weston Razorbrook is in talks for the shoot as well."

Vanessa stops in her tracks, her skirt hem settling on top of a shallow brown puddle. "Weston?" she asks.

"I knew that'd get your attention," Icarus says.

"Weston's our favorite," I tell Mack. "He's, like, sarcastic and quippy, and super brave but also super gentle, and he loves to pick arguments and debates but it's not in an annoying way, it's in a hot, smart way."

She raises her eyebrows, looking thoroughly unenthused. "Oh yeah?"

Wait, does Mack think I'm a bad person for liking Weston and not Vanessa, because that's a really anti-feminist thing to do? "We like Kia, too," I add. "She doesn't come in until season two, though. Just . . . so you know."

Mack nods.

"She's a girl," I add pathetically, and Mack gives me a strange look.

"Cool," she says, and I can tell by her tone that she's indulging me, and has no idea why I'm randomly dumping information about a character from season two on her right now. I'm worried that if I explain my thought process, she *will* think I'm a bad feminist if she doesn't already, though, so I just leave it.

We watch for a little longer, and Mack eventually goes back on her phone. After a few more minutes, I realize I have to call it. She tried, and it's not her thing. That's okay. I mean, obviously, I'm disappointed, but it's fine.

"We can watch something else," I say, and Mack looks up, guiltily, again.

"Sorry, it's good. Really."

"Really?" I repeat, and she looks even more guilty.

"Sort of?"

"Seriously," I say, grabbing the remote. "I'll put something else on. It's fine. I've seen this episode a million times, so if you're not into it, there's no point."

"I'm sorry," she moans. "It's not objectively bad or anything. It's just not my thing."

"I know, it's fine, it's totally fine." I hope I sound reassuring. The last thing I want is for Mack to feel bad about this.

"I can't really hang out to watch the new episodes with you, anyway," Mack says. "Sundays are always busy. You know I have family dinner and stuff."

"Oh, for sure," I say. "I know. I was actually thinking, if you were into it, maybe we could've made it a Monday night thing and I could've just avoided spoilers." I see the look on her face, and charge on hastily. "But that was gonna be if you were into it, and you're not, which is totally fine."

Mack is suddenly very interested in the floor. "Mondays wouldn't have worked anyway," she says. "Brianna wants to start training for a half marathon, and she asked me to go on runs with her after school on Mondays."

Brianna. Brianna who was just kissing Shaun a month ago— Brianna, who Mack says she's not into, but is obviously lying or in denial about, given the look on her face right now—just happens to want a long-standing date with Mack, out of everyone on the team she could've asked to practice with her? Cool. Rad. Awesome. That's just so *awesome*.

Why didn't I think to take up running? I could've asked Mack to coach me.

Who am I kidding, though? I can't run for more than thirty seconds without gasping. I'm not the kind of person she wants to be doing that with.

No wonder she's so bored tonight.

A black cloud of jealousy blocks out my vision for a second, and I don't have time to intervene before the scowl settles on my features.

"I'm sorry," Mack says when she notices my expression. "I didn't realize it meant so much to you to watch the show with me."

"It doesn't," I say quickly, but I don't know how convincing it is, and it's not like I can tell her my mood has nothing to do with the show and everything to do with her and her cute, romantic running date with a girl who has the same interests as her and would never ask her to watch some boring TV show. "It's whatever. Um, what else do you want to watch? I could put a movie on, or . . ."

She stretches on the couch and her hoodie rises a little, showing off a smooth strip of stomach. I do everything within my power not to look at it. "I'm restless. Can we go for a walk or something instead?"

I am not in the mood to go outside. It's cold, and I'm in my comfortable sweatpants, and I'm all snuggly in the armchair. Plus, we had gym today, and they made us do laps, and my legs are like jelly, still.

But. If I say no, will Mack want to come over next time? Or

will she choose to spend her night with someone active, and fun, who doesn't make her sit through shows she's never shown any organic interest in?

And since when do I overthink whether Mack wants to hang out with me like this? She's always wanted to hang out with me.

But I've never felt like there were way better options than me before.

Brianna would go for a walk. Brianna would've suggested a walk from the start.

"Yeah, totally," I say, getting to my feet. "Just let me get changed."

Who cares if I don't want to go outside? I'll get over it. As long as I'm with Mack, it doesn't matter what we do anyway.

PRESENT

The first thing that needs to happen if Weston is going to stay here is a room cleanout. Specifically, I need to hide every piece of *H-MAD* merchandise *now*. I'm just guessing here, but it seems likely to me that Weston might have a few difficult-to-answer questions if he discovers he's the star of a teen TV show. As would I, to be fair.

So, excusing myself from the living room where Weston remains perched on the couch, I hurry down the hall. There, I do a sweep of the room and find every damning piece of *H-MAD* merchandise I can. Anything that includes Weston's name or image has to go, which means . . . basically all of it.

For the first time, I'm grateful my parents never let me put posters up for fear of ruining the paint, because there's no *way* he would've missed his own face plastered on my walls. Lucky for me, he didn't pay much attention to my desk this morning, or he would've noticed my pencil case, and laptop stickers, and key rings. The stickers come off, and the rest go in my desk drawer under a school folder. I change my phone background, then dig through my chest of drawers, find the *H-MAD* pajama set Henry got me for Christmas, ball it up, and throw it under the bed. I'm about to go back to the living room when I remember the Weston tote bag hanging on the back of my door. It goes in the bottom of my closet, and, finally, I'm ready to rejoin Weston in the living room. He's waiting patiently for me, and his face lights up as soon as I arrive.

"I'm going to make you up a bed, if you wanna help me out," I say, and he jumps to his feet to follow me to the hallway.

"You don't need to trouble yourself," he says as I fling open the linen closet. "Your bed was perfectly comfortable last night."

I whirl around and give him a *look,* and my issue seems to click in his mind. "But if your boundaries preclude bed sharing," he says, "a makeshift bed of my own sounds more than adequate. As long as I'm with you, I could sleep on a bed of molten coals beneath a blanket of thorns, and I'd cry out not in pain, but in ecstasy."

I shove a bundle of blankets into his arms in response, and, with me ducking my head so he can't see my furious blushing, we lug the bedding and a blow-up mattress to my room.

"By the way," I say as we walk. "For the next . . . until I say so, it's really important that nobody knows you're here. So if you could be quiet if people are around, and stay inside, that'd be really helpful. And necessary."

"Oh." Weston gives a small jump to adjust his grip on the blankets. "Why?"

"Because . . . because you could be in danger if anyone sees you," I answer. I mean, it's the truth. "No one expects you to be here."

Weston scoffs. "Ivy, if there are dangerous people around, I don't want you speaking to them alone."

"They're not dangerous to me."

"You don't know that. Anyone can betray you at any time. I thought I was safe with Matthew Judas, until he turned out to be working for the shadow demons!"

Well, on one level, he has a point. I thought Mack would be my friend for the rest of our lives, until she discarded me. On another level, I wouldn't trust someone with "Judas" in his name, so I'm already several steps ahead of Weston in the judge-of-character arena. And even if I was wrong about Mack, I can't be wrong about Henry. There's just no way Henry would ever throw me under the bus.

Speaking of Henry, I still haven't explained my absence to him. While Weston attaches the mattress to its pump, I sit heavily on my bed and shoot Henry a quick text. His response comes almost immediately.

> That sucks! I hope you feel better soon. Do you think Mrs. Rutherford will let us do our oral presentation next lesson instead?

I cringe. I forgot all about our joint presentation. Apparently, it wasn't me who should've been worrying about my best friend throwing me under the bus. It was Henry.

> I'm so sorry!!! Maybe she'll be in a good mood today.
> Stranger things have happened.

> Totally
> Like what

> Shh I'm thinking

Yeah. Henry's screwed. I'm officially the worst friend ever. I'll have to find a way to make it up to him tomorrow, though.

For now, I have Weston Razorbrook in my house. It's literally the dream. Or, at least, it's my dream. And if you have Weston Razorbrook in your house, you don't spend your time texting your friends. You ask Weston Razorbrook every burning question you've ever wanted to know about *H-MAD*. Honestly, I'm doing this for Henry as well as me, anyway. This opportunity is worth failing a thousand oral presentations. Well, maybe not a thousand, because that sounds like the sort of thing that would *really* tank your GPA, but at least several of them.

"Weston," I say. "What's it like? Being thrust into a position of power and responsibility, when all you wanted to do was complete a modeling job?"

Weston rests his elbow on his knee, looking deep in thought. "Well," he says, "at the time, it was the biggest change in perspective I ever had. Dwarfed only by the experience of falling in love." He locks eyes with me intensely at that, and I find myself blushing, to my chagrin.

"And," I go on hurriedly, "I've always wondered. Why do you always use your air powers on the ground?"

"How do you mean?" Weston asks.

"You're always wielding them like they're a gun or something. But you never use them to do out-of-the-box things, like flying, or stealing the air from your enemy's lungs so they can't breathe. Stuff like that."

Weston stares at me with bulging eyes. "Your mind," he says. "It fascinates me. You know, I think it's possible you're a genius, Ivy. I really do."

"Oh," I say, flushing hotter still. "No. Henry had the same question."

"Who?"

"My friend. It doesn't matter. I just . . . can you show me?" I ask in a rush. "Your air powers?"

Weston grins, like it's the most flattering thing I could've possibly asked of him. "Of course," he says, straightening. "In fact, here's the perfect vessel. We have no need for a pump. I can fill this mattress by hand."

I shuffle forward to get a better view and watch eagerly as Weston holds out his palm toward the mattress.

We stay like that for several silent seconds.

Nothing happens. "My . . . my powers," Weston says haltingly. Then, with a gasp, he drops to his knees as though his legs gave out beneath him. "They've been stolen," he says in a thin voice, eyes wide and wild.

I climb off the bed and crawl to his side, grabbing his hands in mine. "Weston, breathe. It's okay. Don't jump to conclusions."

"What other conclusion *is there*?"

Good question. This has never been a storyline on the show, so I don't have much to go off of here.

But Weston is doubled over gasping for air now, and I think he's hyperventilating, and I am a fanfic writer, right? So . . . write, Ivy, write.

"I heard Vanessa had a similar problem last week," I say.

Weston grips my hands tightly, his eyes bulging. "She did?"

"She didn't tell you because she didn't want to worry you. But it turned out, uh—she'd just overworked herself. After she stayed inside and rested for . . . I don't know, it was a few days, or a week, or something . . . they came back by themselves. I bet the same thing is happening to you."

Weston relaxes his grip on me and falls backward, thumping his back against my bed frame. "Okay," he says. "That makes perfect sense."

As far as reviews go, I think it's just about the best one I've ever gotten. That's not saying much, given that most of my reviews just ask for an update and then gently criticize my poor spelling and grammar, but still.

"Don't feel like you need to verify this with Vanessa or anything," I say. Oh, good line, because *that* doesn't sound suspicious.

Luckily for me, Weston doesn't notice. "I wouldn't, anyway. I have no interest in speaking to Vanessa."

Now, this is news to me. "You don't?"

Weston runs a hand down his face to collect himself, then draws his knees up. "God, no. She's bland, she's never around when you need her . . . overall, she's useless, and I don't know why I ever liked her."

I stare at him for a long time before breaking into a delighted laugh. I tip my head back until it hits the edge of my mattress. "Oh man," I say. "I think I just fell in love with you a little bit."

"I love you, too," Weston says immediately.

"Okay, buddy," I say. "Take me to dinner first, okay?" I pause. "Wait, do you eat?"

I realize too late that it's not the sort of question you ask a human, which Weston, by all accounts, thinks he is. And for all I know, he might be right. What is a human, anyway?

Weston furrows his brow. "Why wouldn't I?"

"Why wouldn't you!" I agree brightly. "You're real, after all. You've got a physical mass. Chances are you've got a functioning stomach."

"Right on all counts," Weston says calmly, like this is a perfectly normal conversation. It's not going to be nearly as hard to keep him from being suspicious as I feared.

"Do you like pancakes?" I ask.

"I love them."

"Great. Do you like burned pancakes? Just checking in advance, because I can't guarantee anything here."

Weston gets to his feet, then helps me to mine. As my eyes

become level with his, he grins. "I can make pancakes," he says. "Come on."

I soon find out three things about Weston. One, he has an almost supernatural ability to make the perfect golden pancake stack, which is, I might add, something I've always thought was very important in a life partner. Two, he shares my preferences in toppings exactly: lemon and sugar, followed closely by maple syrup. The real kind. Three, he cleans as he cooks, which, as a self-confessed slob, is exactly the kind of person I need in my life. The peanut butter to my jelly, shall we say?

Not that I'm getting ahead of myself or anything.

While Weston cheerfully mixes the pancake batter, I ask him to stay quiet while I go down to the other end of the house to give my parents a call. I'm pretty sure Mom's going to send over the FBI if I don't get back to her soon, judging by the state of my texts.

"Ivy, my god," she cries when she picks up. "Did you *just* wake up? Mack's going to be there any second to pick you up."

"Morning," I say, already feeling a headache coming on. That's good. It makes the next part less of a lie. "I didn't just get up, but I'm actually feeling really sick, Mommy."

The "mommy" part is blatant emotional manipulation, but right now, I couldn't care less.

"What? What's wrong?" Mom's voice is sharp and concerned, rather than suspicious, which is a good sign. Clearly, I've cultivated a relationship of honesty and trust with my parents. If I weren't so desperate, I might feel so overcome with guilt I couldn't continue. But as it stands . . .

"It's my period," I say in a small, pathetic tone. "The cramps are really bad today."

"Oh no, again?" Mom sighs. "Oh, honey. We need to take

you to the doctor about that. That's the second month in a row. I left you bananas. They should help with the cramps. Have you had a banana yet?"

"Not yet."

"I want you to eat a banana right now. Two, even. Two bananas, minimum."

"I'm not hungry," I lie, because I can't exactly tell her about the pancake feast being prepared down the hall.

"*Ivy.* You can't just not eat breakfast. You won't be able to focus on your schoolwork."

Okay, it's time to spell it out. She is not gonna like this. "I can't go in to school, Mom."

"Ivy . . ." Okay, now there's a note of suspicion. "The *first day*?"

"I promise I'm not lying," I lie. "It feels like my uterus is eating itself. And I'm nauseous. And I have a headache."

"Okay, okay," Mom says. "You can stay home. But I'm trusting you here, Ivy. If this becomes a pattern while we're away, we are gonna have a problem."

Well, it won't be the biggest one in my life at the moment, so. "Thank you."

"Do you have ibuprofen? Something for lunch?"

"Yeah. Both."

In fact, Weston has a whole suite of medication at the ready for my personal use, should I need it. Something tells me this information wouldn't comfort her, though.

"If you run out of pads, there's more in the en suite drawer. Is everything okay otherwise?"

The lies. They just keep building. "Yeah, no disasters at all."

"All right, honey. How was last night? Did Henry come over? What did you two have for dinner? Did you finish your presentation?"

"Yeah, we—"

"Oh, the presentation. You won't be able to go in for that. Ivy, honey, let me call the school. I'll tell them you need your presentation date moved."

I snort. "Mrs. Rutherford won't be down for that."

"Well, *Mrs. Rutherford* can kick rocks. I'll tell her that myself."

"Don't do that, Mom. It'll just make her pick on me more."

"Well, let me know if she moves the date. If she doesn't, I *will* call her tomorrow, Ivy. In real life, sometimes you get sick. Sometimes you have your period. Sometimes you get a *headache*. And you shouldn't be failed simply because—"

"Hey, Mack's just knocked on the door," I lie yet again for good measure. "I better go tell her I'm not going in."

"Okay, baby. Love you. I'll give you a call around lunchtime to see how you're feeling. *Don't forget the bananas.*"

All right, all right.

Hopefully Weston likes his pancakes topped with fruit.

The rest of the day passes in a bizarre sort of haze. I give Weston a tour of the house—which he already inexplicably turns out to know his way around—serve him leftover casserole for lunch, and teach him to play *Mario Kart*—another skill he already seems to possess. He beats me almost exactly 50 percent of the time. After that, I decide it's time for a mindless movie, to give me the chance to clear my mind and attempt to process all of this.

In fact, Weston and I are just sitting on my bed to watch a rom-com on my laptop—romance movies, it turns out, are his favorite—when a surprise knock on the front door echoes down the hall.

"Wait here," I say to Weston. "I'll be one minute."

Weston, apparently much less concerned for my safety than he was this morning after a whole day of successfully keeping me alive, nods brightly before turning his attention back to the screen.

Mack has come bearing gifts. A tub of thick, steaming soup, to be exact. Apparently her parents just couldn't help themselves. I have to admit, I'm a mixture of touched and guilty for lying. Not to Mack, but to her parents, even if indirectly.

"I dunno if you're feeling better, or whatever," Mack says as she hands the tub to me. "But here."

"Tell your parents thank you for me, please," I say. "Seriously."

"Sure."

We stand there in an awkward silence. As much as I want to get rid of her and rush back to Weston—it isn't, after all, every day you get to hang out with your favorite character—it feels a step *too* rude to shut the door in her face after she brought soup for me. Even if it wasn't technically her kind gesture. "Did I miss much today?" I ask. When in doubt, small talk always works.

"You missed your presentation," she says with a shrug.

"Wait, did Henry have to do it alone?" I ask, aghast.

Mack doesn't quite roll her eyes, but she *does* look to the sky, which is close enough. "He was fine."

Oh, that was a *tone*. "What?"

"*What?*"

"You rolled your eyes."

"I did not roll my eyes, Ivy."

"You did. You rolled your eyes because I was worried about Henry."

"No. But you are a little obsessed with him."

I gape in outrage. "I am *not* obsessed with him!"

"He survived without you. That's what normal people do, Ivy, they can get through stuff without their friends holding their hands the whole time."

"Oh, *oh*, right, because this is about me and my flaws."

"No, it couldn't be that, because you don't have any flaws, as we've established many times."

I can't believe I even *thought* about wishing we could make up this morning. Clearly I was in shock. "Oh my god. Cool. Thanks for the soup, Mack."

"You're welcome, though, to be honest, you sure don't sound sick."

"I was *so* sick, I was basically on death's door, actually, and—"

"Ivy?" Weston calls from a distance. "It's been well over a minute. You okay?"

Mack's eyes flick sharply in the direction of his voice. God, I was so close. *So close.* Although, I'm becoming less and less sure there is a god at all. Or maybe humans have been the gods all along? Either way, my grip on reality is fast unraveling, and I truly do not need another wrench in the works.

"That's not Henry," Mack says, mostly to herself. I see the cogs working in her brain. If I have a guy here, and it's not Henry, and I've been home all day, with my parents out of the house . . .

I panic. "Uh, no, it's . . . WAIT, I'LL BE THERE IN A MINUTE, DON'T COME OUT, OKAY?"

"Okay, babe!"

I turn back to Mack with the most pleasant, nothing-is-wrong-here grin I can muster. Mack's eyes are so round I can see the full, dark circles of her irises. "Wait, is *this* why you didn't come to school today?" she demands.

"It's complicated, so let's never bring this up again, okay? Thanks for the soup—"

"My mom made you soup because you wanted to turn your house into a sex cave the day your parents leave?" Mack's gritting her teeth so hard a muscle in her jaw has popped out.

"Okay, one, oh my god, keep your voice down. Number two, it's not a sex cave, it's just a friend."

"Who? You've only got one friend."

"I do not. Anyway, you don't know him."

"I know everyone."

Annoyingly, it's the truth. I can't remember the last time I met someone in person for the first time, and I'm nowhere near as outgoing as Mack. Small-town problems.

"I met him online, okay?" I say, a little desperately. "He lives in Southfield."

As far as cover stories go, it's the most realistic one I've thought of yet. Southfield is about twenty minutes away. Far enough that Mack could conceivably not know someone from there, but close enough that someone from the town might pop on over if their crush's parents were ever in Los Angeles. For example.

Mack looks extremely annoyed at this, but she doesn't seem to disbelieve me. She's probably just jealous she doesn't have a girlfriend from Southfield she can have a sexy secret rendezvous with. Or whatever she assumes is happening here. "So, I'll just be getting back to him, then," I say, when Mack refuses to fill in the awkward silence.

Mack sweeps her arms to the sides. "By all means."

"Thank you."

"You should probably try to make it to school tomorrow, though," she says coolly. "I'm not going to lie for you."

"I didn't ask you to," I say.

"Good."

"*Amazing*." I close the door quickly before Mack can reply so, technically, I get the last word in.

Okay, so. A minor speed bump, but I'm pretty sure Mack bought my story.

One thing's for sure, though. If I don't want Mack storming around here with her very disappointed parents tomorrow, I'd better have a miraculous recovery from my mysterious illness slash period cramps.

Which means I have to leave Weston here alone.

But he can cook, he can clean, he can follow instructions, more or less. By all accounts, he's at least as competent at keeping himself safe and alive as I am, and my parents barely hesitated to leave me alone.

What could go wrong?

Chapter Six

PAST

"You know," Mack says, nodding at Henry Paramar across the school hallway. He's talking with a girl from the grade below us, and she's flirting with him about as subtly as Mack flirts with Brianna. "At least half the girls on the team have had a crush on Henry at some point, and I have come to the conclusion that I do not understand the standards of straight women."

"What's not to understand?" I ask, and Mack adopts an expression of intense concentration.

"Well," she says, "I always thought the ideal hetero guy is, like, super jacked, and broad-shouldered, and really cocky or whatever. But that guy looks like some sort of magical woodland nymph or something."

A grin touches the corner of her mouth when I break out in laughter. "What?" she demands. "Am I wrong?"

"I think lots of girls like that look," I say when I compose myself. "I see the appeal."

"Explain it to me."

"He's pretty. He's symmetrical, his jaw could cut glass, he's got those loose black curls. I mean, I could be misleading you here, because I like the androgynous look, but it's not just me."

"Clearly."

"Look at Timothée Chalamet." I shrug. "He could totally be a faerie prince, and girls go crazy for him."

"I used to have a crush on Timothée Chalamet," Mack says.

"Was that an actual crush, though, or was it compulsory heterosexuality?" I muse.

"Oh, the second, definitely the second."

"Exactly."

"I get being attracted to prettiness," Mack says. "I can relate to that."

"Lots of straight girls love pretty," I say. "Plus, he's super sweet and approachable."

"Is that your type?" Mack asks lightly.

"Um, I don't know. Probably, I guess?"

"In-ter-esting," Mack says, but I don't really get what's so in-ter-esting about it.

Before I can ask, Mrs. Rutherford passes us and stops in her tracks. "Girls, get to class," she says. "What are you standing around for?"

I notice at that moment most of the hallway has emptied out. Henry Paramar and his girl-of-the-day included. Mack and I mutter hurried apologies and set off to class at a jog.

"Hey," I say, changing the subject before I run out of time to bring it up. "Tickets to the *H-MAD* convention in the city go up tomorrow. Are you still okay to go with me?"

Mack picks at one of her nails. "Sure."

"Okay. I mean, you don't have to," I say quickly.

"You've said that so many times now, you're making me think you don't want me there," Mack says. There's a sudden edge to her voice, and I backpedal as fast as I can.

"Of course I want you there. I definitely do. I just . . . they're expensive tickets, so . . ."

"You only want me to commit if I'm actually going to commit," Mack finishes for me, and I nod, relieved. "I get it. Yeah, of course I'll go with you."

We walk a few steps in silence, then Mack says, carefully, "Who else would you go with if I didn't go, anyway?"

I think carefully as we start ascending the stairs. "No one, I guess. I'd just skip it."

Mack shakes her head, frowning. "That's not happening. We're getting you to that conference."

I know she doesn't want to go. I'm not completely dense. But I love her for going anyway.

After all, like she said, if she doesn't, who would?

PRESENT

The next morning, I wake up to find, to my surprise, yesterday was not just a dream. I guess at some point, sooner or later, this is going to have to stop feeling like an impossible thing, but for now, my brain is still resisting my reality.

Weston blinks blearily in his nest, where he's lying cocooned in the blankets we piled on it together yesterday. When he stretches and kicks the blankets down, I notice he's wearing an entirely new outfit today; a black button-down shirt, a sterling silver necklace, and charcoal cargo pants. Yesterday's clothes are nowhere to be seen. Presumably, they've gone wherever it was Weston came from in the first place. Another dimension? Thin air? Energy converting itself into new forms at the whims of the universe? I'm pretty sure it's one of the above.

"Good morning," Weston says, smiling up at me. "I have to say, I've woken up to worse views."

I'm sure he means it as a compliment, but it only reminds me that I'm makeup-free, with bed hair and drool on my pillowcase. I'm wearing my nicest pajamas at least—a checkered, pastel green shorts set—but they're still, you know, pajamas. My cheeks heating, I lift my hands to smooth my hair down (it gets way messier overnight than it used to now it isn't weighed down by all that length), and that's when a black mark on the soft underside of my wrist catches my eye.

Someone's written something there.

Ivy? Is scrawled in black cursive, complete with a question mark and all. I'm not sure why the question mark is necessary. Was whoever graffitied me not 100 percent sure about my name?

"Did you write this on me?" I ask, brandishing my wrist. Weston glances at it, then gives me an indulgent look, like a parent whose child just said something both idiotic and endearing all at once.

"It's your soul mate marking," he says.

"My soul mate marking," I repeat flatly. Of course it is. Sure, why not? It's no weirder than anything else that's been going down.

"Yes," Weston says, mistaking my tone for confusion. "It's the markings that appear on the skin of those who are bound to another at birth. They bear the first words spoken to the host by their soul mate. It's how soul mates recognize each other upon their first meeting."

"Yeah, I'm familiar with the concept," I say. As is anyone who's even briefly glanced at a fanfiction website. "But aren't you meant to be born with those markings?"

"Yes."

"I didn't have this yesterday."

"I suppose you've never noticed it before," Weston says by way of explanation. He makes a great point. Seems perfectly logical to me. "I have one, too."

He rolls up his sleeve, revealing his own tattoo-like marking. Inexplicably, his is written in my handwriting. I'd recognize it anywhere. It reads:

Holy fuck, holy shit, what the fuck?

"Yesterday, you spoke those very words to me. You know what that means, right?"

Well, by way of deduction, I can be pretty sure it means Weston and I are soul mates. I think. Or not, given I definitely didn't have this tattoo yesterday. But I'm pretty sure it's what he's implying either way.

I realize that, since Weston was wearing a jacket all day yesterday, it's entirely possible he was, in a manner of speaking, born with this tattoo, as is the case with soul mate markings in all the fanfics I've read about them. A fanfic I *wrote* once, even. I guess he did remove the jacket for those few brief moments, and his arms would've been bare then, but I was in way too much shock to notice whether he had a tattoo on his wrist. So, if he *did* have those words on his arm when he sprang into existence—before I'd had the chance to utter them—then that means free will is also an illusion.

No problem. I'll add it to the list of broken things.

He's looking at me expectantly, so I give him a small smile. "That we're soul mates?" I offer.

He breaks into a grin. "You said it, not me."

I get to my feet and start putting together an outfit for the day. "And, so, what if we are?" I ask as I work my way through my wardrobe. "Yesterday was kind of wild, so I didn't really get a chance to ask this, but where do we go from here? If you're staying . . . here, instead of going . . . back home"—another dimension, presumably—"what does that mean for you? Where will you work? Where would you live?"

Weston takes a long time to answer. Long enough that I turn

around to check on him. He's staring at me with a troubled expression. "Do you . . . not want me here?" he asks finally.

I shake my head frantically. "It's not like that. It's just, realistically, my parents are going to be home in a few days, and there's no way in hell they're gonna let me have a guy stay here. I *do* want you around. But I don't know what that would . . . mean."

I also don't know how much of a choice I'll get in the matter. Yesterday was dreamlike enough that the future didn't feel important. If I'm honest, I expected that I would wake up to find Weston vanished, with little to no proof he was ever here. But he *is* here, and even though I'm not exactly mad about it, it raises some questions. Does that mean he's going to be around forever now? And if so, will he be with *me* forever? I *am* the reason he's here at all, so, it sort of seems that way. It's all a little overwhelming to think about, but I know I need to, or my parents are going to come back from their trip to find me fostering a glowing blue teenager, and I can't see that working out for anyone involved.

Weston, at least, appears to take the question seriously. He frowns, then runs a fingertip over the tattoo on his arm. "That," he says, "will be my task for the day. I will solve this conundrum for the two of us. Please don't concern yourself with it, Ivy. Nothing as simple as accommodation or income or the law can keep the two of us apart. We're fated. Written in the stars."

It's hard to argue his point given the circumstances. In any case, it's something I'm going to have to leave with him, because I need to get to school. I explained that to him last night, and he assured me he'd be more than fine here, but now that I'm faced with leaving him, all I can think of is what can go wrong. What if one of the Gleasons see movement in the house and investigate? What if Weston snoops around and discovers all my

H-MAD stuff and has a breakdown? What if he wanders off? How am I going to make it through eight whole hours without knowing for sure?

Unless I don't have to.

Struck by a sudden brain wave, I run to the study and dig through the cabinet near Mom's desktop computer. When I find what I'm looking for—Dad's old phone, and its charger—I bring it back upstairs with a sense of victory.

Weston regards me with curiosity as I start up the phone. "You know how to use these, right?" I ask.

"Of course," Weston says. "It's a y-Phone."

"Close enough." Thank god *H-MAD* is a contemporary fantasy. He understands phones, money, the general structure of American society. Maybe it won't be too hard to settle him into a life here in the long term.

Luckily, y-Phones seem to function much like regular phones, because Weston has no problem following my hurried tutorial. In the end, I use an old burner email of mine to quickly create him his own social media account under the name John Doe for easy direct messaging, given there's no credit on the phone, and it's not on a plan anymore.

"As long as you're connected to Wi-Fi," I tell him, "we can reach each other."

"Thank goodness," Weston says. "I don't know how I would go eight hours without hearing your voice."

"You won't hear my voice. I can't call, only message."

"Well, it'll tide me over, I suppose."

I can't help but give a self-conscious grin at that. I have to admit, it's *nice* to have someone so eager to be around me. It almost makes me consider skipping school again. Almost.

"I need you to promise me something," I say seriously.

"Anything." He clasps both of my hands in his, his skin

warm against mine. He touches me so freely, like we've known each other forever. I guess, for him, we sort of have.

"There's . . ." I consider my words. "A lot going on that you don't understand. I want to explain it, but there's no time. You have to trust me."

"I would follow you blindly over the edges of the earth itself, Ivy."

"Well, that's physically impossible, because the earth's actually round, and . . . not the point. Weston, I know I said this last night, but seriously, I need you to stay in this house until I return. Don't leave no matter *what*." I pause. "Unless there's a fire or something, then you can go outside to avoid the flames or whatever you need to do, but only, like, fifteen feet away at most. And *only* if there's a fire. But also, please don't start any fires to get around the promise."

"I don't start fires, that's Vanessa's element."

"Right. And Vanessa barely starts any fires, because she's useless."

"Completely useless, Ivy, that's right."

There's that loving feeling again. Maybe all I ever wanted in a partner all along is someone who hates the same things—and people—that I do. Maybe that's what love is at its core, and no one ever acknowledges that, because it sounds sort of mean-spirited. It's not something I'd ever include in a romance novel, but maybe in real life, love plays out differently from fiction.

"We agree, then," I say.

Weston raises our joined hands to his chest and looks deep into my eyes. "Our souls were crafted of one. There is nothing you could believe that I have not already determined myself."

"So, you get it's important to stay inside?"

"If you believe it is, it must be."

"Okay." That sounds promising to me. "Also, I want you to take a new photo of yourself every fifteen minutes, and send it to me. Just to show me you're still all right. Can you do that?"

Weston's smirk is undeniably flirty. "Is this your way of telling me you'll miss me?"

I might have been joking about the love thing, but if he keeps talking like this, he'll be my first crush since Mack, guaranteed. Fighting another smile, I remove my hands from his.

"It's my way of begging you to do exactly what I'm asking you to do, no questions asked."

"Ivy," Weston says. "I will start not one fire. I will wander not outside. I will take a photo every second—"

"That's probably a bit excessive."

"—and send it to you as proof of my continued safety. Is that all?"

"There's some casserole in the fridge if you get hungry."

"Oh, wonderful, I love casserole!"

"I'll try to get you some, um . . . protein . . . salad . . . after school," I say. Truthfully, I'm not entirely sure what people like Weston eat to look like he does, but that sounds about right.

"Oh, don't trouble yourself," Weston says. "I'll just eat whatever you're eating tonight. It takes literally zero effort to look like this."

"That seems fake."

"Have you seen me eat a vegetable?" he asks. "Or go to the gym?"

I think through the *H-MAD* episodes. "Well, no, but fantasy adventure stuff looks pretty tiring. You do a lot of walking. And you wave your arms a lot when you're lassoing the wind."

"I do. But even in my off weeks it just . . ." He raps a knuckle against his washboard abs.

Why do I doubt it comes quite that easily to Chase Mancini?

I don't have time to argue the point, though. In fact, I barely manage to throw some clothes on and brush my teeth before Zeke beeps outside. Maybe they figured if Mack doesn't come to the door this morning, I won't have a chance to make an excuse to get out of school. With one last plea to Weston, I take a deep breath and jog to the car like it's an ordinary morning.

Zeke turns his music down when I slide in the back seat and beams at me. "Ivy! How have you been? It's been a thousand years."

Mack glances at me in the rearview mirror. I have no idea what she's told her family about our friendship breakup, if anything. "Uh, you know, same old," I say.

Bar one or two small changes.

"I was looking forward to seeing you yesterday, hearing about what's new and all that. You broke my heart." He says it in a casual way that makes it clear his disappointment was mild and fleeting at worst, and his eyes are glinting the way Mack's do whenever she's gently ribbing someone she knows well. In a weird way, it means a lot that even after a year of barely speaking, Zeke still feels familiar enough with me to tease.

"Sorry about that," I say. "I didn't mean to hold you up."

"Nah, you didn't. Besides, you were sick. You couldn't have planned it."

"True," I say weakly. Mack sighs audibly, and digs through her backpack for something. At least she didn't contradict me.

"You feeling better?" Zeke asks.

"Yeah, much."

"It's because you spent all day in bed, I bet," Mack says with an edge to her voice. "Fastest way to get over something is to get under . . . the covers. Isn't that what they say?"

I'm never forgiving Mom and Dad for forcing me into a car with Mack every morning this week. They could've left me money for a cab and saved my sanity. I shoot her a death glare in the mirror, but don't dignify her jab with a response.

When I find Henry, I launch into another apology for abandoning him for the presentation. I already apologized a ton over messages last night, but it feels like an in-person-apology sort of screwup.

"You have nothing to apologize for," Henry insists. "You can't help being sick."

That's true. But I could help being a lying liar, and I went ahead and did that anyway. I'm an awful friend, and an awful person, and I'm hiding Weston in my house, and I haven't even told Henry, the person who would *most* want to know that information, all because I'm scared it might go badly.

"Hey, did you see Chase is gonna announce something soon?" Henry asks. "What do you think? I was thinking maybe a renewal, but usually they don't announce that so early, right?"

It takes me an embarrassingly long time to catch up. Right. Chase Mancini did that announcement thingy yesterday. Sure. "I don't know," I say, a little vague. Maybe I should ask Weston. Is that the sort of thing he'd know? No, he'd know fictional things, right? Not production information. He doesn't even know he's *part* of a production.

Henry gives me a funny look before launching into his other theories, which include a guest appearance, a musical episode, and—most exciting of all—a potential movie. I should be excited. I should be theorizing along with him. Instead, I keep dwelling on everything I'm not telling him. That, and what Weston is up to at home without me.

By midday's history class, I'm just about ready to crack. All I can think about is Weston, and how this happened, and what's going to happen next, and I don't know the answers to any of it. I'm desperate to tell Henry and ask for his advice. Like all things with me, apparently, I can't face this alone.

So, I decide, Henry needs to know. I'll have to bring him home to meet Weston first, though. If I tell him at school, I'll just sound like I'm either delusional or playing the world's strangest prank. Henry might be good-natured, but that doesn't mean he's naive. He'll need proof.

"Ivy?" Henry whispers under his breath. "Are you sure you're feeling better today?"

I blink back into the present. "Yeah, I'm fine. Why?"

"Oh, no reason, except for the fact that you're pale enough to blend in with the walls."

"I'm fine, promise," I whisper back, which is, I guess, yet another lie. But as far as lies go, "I'm fine" is famously up there with the most common and least offensive, as long as it isn't followed up by an overreaction. Less of a lie, really, and more of a time-buyer.

Henry, apparently, buys the lie, and goes back to his essay outline. I do, too, keeping an eye on our teacher, Mrs. Rutherford. When she approaches Viktor to help him with a question and her back's turned, I whip out my phone from my pocket and check it. To my relief, there's a new photo from Weston in my messages. He's smoldering in the bathroom mirror, and has taken a photo of his reflection. There's a message waiting beneath it, too.

> Every hour without you stretches out thinner and thinner, like a piece of gum long enough to wrap itself around the hearts of every lover in the world.

No one's ever written me poetry before.

I don't have time to reply to it, though, because Mrs. Rutherford glances back up. Not before I shove my phone back in my pocket, though.

So far, so good.

A few minutes later, Mrs. Rutherford is distracted again, and I'm not the only one who notices.

"Ivy," Henry whispers. He's digging through his bag with a furrowed brow, and at first I think he's looking for something. Then he indicates for me to take a look, and I duck down beside him to find my own face staring back at me. Henry's holding his phone inside his bag, away from the prying eyes of Mrs. Rutherford. Henry makes a horrific face at the camera, and I dutifully roll my eyes back as far as they'll go. I'm pleased to see only the whites visible in the photo.

I return to my work, watching Henry out of the corner of my eye as he continues to busy himself in his bag. I guess he's posting the selfie online somewhere. If he doesn't hurry up and finish, Mrs. Rutherford's going to catch on, though. I clear my throat once, then again, louder. Henry glances up now, and, at my pointed look, reemerges from his bag. Keeping an eye on Mrs. Rutherford in my peripherals, I check the post as subtly as I can on my own phone.

It's not subtle enough.

"Ivy," Mrs. Rutherford snaps, and I jump a mile. I look up at her guiltily, and she holds her hand out. With the whole class's eyes trailing after me, I get up and do the walk of shame across the classroom to hand my phone over.

"You can pick this up after class," she says. "I don't know why you bother. There's nothing important enough it can't wait until after class. And I *will* catch you. I *always* catch you."

She didn't catch Henry. But, it's true. She will always catch *me*. She has a sixth sense for it. All teachers do.

As I head back to my seat, Mack stares me down. I can almost hear her thoughts from here. *What did you think was going to happen?*

"Why is she so obsessed with you?" Henry mutters as quietly as he can, apparently sharing my sentiment. "Put less effort in, woman, it's really not that serious. What is she doing here, vying for principal of the school?"

Needless to say, by the time the period's over, I'm a mess of nerves, after managing to visualize no fewer than ten catastrophic things that might have happened to Weston without me.

Luckily, I don't have to check my messages without Henry seeing, because he immediately announces he needs the bathroom. I urge him to go on ahead, check the halls for a teacher, and then angle my body against the wall so I can check my messages somewhat out of view. There's several photos waiting from Weston. I open and flip through them. Kitchen selfie, living room selfie . . . oh no. Front door selfie.

Below the last photo is a message from Weston.

> I got your distress message. Help is coming. Hold on.

Distress message?

Wait, Weston is coming? Here? To school?

Looking exactly like Chase Mancini?

Okay. Cool.

There's a dozen ways this can end and none of them are good.

Chapter Seven

PAST

I can tell from Mack's face when she meets me at the school gates that something's wrong. She doesn't beat around the bush, either. Just jumps straight into the bad news.

"Something happened," she says. "I thought Brianna's birthday lunch was next Saturday, but it's actually tomorrow. I got confused."

Tomorrow. *Tomorrow.* She can't be serious, can she? My stomach clenches. "Okay . . ." I say, making her spell it out. I know exactly where it's going, even if I can't believe it.

"I'm so sorry, Ivy," she says. "I committed to going already."

I keep my voice even, and icy. "You committed to the conference already."

"You don't understand," Mack pleads. "The whole team's going to be at Brianna's lunch."

"It's a lunch."

"A lunch plus an afternoon at Sky Zone."

"Oh, well that changes everything," I snap.

"It's basically a whole day, Ivy," Mack says. "If I'm not there, I'll miss out on so much. It'll affect my chances of getting captain next year."

"Bullshit," I cry, and Mack stares at me, shocked.

"What?"

"Bull. Shit," I say. "One birthday lunch won't stop you from making captain. You just don't want to come to the conference. You want to spend the day hanging out with your fun friends."

Mack looks hurt, and then she darkens. "That's not true."

"Of course it is," I say. "You can't tell me you wanted to go to the conference. I know you didn't."

She doesn't disagree, because she can't. It'd be lying.

"And now there's something you want to do more. You have to choose between hanging out with Brianna and the girls and jumping around, or following me around bored out of your brain. Of course you're going to choose that."

"It's not that I want to go to the lunch, I have to go," Mack says. "And besides, I'm not bored out of my brain with you, Ivy. I wouldn't have said yes to the conference if it was like that."

"But you did say yes," I say. "And now it's tomorrow, and you're backing out, and now, what, I just can't go?"

"You can still go. You don't need me."

I glare at her. She knows I can't do something like that alone. She knows it. She didn't meet me yesterday. Just because she can't see the big deal about doing something like this alone is not a good enough reason to abandon me.

"You can have my ticket," she adds a little desperately when I don't reply. "Maybe you could bring your mom, or . . . someone . . ." Apparently she hears how pathetic that sounds as she says it, because she looks to the ceiling and steels herself. "You know what? You're right. I'm sorry. I'll tell Brianna I made a commitment to you."

But it's too late. Tomorrow's ruined either way now. Either I miss out on it, or I force Mack to come with me and she resents me for it the whole time, and I'll know she's resenting me the whole time.

"No," I say firmly. "I don't want you to come."

"You don't want me to come?"

"Yup." I set my jaw. "I'm not going with you tomorrow, so you might as well go hang with Brianna."

"What is your preoccupation with Brianna? It's not just her. It's the whole team."

"Okay, go hang with the whole team, then. Either way, you're uninvited to the conference."

Mack gives me a pitying look. "So, now you're throwing a tantrum?"

"Screw you," I snap. "And, by the way, next time you don't want to do something with me, just tell me up front. To my face. Don't pretend to commit to it and hope something better comes along."

"I never said I didn't want to do it."

"No, this is totally the behavior of someone who really wants to hang with me." I scowl. "You know what? It's fine. The conference would've sucked with you anyway. You would've been bored the whole time, and you would've ruined it for me."

Mack throws her hands in the air. "Then why did you even invite me?"

"Because I don't have anybody else."

I don't mean it to come out the way it sounds. But once I say it, it's out there. And I don't know how to take it back, because it's true. I don't have anybody else. That's not why I want to hang out with Mack—not even close to why—but facts are facts.

"Nice, Ivy," Mack says coldly. "Maybe if you tried making conversation with people once in a while, you wouldn't have to resort to me. Have fun at the conference. Or don't. Either way, I will have fun with people who actually want me there, even when they have other options."

With that, she turns her back on me and storms into the school building, leaving me staring after her in shock.

PRESENT

Pushing down a wave of desperate panic, I try calling Weston on the app, but there's no answer. It doesn't take me too long to figure out why. Duh. He's off the Wi-Fi by now. I try him again on Dad's old number, but he won't pick up. I don't even know if the phone's off silent, now that I think of it. I didn't bother to go over that in this morning's tutorial. Stupid, stupid, *stupid*.

I power-walk into the hallway, joining the throng of students, and speed against the grain. I dodge and weave, trying to make it to the entrance while also listening out for any screams of surprise or joy that might indicate a student's spotted a B-list celebrity at our school. But nothing seems out of the ordinary.

I'm almost at the door when someone grabs my arm to slow me down.

"Ivy?"

Of *course* it's Mack. "Oh my god, stop stalking me, please!" I exclaim, wrenching my arm back. I've seen her more in the last two days than I have in the last *year*, and not only does it wrench my heart apart every time I talk to her and see the disdain in her eyes, but it's making it extremely hard to keep the world's biggest secret a freaking *secret*.

Mack drops her arm to her side, and has the gall to look wounded. "I was just wondering where you're going."

"This way."

"I can see tha—Wait, Ivy!"

"If I tell you, you'll tell your parents," I say as I continue down the hall. Unfortunately, Mack takes it upon herself to follow me.

"I didn't tell them about your sex thing yesterday, did I?" Mack asks.

"You might as well have told Zeke this morning."

"Yeah, but that's *Zeke*," Mack says. "Who's he gonna tell, the IT club? And I wouldn't tell Zeke about something important like this."

"What makes you think something important's happening?" I ask.

Mack shrugs. "You look kind of like you did the day you lost your diary."

"It wasn't a diary," I snap. "It was a fictional story with fictional people having fictional romances. I just didn't want anyone reading my work before it was ready."

"Right, but one of the characters was, like, one thousand percent based on Alice Kennedy, though. And the main character *was* called Evie."

What, I can't call a character a *vaguely* similar name to my own without it automatically being a stand-in for me? "What's your point, Mack?"

She slows her step, her arms hanging helplessly by her sides. "My point is, is everything okay?"

Of course. Of *course* she picks today of all days to be an actual, caring human being toward me.

She picks up speed again and turns around to face me. She's slowing me down, and every second counts right now, but I am not going to lose my cool.

"I'm fine, I just have an urgent thing to take care of."

"What sort of thing?"

"A none-of-your-business thing. Besides, if you don't know, you have plausible deniability if your parents grill you. It's win-win."

As far as I'm concerned, it's a flawless argument. And yet, Mack continues to follow me, even as I charge out the entrance and down the steps.

"Yeah, so, the thing is, I know you," Mack says wryly. "And I know something's up."

"Then you should also know I can handle it."

"Not while I'm responsible for you."

At this, I lose focus on my find-Weston journey for a second, and stop in my tracks. "Responsible for me?"

"Yeah. Your parents are trusting us to make sure you're okay."

"Uh, no." I laugh. "My parents are trusting *your parents* to intervene if the house burns down. There was nothing in the job description about sending their kid to do recon on me twenty-four hours a day."

"Huh. Guess I just assumed you'd want it, considering how much you like people's company."

She says it with a smugly raised eyebrow that has me clenching my jaw before she's even finished the sentence. She'll literally never let the conference go, will she?

"I like my *friends'* company," I correct icily.

Without even flinching at the jab, she tips her head to one

side and sticks out her bottom lip. "Maybe if you didn't so obviously require recon, I wouldn't be worried."

"Worried?" I repeat.

"Nosy," Mack corrects quickly.

Yeah, that sounds much more plausible.

We're still too close to the school. If a teacher drives past on their way back from a lunch break or something, it's over for my plan to intercept Weston. I need to get rid of Mack.

The problem is, when Mack gets set on something, it's not easy to get her to let go. Her mind can have a death grip.

"Look," I say. "You've shown zero interest in my life over the past year, there's no need to start now." I nod toward the school to drive my message home. Time for her to *go*. But either Mack doesn't notice, or she just doesn't care. I'm inclined to assume the latter.

"Is that fair?" Mack asks.

"Why wouldn't it be?"

"I haven't exactly had the impression my interest was welcomed," Mack says with a frown.

Right. The thing is, I've hoped Mack might initiate a conversation like this. Preferably, one that ended in some sort of apology from her, given I've yet to receive one. But Weston is going to come around the corner any minute. That is, assuming he took the route I'm familiar with. But he did know his way around my house without needing to be told. It makes sense that he was born with a general sense of direction around my town, given I'm the one who gave life to him. Well, maybe "sense" isn't the right word. Nothing about this makes any goddamn sense. But out of all the theories, that one seems the least bizarre to me.

"Well, today," I say thinly, "your impression is spot-on."

I start walking again, and, finally, Mack doesn't follow me.

"Got it," she mutters, and oh god, she's *hurt*. I can hear it in her voice. Really? *Really?* After a year of verbal sparring, I somehow push things too far by asking for some space? I slow my step, with the intention of softening the blow to Mack, and maybe giving her an open invitation to follow me around, annoying me sometime in the future when I'm not handling a major crisis. But I don't get the chance, because at that moment, Weston rounds the corner.

His sleeves are rolled up to reveal his expletive-ridden soul mate tattoo. His glowing eyes are wild, and his waves are plastered to his forehead from sweat, turning them from an icy blue to an almost desaturated robin's-egg color. He must have sprinted here.

"Ivy!" he shouts. "Are you okay? What's happening?"

"I'm okay, nothing's happening, no one's hurt me," I say quickly, suddenly afraid Weston might put two and two together and assume Mack's the person I apparently need "help" around. And technically, I do, but not the kind of help Weston can give.

Weston jogs up, relief overwhelming his expression, as Mack reaches my side, apparently invested again.

It's all over now. If Weston somehow avoided being spotted on his way over here, now Mack knows everything. Unless I can come up with a good explanation, fast, I'm no longer alone in this. For better or for worse.

And weirdly, I'm relieved about it. Maybe Mack isn't wrong about my need to face new situations with someone else by my side.

I steal a glance at Mack and wait for the confusion. The shock. The accusations.

Mack does have a weird expression on her face, that much is undeniable. But, to my surprise, it's something a lot closer to dislike than disbelief.

"So," Mack says. "This is the guy you had over yesterday?"

I study her as I reply. "Yes."

"And he's back in town already?" Mack says. I don't miss the implication that he spent the night at my house. Which he did, but it's so not the point right now.

"It's not . . . like that," I say.

"We're soul mates," Weston explains helpfully, raising his arm so Mack can take a closer look at it. "We have tattoos to prove it."

Mack's eyebrows shoot up.

"Temporary ones," I lie, hoping to god the words disappear as randomly as they appeared so I don't have to explain them to my parents in a few days. "And we're . . . platonic soul mates. The dude just gets me."

Weston beams at me. Mack folds her arms across her chest. "Uh-huh. And, uh, does 'the dude' have a name?"

"Wes . . . ley," I say. Amazing save. Ten out of ten. Better than John Doe, though, I guess.

"If that's what you want it to be," Weston says with a shrug, not at all suspiciously. Fantastic.

"Cool, and, uh, what's with the eyes, Wesley?" Mack asks coolly. "Are you one of those dress-up people?"

"My eyes?" Weston asks, somewhat confused. "Do you . . . like them?"

"Mack, it's called cosplay, and don't be judgmental," I jump in, and Mack looks suddenly ashamed. Not that I think she should be. I just want to redirect her attention away from *exactly* how much this guy looks like Weston. As in, much more than any normal cosplayer would be able to pull off.

Actually . . . now that I think about it, maybe I *do* want her to notice that. When Weston rounded the corner, I was hit by relief, right? Relief that, suddenly, I wasn't alone in this bizarre life plot twist. So, why the excuses and explanations? Why don't I just tell Mack the truth? She might be my nemesis, but she's also smart, and good in a crisis, and much better at thinking on her feet than I am. I might not like her, but that doesn't necessarily mean I don't trust her. And yes, both can be true at once.

"Mack, do you think there's anything . . . interesting about Wesley?" I ask, a little desperately.

Mack furrows her brow, and I wonder if she's noticed now. She's seen Weston's face on my walls, and phone, and T-shirts enough times to know that this guy is his absolute twin. Does she at least suspect that something's off? She has to, right? She at least has to remark on it.

"Nice shirt," Mack says.

Oh, for *Christ's sake.* The one time Mack chooses to be utterly dense about things.

"Mack!" I cry.

"What?" Mack asks, defensive. "I like the shirt."

I laugh and hold my hands up in surrender. "Don't worry about it. This is obviously normal to you. Don't even worry."

If she doesn't even *notice* how similar Weston looks to, well, himself, she's never going to believe me if I try to tell her the whole story. I'm on my own, still, and the disappointment of that hits surprisingly hard.

"I am so lost," Mack says, and I take the slowest, deepest, most calming breath ever inhaled by a human.

"That," I say, "is evident. Come on Westo—ly. Westerly. Wes . . ."

"Wesley?" Mack supplies.

"*I know his name!*" I screech. "And he and I are leaving. Right now."

Weston, who's been waiting patiently throughout this entire exchange, snaps to attention and follows me like a well-trained collie. The sort of collie that would for sure know all his basic commands. Like *stay*, for example.

Weston had better have a very good explanation for why he did this.

And I had better figure out how the hell I'm going to stop it from happening again, before he gets hurt.

Chapter Eight

PAST

It's coming to the end of history class—which is the last lesson before lunch—and Mack and I still haven't resolved the argument we had at the school gates this morning.

So, what happens now? Normally, I'd head straight down the hall near the nurse's office after history. Mack would meet me halfway to walk to the cafeteria together, even though she has Spanish right now and so the nurse's office isn't even on her way to lunch. It's a routine we've got down to a fine art, and there's a comfort in that. Knowing what to expect.

Today, though, it's all up in the air. Will Mack be by the nurse's office? If not, should I wait for her, in case she just got held up? How long? What if I don't wait, and she is late, and then she gets there and thinks I didn't want to meet her because I'm too mad at her, and I accidentally escalate our whole fight? Or what if she does come, but we're both still too mad to act normal, and we have to go through the motions of our normal routine in icy silence? If that happens, should I be the bigger person and act like nothing's wrong, even though a lot's wrong? Or should I stand my ground, and not be a pushover?

What's more important, our friendship or my principles? Can I have both? I don't know, I don't know, I don't know.

I don't take in a word of history. Luckily, I figure that's not the end of the world, since Mack always says half the stuff taught in class is basically just biased propaganda written by the victors anyway, but I digress.

By the time the bell rings, my stomach's executed a flawless sailor's knot, and my throat feels like it's being pulled toward my gut. Students shove past me in droves as we spill into the hall, but no one stops to ask if I need an ambulance, which I assume means I look much calmer than I feel.

That, or I'm invisible.

As I reach the nurse's office, there's no sign of Mack through the throng. I stand there for a minute, hoping even when I know I shouldn't, scanning for the sight of her voluminous black curls—recently removed from her braids—bobbing through the crowd, or the sky-blue hoodie she wore to school today, or her pristine Jordans.

I don't wait for as long as I planned to when I thought this through in history. Now I'm living it, I know exactly what's up. She's not late. She just doesn't want to see me. Obviously.

As much as I knew there was a good chance this would happen—and as much as I told myself I don't want to see her, either—now that it's happening, it's hitting hard. I'm totally certain, now, that if she had just met me here, I would've happily acted like everything was fine. Hell, I would've even apologized if she'd said she wanted me to, even though I don't think I did anything wrong. I'd have done whatever I needed to in order to hold on to her.

I need to fix this.

By the time I enter the cafeteria, I have a hurried plan in place. I'm going to find Mack in the line and jump in with her, super friendly and casual, and act like I think she just forgot to meet me. Then, if she matches my energy, we'll be fine and we'll never bring this up again. And if she doesn't, I'll tell her I love her and I don't want to fight, and I don't care if she won't come to the conference with me, and then we'll be fine and never bring this up again. It's foolproof. It'll only cost a little of my dignity—to grovel like that after she did something kind of shitty to me—and that's worth it, right?

But as I scan the line, snaking from the heat lamps and food through to the entrance, I realize Mack isn't there, either. For the tiniest, breathless second, I wonder if I was too hasty. Is she waiting for me by the office after all?

That's when I spot her. She's sitting already, spaghetti in front of her. Not at our usual table near the windows, but with a group of her volleyball teammates—my now ex-teammates—in the center of the room, Brianna at her right-hand side. She must have all but sprinted here to be eating already. Which means she didn't even hesitate about whether to meet me or not. Didn't even start walking toward me, before reluctantly joining her other friends.

There's space at the table. I could theoretically grab my own lunch and join her, like I do it all the time. It's not like I don't know the other girls or anything. Even if we were never close, they wouldn't mind me joining, would they? They don't hate me or anything, right? They just . . . aren't crazy about me.

But I can't walk up to a group of girls I used to know, and a girl who apparently doesn't want to know me right now. I just can't. So, tears pricking at my eyes, and swallowing fiercely to avoid the extra humiliation of crying in public, I line up by my-self, grab lunch by myself, and sit in our spot, by myself.

It feels as though everyone in school has seen me sit alone, that now they all know Ivy Winslow got ditched by the one person in school who thought she was worth hanging out with. But, in reality, no one even glances at me. Even Mack hasn't looked over at me once. I'm as invisible to her as I am to the rest of the school now, apparently. They don't want to gossip about me, and they don't hate me, because they just don't care about me.

Somehow, that feels worse than being hated.

As I look around the cafeteria—because there's nothing else to do while I eat except feel sorry for myself, which is getting old, fast—I find out that I was wrong. Someone is staring at me, with a humiliatingly concerned look. Henry Paramar, who's sitting two tables over with a group of gamer kids. Even though he's in a few of my classes, we've never really spoken, so I'm surprised that he's noticed me here.

And I'm downright shocked when he stands up, grabs his tray, and makes a beeline to join me at my table.

"Hey, Ivy," he says, like he says my name all the time. Like we talk all the time. "Question. Are you and Mack going to the *H-MAD* conference tomorrow?"

It's not that I don't want to reply. Honest. It's just that my shock level has exceeded critical capacity, and as a result I've actually forgotten how to speak English, so all I do is blink at him in response.

He seems to take my silence as confusion, because he continues on without missing a beat. "There's an *H-MAD* conference tomorrow at the convention center in the city. Tickets sold out a while ago but a few popped up online today, and I'm thinking of going, but I don't know anyone else who is."

I stare at him some more.

Henry has finally started to falter. He's squinting a little as he studies me, like he's trying to figure out if he's put his foot in it, or if I'm having a medical emergency. ". . . You did post about *H-MAD* last week, right?" he asks. "I was pretty sure it was you."

I didn't even realize Henry Paramar followed me on socials. Hopefully he isn't offended I never followed him back. I make a mental note to do so as soon as I can, and take a deep breath.

"You like *H-MAD*, too?" I ask, just to make sure I'm following the conversation correctly. I think maybe I have some internalized sexism, because for some reason it seems impossible to me that a guy from my class goes home after school and watches Weston fight the forces of darkness with his elemental powers, while simultaneously fighting for Vanessa's heart.

Wait, what if Henry watches for Vanessa? I can't go to a conference with him if he's a Vanessa fan.

"Who are your favorite characters?" I add to double-check, realizing too late it sounds like I'm accusing Henry of lying about liking the show.

Luckily, he doesn't seem bothered. "Kia, Weston, and Astor."

"What are your thoughts on Vanessa?" I ask evenly.

He shrugs, sticking his bottom lip out. "No thoughts. Head empty."

Oh, thank god.

"Shakira Johnson's gonna be there tomorrow," Henry says, naming the actress who plays Kia. "I think I'd really like to go, but I don't wanna go alone, you know?"

Oh, I do know. I know very well. And if Mack and I were talking, I would march over to her and tell her Henry Paramar agrees with me, and it's actually not pathetic to be afraid to go to things like this alone, and it really was a dick move on her part to pull out of it the morning before to hang with her precious Brianna after committing to it months ago.

But we're not talking.

"We were going to go, but Mack doesn't want to anymore," I say.

Henry's face falls the slightest amount. "Oh. That's cool. So, you're pulling out, too?"

I don't really know Henry. But the little I do know of him, I like already. Do I want to spend a whole day alone with him, though? What if we run out of things to talk about? What if he's secretly a terrible person? What if he decides I'm a terrible person, and tells everyone at school how boring I am to be around?

Well, any of those things could be true. But one thing's true for sure, and that's that I am not brave enough to go to the *H-MAD* conference alone tomorrow, no matter how badly I want to be that kind of person.

Across the cafeteria, Mack finally, finally glances at me. Then, her eyes flicker to Henry, and something flashes across her face. I can't tell if it's curiosity, or confusion, or both. My cheeks heat, and my chest clenches, and I tear my eyes away before she can look back at me. A part of me is relieved she didn't look over until Henry arrived. As far as she knows, I'm totally unbothered by her abandoning me for the volleyball girls, and launched right into making a bunch of new friends.

I mean, she does know me pretty well, so that might actually not be the conclusion she jumps to. But maybe I could be the kind of person who just casually makes a new friend in her absence. Why shouldn't I be?

I realize it's been at least five seconds, and I still haven't answered Henry's question. *So, you're pulling out, too?*

"No," I say, to both Henry and myself. "I'm going. But it means I have a free ticket, if you want it?"

Henry shoves a fork into his spaghetti and nods, a smile spreading across his face.

For once, I push aside all my fears and anxieties and what-ifs, and I simply smile back.

PRESENT

I'm struggling to hide how exasperated I am while Weston explains the—in his view—completely reasonable misunderstanding that led him here.

"It specifically says 'help me,'" he grumbles, pointing to the caption beneath the photo Henry uploaded. "And you are quite patently possessed in the photo."

"I wasn't possessed, Weston, I was bored," I promise as we head along the sidewalk in the direction of my house.

"Can you blame me for the confusion?"

I sigh. "No," I admit. "But I'm still probably going to get in trouble at school now."

Weston considers this, then brightens. "No, you won't," he says.

"Uh, yes, I will. You can't just walk off school grounds in the middle of the day without signing out. They'll call my parents."

"No, they won't."

I fight the urge to roll my eyes at him. "And how do you know that?"

"Because I just fixed it."

I slow my step. "Fixed what?"

"I made it so they won't call your parents. It's fine now."

I stop altogether now, studying him. He looks calm and completely sure of himself. Against my better judgment, there's a spark of hope in my chest.

"What do you mean? How did you?"

He shrugs, smiling. "I'm not sure. But I can tell you I did."

A part of me wants to continue arguing with him. But then I think of how he appeared in my house. How his clothes defy all the laws of physics. How quickly he seemed to conjure his first-aid tray yesterday morning. If he says he just altered reality without lifting a finger, who am I to disbelieve him?

Still, he must notice the look of bewilderment on my face, because he goes on.

"It's like . . . there's certain things that are necessary for you and me. For us to be happy, I mean. And if I know something needs to change for us to be happy, I can change it."

I guess that makes sense. Sort of. At least, it explains why he can't use his air elemental powers, but he can conjure up a bottle of painkillers from the ether. I don't know if it explains everything—for example, our happiness doesn't seem particularly contingent on whether or not his clothes stay on his body at all times—but it *is* an extra clue as to what's going on here. And the more information I have, the better.

"Wait," I say. "Is that why Mack didn't recognize you?"

"Your nemesis?" he asks. "I minimized all cause for alarm on her end and sent her back to school."

Well, it's safe to say she would've been alarmed if she'd known I was hanging out with a fictional character, so I guess he *must* have erased her ability to recognize him. The realization comforts me. I could understand Mack not knowing intricate details of *H-MAD* lore, but not recognizing Weston is a bit of a stretch. His face is on half of my belongings.

"Can I put in requests?" I ask.

Weston sticks out his bottom lip. "I don't know. Want to try it?"

"Okay. Umm . . . it would really help us in the romance department if we both gained the ability to fly right now."

It's the first thing that pops into my head. Weston squints, concentrating. I wait, hoping a little despite myself. Then, I think floaty thoughts, and give a hop in place for good measure, but I land straight back on the sidewalk.

"Nope," Weston says, sounding more than a little put out.

"It's okay," I say. "I figured it would've been too good to be true."

I check my phone as we walk to find a ton of texts from Henry.

Hey where'd you go?

Are you ok? Class is about to start.

Are you ok??????

I told mr s you're sick again.

Please reply I'm worried.

My stomach sinks, and I message back a hurried reply, asking him to come by after school. If the run-in between Mack and Weston taught me anything, it's that I need an ally, desperately. And even if he weren't my best friend, there'd be no one better for the job than Henry.

The only thing is, I'm not quite sure how to bring up a topic like this. And I have about an hour to figure it out.

When Henry messages that he's close, I decide to meet him a few houses away from mine so I can brace him in person. I spot his fluorescent yellow sweater a mile away. It's hard to miss your friend when he's dressed like a stylish highlighter.

"I want to tell you something," I say when I reach him.

Henry falls into step beside me with a curious look. "Okay. What's up?"

"I think the universe has ripped open at the seam." I pause. "The fabric has been torn, at least. Frayed, maybe?"

"The fabric of the universe?"

"That's my working theory, yes."

"Christ," Henry says mildly. Then he runs a finger across his bottom lip. "Quick question. How is it that, since we saw each other three hours ago, you've come to the conclusion that the hem of the universe is fraying?"

"The *seam*, Henry."

"The seam, then!"

I fold my arms and look to the sky for strength. "We're at a crossroads."

He glances sideways at me. "Who is? Humankind?"

"No, you and I. What you say to my question will drastically alter the trajectory of our friendship, so consider your words carefully."

Henry's eyes widen. I wait for a response—maybe an appropriate exclamation of awe or trepidation. A question, maybe? Instead, I'm met with a long silence that drags on even as we pass an elderly couple walking their golden retriever.

"What?" I ask when we're out of anyone's earshot and he still doesn't speak.

". . . I was considering my words too carefully," he says finally. "It was too much pressure."

"I didn't ask you the question yet!"

"Oh, sorry. Go on."

I suck in a frantic breath. "The question is, can you keep a life-or-death secret?"

"No, Ivy, you know I can't," Henry says.

"But *Henry.*"

"Remember when I told Robbie you weren't too sick to go to his birthday party last year, you just didn't like him?"

"Yes, but—"

"Or when I told Rachel Mueller she was getting a chocolate cake at her surprise party in sixth grade?"

"Not really, but Henry—"

"Oh, or when you begged me not to tell anyone you liked Mack, and then I told your mom and—"

"Okay, Henry, I remember vividly." That particular slipup was followed by weeks of Mom sending me "how to win them back" videos, and trying to convince me to rejoin the volleyball team "for my fitness," and dragging me to the front yard to help her with increasingly convoluted tasks just around the time Mack and Keisha returned home from volleyball practice.

"The point is," Henry says, "if you need someone to keep a secret that big, I'm not your man. I urge you to consider someone else."

"Like who?"

"Literally anybody, Ivy. The mailman, maybe?"

Oh for god's sake. "You're supposed to be my best friend," I cry.

"Oh, I am. I would throw myself onto a fire for you. I would jump off a cliff for you. I would give you my last slice of pizza, even if it was a good flavor, like barbecue chicken. But keeping secrets is a skill I literally don't have. I will crack, and I will crack immediately."

"Fine."

"It's not personal."

"Yup."

"The mailman seems quite nice, actually. You should strongly consider telling him."

"I'll put it on my 'never gonna do' list."

"But good luck with that secret of yours."

I stare at him.

He gives me an innocent smile.

"God, screw it, come on," I say, tugging on Henry's arm.

"Where are we going?"

"To the secret."

"Okay, it's just, I thought we'd come to an understanding?" Henry pleads. "Shouldn't we be walking directly away from the secret?"

"No, it's cool. I just had a thought."

"What?" He slows his step, looking suddenly concerned. "I don't respond well to torture or blackmail. It'll only make things messier, just so we're clear."

"Oh my god, Henry, I'm not going to torture you. It's just . . . if you believe the secret—"

"Why wouldn't I believe it?"

"If you tell people the secret, they're just going to think you're a total weirdo. They'll never actually believe you. Plus, bear with me, but I think we might be able to alter reality so they couldn't find proof themselves, either way. So, I think it's safe to tell you after all."

"Wait, what?" Henry asks. "What kind of secret is this?"

"You're about to find out."

Henry frowns as we press on. "Hold on, let me clarify. We've established that I'll tell your secret, right?"

"Yeah."

"And that if I tell people your secret, they'll all think I'm a lying weirdo, apparently."

"That's right."

"So, you're happily putting me in a situation where every-one's going to think I'm a weirdo, just because you have a com-pulsive need to do everything in your life with someone else by your side? Is that where we've landed?"

I roll my eyes. "Well, if you just don't tell people—"

"But I *will*, Ivy, I *will*."

"That," I say, "sounds like a 'you' problem. And an incentive to learn how to keep your damn mouth shut."

"This is callous."

"Call it revenge for telling Mom about Mack."

Henry glares at me. "Oh my god, Ivy, that was, like, eight months ago. Let it go."

We're at the front door now. I draw a deep breath. It's now or never.

"Okay," I say, pushing open the door.

Inside, Weston is sitting on the couch, fiddling with his phone. When he hears us enter, he looks up with a friendly smile.

"You're back!"

I look right at Henry, waiting for his reaction. At least Henry, I know for a fact, notices how much this looks like Weston. Henry scans from Weston's icy-blue waves to his silver tornado necklace to his cargo pants.

"You hired a Chase Mancini lookalike?" he asks slowly. I can tell from his expression he's fighting and failing to keep the judgment off his face. "Why?"

I fold my arms across my chest and shift my weight. Okay, so, he definitely notices the resemblance, at least. It's just the wrong conclusion. A sane conclusion, I'll give him that, but the wrong one. "It's not a Chase lookalike," I say. "It's Weston."

"Who's Chase?" Weston asks sharply.

"When you say 'it's Weston' . . . ?" Henry asks, raising a sin-gle eyebrow.

"I mean that in the strictest sense of the phrase," I reply.

"Is this meant to be funny?" Henry asks. He starts looking around the room suspiciously, like he's searching for something tucked away on the shelves or beneath the coffee table. "Because it's not. Is this a hidden-camera thing? If it is, you do not have my permission to upload the video. I *do not consent*."

"*Who's Chase?*" Weston repeats, standing up from the couch in a bid for attention.

"No, Henry, there's no hidden—" I sigh, and take a deep breath. "Weston, would you please excuse us for one second?"

Weston gives a bewildered sort of nod. Henry, looking even *more* bewildered, follows me into the kitchen, where I face him and lower my voice.

"Listen. Yesterday, I woke up, and he was in my bed. He just appeared."

"Wait, that guy broke into your *house*?" Henry asks, alarmed.

"*No*. I think he just sort of appeared inside my house. Like teleportation."

Henry guffaws like that's the stupidest thing he's ever heard. Which, come to think of it, is not entirely unfair. "Teleporfucking-tation? Ivy, what are you *talking* about?"

"Hear me out. He has these clothes that change every day. One second they're on him, the next morning, out of the blue, brand-new clothes!"

I hear how ridiculous it sounds as soon as I finish speaking, but it's too late to self-edit, because Henry is laughing shrilly.

"Oh, well, in *that* case. How can I argue in the face of evidence *that* compelling?"

"Henry—"

"People change their clothes, Ivy," he says. His tone is teetering on the edge of hysteria. "As often as every day. Also, I'm still trying to process the fact that this guy showed up in your bed, while you're at home alone, and you *didn't call for help*. You could've told the Gleasons, or me, or even the mailman, but *nooo*."

"Why is your solution always to turn to the mailman?"

"I told you, he seems nice."

I let out a sigh of frustration. "Henry, the clothes *appear* on him! Like, before your eyes!"

I realize from the look on Henry's face that I'm going to have to do better than that, because apparently a year of unwavering friendship isn't a good enough reason to take me at my word when I start insisting on the impossible.

"Look," I say, leading Henry back into the living room. "Weston, can you please take your shirt off for Henry?"

Henry balks. "Can I just say, for the record, I did not ask Ivy to ask you to take your shirt off. This is not *for* me."

Weston raises and lowers his eyebrows in a suggestive way that makes Henry press his fingertips to his forehead, before stripping. I take the shirt and hand it to an incredulous Henry. Weston crosses his arms in a way that makes his biceps bulge and flex, and I don't think that's an accident.

"Get a good look at it. Confirm to me that it's a real shirt. It's not a prop. Right?"

"Yes, it's a shirt, Ivy," Henry groans. "This guy's clothing isn't the problem, though. You get that, right? Like, the fact that he's now partially naked actually makes this whole thing even *more alarming.*"

I push on valiantly. "Good, now let's get rid of it. Oh, I've got it. The mud. Throw it in the mud. Come on, guys."

I start toward the backyard, with Weston following at my tail. Henry hesitates, then scrambles to catch up.

"Throw it in the mud," Henry mutters to himself. "Of course. This is normal. What a normal after-school activity this is."

"There's nothing normal about Ivy," Weston assures Henry. "She's not like other girls. That's what makes her so enticing."

I don't turn around to check Henry's reaction to that one. His extended silence is enough, though.

In the backyard, under the tulip tree, is a patch of dirt left over from our old dog, Billy, who used to dig up the grass there every day before he passed. Even though that was ages ago now, the grass still struggles to grow there. Today, it's basically a mud puddle from the storm, still.

I clear my throat. "So, Henry, he's not wearing a shirt, right?"

Henry scowls at me, refusing to look at the half-naked Weston again. "Evidently, Ivy."

"You're holding his shirt?"

"I'm holding his shirt."

"Okay, now do it. Throw it in the mud."

Henry hesitates, and Weston places a reassuring hand on his shoulder.

"Even if it doesn't work, it's not a problem, I promise," Weston says in a soothing tone. "I'll get a new one tomorrow. It's what happened today."

Henry looks at me like he might hate me just a little bit, then steels himself, and delicately drops the shirt on the muddy grass. I trot forward and stomp on it for good measure.

"Was that necessary?" Henry asks.

"Yes. Okay, now, turn your back to the shirt with me. Let's look at the fence. Good. Now, look at Weston."

Henry lets out a gasp of alarm before I can even turn back all the way. "What the *fuck*?" he asks.

Weston is wearing the very shirt we just threw in the mud, perfectly buttoned, clean and uncreased. The spot of muddy grass where the shirt lay only seconds before is now bare.

"Believe me now?" I ask.

"I'm not sure," Henry says, approaching Weston. He circles him like a vulture, eyes narrowing, like he's searching for the trick.

"You're not *sure*? What else do we need to do to prove he's magical? Look at his eyes."

"They could be contacts," Henry says.

"Contacts," I repeat flatly. "They're glowing."

"Expensive contacts."

Weston looks at me hesitantly. "Do you need me to touch my eyeball?" he asks, sounding less than thrilled about the idea. "I will if you really need me to."

"No," I say quickly. "Henry's just in denial. He'll be okay in a minute."

"Look, Ivy," Henry says, holding his hands up. "I saw a magician make someone float once, and they used hoops around her and everything. Magic, like, *actual* magic, is never the most likely explanation. If he's a trained actor, he probably knows a quick-change technique or two."

"Henry," I say in exasperation. "Quick-changes don't get rid of mud. Did you not just see me stomp it into the mud?"

"Okay!" Henry snaps, laughing a little. Then, he laughs more than a little. I'm suddenly concerned. "All right! For the sake of argument, let's say this is, somehow, Weston. I still say we call the police."

"No!" I yelp. "We can't call the police on him. I gave life to him! You don't give life to someone and then call the police on them, Henry, it's not cool."

"Ivy, you have a *stranger in your house*. In your *house*. He needs to leave!"

"We're not strangers," Weston cuts in. "We're actually soul mates."

"*What?*" Henry shrieks, whirling around to face Weston.

"And where's he gonna go, Henry?" I ask.

"Not here! That's all that matters. Not! Here!"

"I don't want him to leave. He's nice, and he's good to talk to, and he was with me all day yesterday and he didn't try to hurt me once. And he thinks I'm beautiful, so."

"I think you're breathtaking," Weston corrects.

"Are you listening to yourself?" Henry asks. "You know how the story ends when a guy follows a girl around all day telling her how beautiful she is, and shows up in her bed? Murder, Ivy, it ends in murder. Always. He's going to stab you, and I'm not sure I'll be much help if he does. I'm *not good in a crisis*."

"Who's going to stab Ivy?" Weston asks, leaping forward to place himself in front of me. "Let him try. He stabs Ivy, he stabs me. And trust me. He doesn't want to stab me. I'm rock solid."

I step to the side so I can see Henry again. "The *really* unbelievable thing is he insists he doesn't work out," I say wryly. "If you need proof something strange is going on, that's plenty."

Henry stares Weston down, then glances reluctantly at me. "You really think this is Weston?"

"I really do."

"Okay," he says, before turning on his heel to head back inside. I follow, Weston close to my side. "Okay. I'm going to give you the benefit of the doubt for a minute. But you're gonna have to tell me everything you know. From the start."

Henry and I set Weston up with another rom-com and some snacks before we escape to my room, where we close the door and speak in hushed tones as I tell him everything. The thunderstorm, the wish, Weston's appearance, the soul mate markings, the spare phone. Mack not recognizing him. Weston's assurance that the school won't know I left early.

When I finish, Henry rests his chin on his hands and stares at the carpet for a long while. Processing, I suppose. Eventually, he cocks his head. "What are you gonna do if the marking doesn't vanish?" he asks. "Your parents will kill you if you get a tattoo."

I rub the spot and raise my eyebrows at him. "I get what you're saying, but it's low on the list of things to fix before my parents come home."

"Right. Which is when, again?"

"Thursday night." I gesture toward the calendar on my desk, which marks their return with a large red X.

"So we have two days to figure out how to send him back to . . . wherever he came from, right?"

I reel back. "Who said I want to send him back?"

Henry looks at me like I've grown an extra nose. "What? Why wouldn't you?"

"Well, for a start, what does that even mean? Will it be killing him?"

"No," Henry says, fluffing one of my pillows casually, like he's not talking about doing away with a whole human. "Just forced relocation. I think."

I check my drawers while I have a rare moment without Weston, just to make sure my merchandise is as hidden as I remember it being. It's effectively buried under several boring-looking notebooks and various receipts. Good.

"Even then, I like him here. He's my friend."

Henry scoffs and falls back onto the pillows, bouncing in place. "Is this because he called you 'breathtaking'?"

"*No.*" I shut the drawer a little harder than I mean to. "He's nice, and he's easy to hang out with, and he doesn't have a mean bone in his body. He gets a little . . . enthusiastic sometimes, but he's just come from a reality where people get legit murdered every day. He'll calm down soon."

"Uh-huh, and what do you foresee happening? The guy who thinks he's a character from a fantasy show puts on a pair of sunglasses and gets a job somewhere without any ID, or a bank account, or anything?"

"We're figuring that out," I say.

"How?"

"I don't know yet. I was hoping you might be able to help me." I don't mean to sound so defensive, but I'm a little taken aback by Henry's lack of enthusiasm. If I'm honest, I expected him to be starstruck, asking Weston about the show or maybe brainstorming some fun things to do with him, given he looks *exactly* like the character. Not to immediately jump to erasing him from existence.

Henry softens. "Look, we're in this together. I just think we need to be careful. Maybe I'm in shock still, I don't know. How long did it take you to wrap your head around this?"

"Uh . . ." I say. "To be confirmed?"

He snorts at this, and I giggle with him at the absurdity of it all.

"Okay, if I'm honest, there's one thing that's bothering me a lot," Henry says.

I brace myself. "What?"

"I just . . . don't get mad, but I find it hard to believe that's Weston."

I fight to keep the whining out of my voice. "What's it going to *take*, Henry?"

"No, I think he's magical," Henry says hurriedly. "At least, I can accept that it's on the list of possibilities. And I definitely agree he *thinks* he's Weston. But come on, Ivy, we know that character like the back of our hands. Where's the deadpan humor? Where's the obsession with finding the fourth portal? Has he mentioned that to you, like, *ever*? Also, Weston picks arguments, like, all the time. This guy is too agreeable. It's almost creepy."

"It's not a crime to be pleasant," I say.

"No, but it's not *Weston*. And, no offense, but why is he so obsessed with you?"

I bristle. "Offense taken."

"Weston isn't even single, though, right? Where does Vanessa fit into all of this?"

"He doesn't like Vanessa anymore," I say.

Henry throws his hands up. "*Come on!*"

"What, Weston couldn't *possibly* choose me over Vanessa?"

"Not after knowing you for five minutes, no, I don't buy that. *No offense,* I said," Henry says, in response to my obviously continued offense.

"Okay, so, maybe he's a little different," I admit. "But, I don't know, maybe this is who Weston is when there's low stakes. It doesn't really matter to me, anyway. I like him like this."

Henry studies me, brow knitted. Finally, he shrugs. "Okay. We'll figure it out. But just . . . be careful, okay? And keep me involved. I'll take my phone off silent, so if you need me, call. It doesn't matter what time it is."

"I won't need you, I promise," I say. "But thank you."

I'm confident that Weston wouldn't do anything to hurt me. But now that Henry mentions it, I'm less confident that the person downstairs is strictly Weston after all.

But if he's not, then who the hell is he?

Chapter Nine

PAST

"You can't drop a bomb like this on me the night before you're due to go to NYC, Ivy," Mom says, putting her reading glasses on the kitchen counter.

"I only made the plans today," I say. "It's been sort of last-minute all around."

Mom leans against the counter and presses her fingertips against her temples. "And why can't Mack join you, suddenly?"

"She has some volleyball thing she wants to do," I say, trying not to let the bitterness edge into my voice. Of course, I'm hurt that she ditched me at the last second. And, yes, I'm jealous that she'd rather hang with her teammates—and Brianna—than with me. But I'm trying to be an adult about this and focus on the fact that Henry Paramar is happy to come with me. All's well that ends well, no harm done, yadda yadda yadda. But Mom's doing her best to throw a wrench in my "it all worked out" plans.

"What do you mean 'some volleyball thing'?" Mom asks. "Doesn't she already have a ticket?"

"Yup."

"Well, how important could this volleyball thing be? Have you explained to her how important the conference is to you?"

"Yes, Mom, she knows."

"Well, she should commit to her plans, then."

"She should," I say acidly. "But she's not."

"Did you two have a fight?"

I try to keep my expression neutral. "No."

I clearly failed at keeping my expression neutral. "Wait, Ivy, what happened?"

"Nothing, we didn't fight. Anyway, it's fine, because I have someone else to go with, so it's fine. Just say I can go with Henry, please."

"Ivy, I don't know this boy," Mom says. "I've never spoken to his parents, either. I'm not just going to let you get on a bus with some random boy from your class and head off to the city. You're fifteen. No."

"Mom, please," I say, placing my hands on the dining table. "He's expecting me."

"You shouldn't have committed without my permission. I'm sure he'll understand."

"He's really nice, Mom. And he's, like, popular, but not the douchey, stuck-up sort of popular. He's the 'everyone likes him because he's nice to literally everybody' sort."

Mom stares me down, brown eyes bright. ". . . Is he your boyfriend?" she asks, with the tone of someone who's just solved a great mystery.

"No," I say. "I haven't even really talked to him before today."

Mom throws her hands up. "Great. Now you're definitely not going."

"Mom, I've been wanting to go to this conference for months. Please, please, don't make me miss it. Please."

She starts to make a cup of tea, which means she's about to go to bed, and I'm going to have to get a win in the conversation fast before it's over for the night.

"I know you don't want to miss the conference," she says. "But I'm not okay with my fifteen-year-old daughter climbing on a bus by herself. It was one thing with Mack. . . . Look. How about I drive you up tomorrow? We can go together."

I don't mean to look as horrified as I'm sure I do, but I can't help it. My cheeks start to burn even thinking about it.

It's like Mom can read my mind. "Ivy, nobody is going to be thinking about what you're up to. Everyone's focused on themselves. We'll have fun together. You can tell me all about the show, we can grab lunch. . . ."

Unless . . .

"How would you feel about it if you could meet Henry first?" I ask, desperately. I clench my hand into a fist by my side, willing her to say yes. When she doesn't immediately reject me, I scramble to grab my phone and bring up his profile. "Look at his photos," I say. "Does he look like a bad kid?"

She flicks through the photos, and her face softens. "If we pick him up from his house, and I can meet his parents first. . . ."

When I break into a beam, she rolls her eyes, then smiles back.

PRESENT

I wake up to someone yelling at me, which is one of my least favorite ways to start the day. It's still pitch dark, except for Weston's glowing eyes, luminescent even in the night. It takes a while for my eyes to adjust to the darkness, and my mind to adjust to the ranting.

". . . can't *believe* I have to share a *room* with you," Weston is saying. From the rapid movement of his glow-in-the-dark eyes, floating around the room six feet off the ground, it seems as though he's pacing back and forth at a frantic pace.

"What time is it?" I groan, pulling the blanket up to my chin.

"You have a phone, don't you?" Weston snaps, shocking me out of my dreamlike state. "Figure it out!"

I gape at him. Or, at least, in his general direction. Figure it out? Whatever happened to me being beautiful, and wonderful, and his soul mate? Grabbing my phone, I learn that it's about an hour and a half before I'm meant to get up for school.

"I can't be here," Weston declares before I can ask him what the hell has gotten into him. I flick on the lamp on my bedside table, and he's thrown into dim light. His eyes are wild, his hair is sticking out haphazardly in all directions, and he's now dressed in a white collared shirt with the top buttons undone, beneath a slightly oversized blazer.

"What? Why can't you be here?" I ask, but he's off before I finish speaking. At top speed, too.

It's not the way someone runs when they're planning on staying inside the house. And if I thought Weston looked out of place in the daytime, it's nothing compared to how much attention he'll grab on the street with glow-in-the-dark eyes. And, sure, maybe not many people are awake right now, but that's assuming he plans on staying quiet enough to not draw people out of their homes. And right now, I don't know *what* he's planning.

So, with no other option, I give chase, but he's too fast for me. Within seconds he's made it down the hall, and he unlocks the front door before I can reach him. I fly through the door seconds after him.

"Weston, *stop*," I hiss, and he whirls around in the center of the lawn. The streetlight's lit the yard up enough for me to make out the dew on the grass.

"Stop?" he asks. "*Stop?* It's driving me crazy just to be around you, Ivy. I can't bear to look at you."

"What did I do?" I ask indignantly. He definitely wasn't this pissy at me when we went to sleep. If something went down while I was unconscious, I think it's not entirely fair to hold me accountable for that. Did I say something in my sleep? Was I dreaming about Mack again? That could be it—but I don't remember *what* I was dreaming about.

Wait, maybe he went through my desk and found my *H-MAD* stuff. Crap, I knew I should've thrown it out instead of just hiding it. At a minimum, I should've sent it home with Henry to hide for a while. Why did I insist on living life on the edge?

Weston throws his hands up with a look of despair and disgust. "Don't you know?" he cries to the night sky, and a dog starts barking a few houses down the street.

With a sinking stomach, I check to make sure no one is around. Hopefully, I can get him back inside before he causes more of a scene.

"No," I say, lowering my voice. "But hey, how about we talk about it ins—"

"It's you, Ivy," Weston says over me, sweeping his arms to the sides. He seems not to have noticed it's the middle of the night, on a weeknight, in a suburban neighborhood. Or maybe he's just never had to worry about that before. After all, Weston's held many an epic battle during the night, and has never once had to deal with the police dropping by with a noise complaint. "You and your stubbornness. Your pride. Your obstinate, narrow-minded inability to see—to even *notice*—the effect you have on me."

"Weston, you're being really loud," I plead.

"LET THE WORLD HEAR ME," Weston screams, and I regret speaking. Clearly, my de-escalation skills leave something to be desired. "I want to destroy you," he goes on, stepping backward toward the street. "I want to rip you limb from limb. I want to watch you suffer, and bleed, and beg for a mercy I have no intention of giving."

"Jesus Christ," I say, smarting. "*Why?*"

"Because I love you," Weston explains.

Despite myself, I let out a shocked laugh. "That's not what you say to someone you love."

"Then . . . what is?" Weston asks. He looks genuinely confused.

I take the moment of confusion to step closer to him. Almost close enough to grab his arm and steer him back to the house.

"Honestly, almost anything else. And keep your voice down, *please*."

"I hate you as well," Weston whispers. Well, at least he's finally stopped yelling. We might have the noise levels under control, but the content still leaves something to be desired.

"You still haven't told me what I did," I say. "You liked me just fine before we went to sleep. Right?"

"Hate and love go hand in hand."

"I mean . . ." I hesitate. "Not . . . really. Not like that. Please, can we just go inside?"

"I can't be alone in a room with you," Weston goes on. "I can't be trusted."

I'm not sure *exactly* what he's implying—or threatening, maybe—here, but I can hazard a guess. All at once, I realize Henry might be right. I've known Weston for two days. I don't know what kind of person he is, or what he's capable of. How quick he is to anger, or how safe he is in various circumstances. I might trust Weston Razorbrook of *H-MAD*, but deep down, even I know this isn't strictly him, so what *do* I know about him?

I know he's solid, and strong. I know he has the ability to defy physics, even if it seems a bit arbitrary as to when or why that ability applies. And I know that, until I went to sleep, I felt perfectly safe around him, because he never once showed an inclination to use either of the first two points against me.

But that was then, and this, apparently, is now.

"You're the worst thing that's ever happened to me," Weston says, locking eyes with me with an intensity that makes me feel nervous, and a little itchy. "I rue the day we met. I envy the parallel-universe version of myself, who never had the misfortune of knowing your name."

I swallow. "I . . ."

"Now come here and kiss me," Weston says.

I stand motionless.

Weston waits patiently.

"No, thank you," I reply after a long beat.

It might be because I'm sleep-deprived, but it's harder to follow Weston's train of thought right now than it was to keep up with the season-three finale's plot twist, and that involved time travel and the catalogue model multiverse. "Bewildered" doesn't begin to cover how I feel right now.

"You don't have to fight it anymore, Ivy. Just kiss me. Even . . . just a little one on the cheek."

"No, thank you," I repeat firmly.

"We can give in to our primal urges."

"What if we went inside instead?"

Weston sighs. "You irritate me to no *end*. When will I be free of you?"

Those words seem familiar, but I'm not sure why. "It'll go faster if we head inside. Promise."

"Kiss me first."

"I said no."

"Ivy, come on, I won't murder you," he pleads. "I *promise*."

"I didn't think you were going to, but now you've brought it up—"

I trail off, because that's when it clicks. I know where I heard that phrase, the one Weston spoke seconds ago. *You irritate me to no end. When will I be free of you?* Of course it sounded familiar. It would.

I wrote it.

It's from my enemies-to-lovers fanfic, "Forbidden Hearts." I wrote it last year, after Mack and I got into an argument during history over the details of the French Revolution—long after we'd declared our friendship over in real life—and I needed to vent onto paper. It's easily the most successful fanfic I've ever uploaded. How could Weston know it, though? Does that mean . . . is Weston somehow a fan of mine? Is that why he's acting like this? What is he doing, really committed cosplay of my fanfics? Or is it meant to be some sort of role-play? No, that doesn't make sense, because that doesn't explain the clothes, or the soul mate markings, or—

Soul mate markings.

I wrote an *H-MAD* fanfic with the soul mate trope last year, too. And, specifically, I used the trope of an arm tattoo. Soul mate fanfics come in many forms. I've seen ones where characters are born seeing the world in grayscale, and the sign that they've met their soul mate is the world suddenly exploding into Technicolor. I've seen ones where characters develop scars in places their soul mates get hurt, and stories where characters are able to write messages to their soul mate by writing it onto their own skin.

It isn't a coincidence that Weston and I had markings appear on our arms to the tune of the first words we spoke to each other—the same version of the soul mate trope I wrote about—is it?

This is Weston Razorbrook. But at the same time, it's not.

The person standing by me is Weston Razorbrook as I wrote him.

As I *write* him.

He's mine. I didn't only bring him to life. I created him.

"What in the *world* is going on out here?"

Both Weston and I jump as we hear the whispered hiss. Not far from us, the Gleasons' front door opens, and Mack pokes her head out to gawk at us. I remember too late that Mack's bedroom faces the street, and that she has a habit of leaving her window open a crack while she sleeps. Not that an open window was a necessary condition for hearing Weston. I'm pretty sure astronauts could've heard him if they'd listened hard enough.

When Mack makes out Weston in the streetlight, she starts shaking her head.

"Wesley! Why are you yelling at Ivy?" she asks Weston.

"Because I want her dead," Weston explains helpfully, and Mack freezes in place, turning her head to look at me in alarm.

"Um," I say weakly. "He's kidding. It's an inside joke. I promise. So, if we could all just keep our voices down, maybe head on inside, I'm sure we can figure this out without involving the whole block."

"I'm going to get my parents," Mack says.

"No, please," I say quickly. "They can't know."

Mack half shuts the door behind her, taking a step toward me as she does, but she doesn't let go of the knob. "Ivy, this is serious. No one's gonna care that you snuck him in. You need to be safe."

"I just really need to get him back inside, Mack. Just . . . let me do that, and we can talk."

"Uh, no. No, you are *not* going inside with someone who just threatened to kill you. Are you serious?"

I am serious, because I finally understand what's going on. Which means I know I am at approximately zero risk of death around Weston. A verbal barrage, maybe, but that doesn't hit quite as hard when it's a meaningless script.

Which is exactly what this is. A script. Specifically, a script written by me.

"We're going inside," I say firmly. I beckon to Weston, who finally obeys me, if with a little more attitude than he usually gives.

We're almost at the door when Mack sprints across the road after us.

"No, I'm drawing the line at this," she says, forcing her way around me and inside the house. "I heard him threatening you. It was very loud, and it wasn't a joke."

"It was passion," Weston says, and I shush him.

"Who is this guy, Ivy?" Mack demands, flicking on the living room light.

"It's . . . complicated." I falter, shutting the front door behind me as gently as I can. It's the middle of the night, after all. It'd be rude to disturb the street by shutting front doors at a normal volume.

Mack's laugh is devoid of humor. "Well, you'd better figure out a way to uncomplicate it, or I'm filling my parents in like I should've done yesterday. Who is he? The truth."

On the one hand, I *did* want someone to find out so I wasn't alone in this. On the other hand, Henry knows now, so I have him, and including more people will only complicate matters, right? On the *other* other hand, Henry's reaction wasn't exactly what I hoped for, so maybe Mack—who has zero opinions about what does or doesn't make a correct version of Weston Razorbrook—would be more able to support me.

More importantly than all of that: for some reason, I just want to tell her. Maybe because I know how competent she is, maybe because she's been there for me through a million crises before, or maybe there is no reason. Either way . . .

"He's Weston," I say. "Tell her, Weston."

Mack rounds on him, waiting.

Weston raises his eyebrows, his expression cold. "Weston Razorbrook. Air elemental, shadow demon destroyer."

Mack stares at Weston for a long, long time. Then, without taking her eyes off him, she says to me, "Isn't that . . . he's not trying to say he's an *H-MAD* character, is he?"

It's too bad Weston can't use his magic to convince Mack

and Henry that he is, in fact, exactly who he looks like. It'd save a lot of effort on my end. But as it is . . . here we go again.

"Yes," I say.

"I don't get the joke," Mack says.

"That's fair enough. The thing is, there's no punch line."

"Yeah, that's the problem."

"No, like . . ." I take a deep breath. I might as well cut to the chase. "It's not a joke. That's actually Weston."

Mack looks as though I said the last thing she'd ever expected. Which, I suppose, is fair. I can't say for sure how I would react if Mack had said something like this to me. But this isn't my first "convince someone of the impossible" rodeo. Sure, it might only be my second, but second rodeos are famously more successful than first ones. I think.

"Are you, like, role-playing?" Mack asks.

"It's not a game, and it's not pretend. Look at him, Mack. He *is* Weston. You have to see this is literally Weston. I know you don't like *H-MAD*, but come *on*."

"Okay . . ." Mack says slowly. "Um. Right. Of course he's dressed like the guy from your show. But he's obviously dressing up. What did you call it? That thing . . . cosplay! It's cosplay, right?"

I bite my lip, and Mack cocks her head at me in exasperation. I think she's not sure whether I'm teasing her, or I've simply lost my mind.

Mack tries again. "Ivy, you know there's a difference between dressing up as a character and actually being that character, right? Tell me you understand that."

"I know the difference, but that's not what's happening," I insist. "And to prove it, Weston's going to undress."

Mack starts. "*What?* I don't want that."

"Just the top," I clarify.

"Oh, well, *that* makes perfect sense, then," Mack mutters. "But sure. Go for it, I guess?"

"Weston," I continue, "just do it like you did with Henry yesterday. Minus the mud."

"Don't tell me what to do," Weston says petulantly.

"Oh my *god, please, then.*"

I do *not* like this version of Weston. It'd seemed so romantic when I was writing it, but in reality, it's irritating at best.

With a heaping serving of attitude, Weston peels off his shirt. Slowly. Achingly slowly. Locking eyes with Mack, he flings the shirt as far as he can manage, and it whacks against the wall before crumpling to the floor. Then he stands with his chin raised, flexing his muscles.

Mack raises an eyebrow. "I'm a lesbian," she tells him.

Weston sighs in exasperation. "I'm not flirting with you. I'm showing you my body."

". . . Why?"

"Because I saw the way you looked at Ivy," he says. "And I want you to know you can't compete with me."

Mack chokes. "Buddy, you can have her. Trust me."

I ignore the sharp sting of that, and move on.

"Okay, now turn with me," I say to Mack, and she, surprisingly, cooperates. Probably out of sheer curiosity and confusion. "And back," I say almost immediately. And, of course, the shirt's back on Weston's body.

Mack suddenly seems very, very tired. She trudges to the sofa and sits heavily on the edge of it, resting her chin in her hands.

"Look," she says. "It's late. Or early. Or both. And that wasn't physically possible, but I don't believe you either way."

"Yeah," I say, equally tired, "that's kind of fair enough."

"I'm also really uncomfortable with all of this," Mack goes

on, twirling a hand at Weston. "In fact, could you, like . . . fuck off for a second and leave us alone?"

Weston gives her a scathing look. "You want me to leave my nemesis alone with her nemesis?" he asks flatly.

"I'll be fine, Weston," I say.

"I couldn't care less if you're fine," he says.

"Sure."

"But I *will* be *right* on the other side of that door," he warns icily.

When he's out of sight, I join Mack on the couch, close enough that I can smell the vanilla body spray she always sleeps in. It was a habit she started about a year and a half ago, when she went through a period of insomnia, and the school counselor told her to pair sleep with a certain scent. I guess she never stopped. She turns to me and murmurs under her breath. "You promise you're not lying to me about any of this?"

"I promise."

"Because you know how this looks."

"I do."

"But, also, that shirt thing isn't possible."

"That's correct."

"Was it a party trick? Is he a magician?"

"Not the kind you mean," I say.

"Even if he is magic, he was threatening you. In fact, doesn't magic make him *more* of a threat?"

I have to admit, the fact that Mack's concerned for my safety makes me feel like I've skipped a step going downstairs. I wouldn't have expected her to care all that much if I got murdered. In fact, last week I would've guessed that if someone broke into my house to take my life, she would've cheered them on. Or at least politely acted as though she saw nothing. "I get why it seems that way," I say. "But I promise, he has no intention of hurting me. It's sort of, like . . . an act."

"Like, a fetish?"

"In a sense?"

Mack groans. "This isn't possible. I'm really uncomfortable with impossible shit."

"I know. I *get it*. But I adjusted."

"I don't want to adjust," Mack says. "I want to go back to my house, and pretend I didn't see or hear any of this. And I want you to not turn up dead or anything. Because if I believed you when you said everything's fine but something happened to you anyway, that would be *really* unfair to me."

"Noted," I say. "I can do that. Not turn up dead, I mean."

"Okay."

"Okay."

There's a brief standoff. Finally, Mack bites her lip.

"I'm going to go, then," she says.

"Okay."

"I was never here."

"Gotcha."

"Stay safe."

Her concern sounds genuine. I can't help but smile at it, because there's that funny feeling again. "Thank you."

With that, Mack lets herself out of the house. Not entirely sure this isn't still part of a dream, I shuffle back to my bedroom.

Inside, Weston is sitting on the bed, wearing a pair of checkered pajamas. This is of immediate concern, because I have yet to see Weston in pajamas. Of further concern is Weston's pose: one leg is bent at the knee, his arm is flung across his middle, and he's propping himself up on one hand. His eyes are of the bedroom variety, his lips are parted, and his socks are knitted.

Weston's come-hither pose is startling enough that it takes me a beat to notice the bare floor.

"Where's your bed?" I ask.

"There's only one bed," Weston says. "And I'm furious about it, because the last thing I would *ever* want to do is sleep *anywhere* near you."

I stare at Weston.

Weston blinks back.

"We're not doing this," I say flatly. "I already told you, we're *not* sharing a bed."

"Even if there's only one?" Weston asks sulkily, but I stalk past him without engaging further. Deflated, he drops his knee as I yank open the closet door. "Wait, Ivy, don't go in—"

A pile of crudely folded blankets tumbles to the floor. I look back at Weston, who's staring at the blankets with an open mouth, the very picture of shock.

"Who put those there?" he asks.

I scoop the blankets up and throw them across the bed at Weston, who catches them with a sheepish grimace.

"Rebuild. Your bed," I say through gritted teeth. I'll be lucky to get fifteen minutes of sleep in before my alarm goes off at this rate, and I am *not* pleasant in sleep-deprivation mode.

"Are we expecting company tonight?" Weston asks hopefully.

"No. It's your bed. That's where you sleep. Always."

"But if I sleep down there, it's significantly harder for us to accidentally give in to our latent desires and kiss in the night," he protests, getting to his feet, loaded up with linen.

The more Weston talks, the more unsure I am of why I ever wrote that fanfic to begin with. Let alone why so many people enjoy it. Being adored was great. Having my boundaries respected was lovely.

This is more of a nightmare.

Chapter Ten

PAST

Hey. Did you still go to the conference?

I almost drop my phone when the text comes through. It's the first time Mack's reached out to me since we had words about her ditching me for the volleyball team. I'm in the middle of the convention center with Henry, fighting desperately against a sea of people trying to make our way toward Shakira Johnson's signing table. When I get Mack's text, though, I slow almost to a stop.

"Oh! Did she text?" Henry asks excitedly.

Henry put two and two together this morning around the thirtieth time I checked my phone on the bus, and he'd asked if the reason Mack's ticket was free was because we'd had an argument. I spared him the private details of the argument, but I did admit I was starting to feel guilty over it, but I wasn't sure how to apologize.

"Yeah!" I say.

"What did she say?"

I show it to him, and he gives me a thumbs-up.

"Good sign. See? She's totally not still mad at you."

I start walking slowly again, gluing myself to Henry's back so he can steer us through the mayhem, while I text Mack.

> Yeah! Here right now. I came with Henry actually

Henry from school Henry?

> Yeah. Kind of random and last minute but he's a lot of fun

Very random! I'm glad you're having fun though

> Thank you.

> I don't want to fight any more.

My heart feels like it's about to burst out of my chest while I wait for her reply. Thankfully, it comes through in seconds.

Omg good. Neither do I. Come over tomorrow night?

> Okay!

And just like that, all my stress melts away.

"All good?" Henry asks, as I pick up speed to reach his side.

"Yeah, perfect. I can see the line."

"Holy shit, it's almost out the door."

"It's worth it."

"So worth it."

"Did you bring snacks?"

"I have raisins."

"They'll have to do. Come on."

PRESENT

An hour after Weston's outburst in the street, I'm sleepwalking through my dressing routine. All the while, Weston respectfully faces away from me while loudly criticizing my outfit choices. It's not like it even matters what I wear today—clearly, I can't go into school and leave him alone after yesterday—but I still don't really want to walk around all day in an outfit he just ruthlessly roasted, you know?

"By the way," I say to him as I try on my third shirt—a blue-and-purple checkered button-down—"Mom's going to call any minute now, and I know you think this whole 'we're enemies' thing is romantic, but it's going to be a whole lot less romantic if you yell at me while she's on the phone and they rush home to see what's going on."

Weston looks me up and down and scrunches up his nose. "I know you're not cool, Ivy, but you don't have to *announce* it with that shirt. And do you even *own* a dress?"

None that I wear whenever I can help it. And I am not putting on a fourth outfit. I cross my arms over the print and stare him down.

"And can't you just tell your mom not to call?" he asks sulkily when I don't reply. Because *that's* a simpler solution than him simply keeping his loud insults to himself for sixty-odd seconds.

"No, Weston, I can't," I say. "Because that's just as likely to get them to rush home to see what's going on. You see the problem, right?"

Weston flops in my desk chair lazily and lets his arms dangle over the side as he slouches. He's watching me with a strange look, as though he's waiting for something to happen. My phone buzzes a moment later.

> Hi sweetie. Really busy morning, can't talk unless it's an emergency. Have a good day!

Mom.

"No," Weston says. "I don't think I do see the problem."

I blink at my phone, stunned. Is this what it's like to have parents that trust you not to have messed up your life in the eight hours since you last spoke to them? Did Weston seriously just turn my parents into people with normal boundaries?

"I take it that wasn't a coincidence?" I ask him, just to be sure, and he gives me a noncommittal shrug. So, that's a yes, then.

A knock on the door tells me Mack's arrived early, which is annoying because I was going to text her to say not to bother coming over. Frowning, I start down the hall, and Weston jogs after me to catch up.

"You don't have to follow me everywhere," I tell him.

"You might need protection."

"The only person I need protection from today is you,

evidently," I grumble, ordering him to my bedroom by way of pointing firmly.

"See, this is why people don't like you," Weston says. "The endless attitude."

"People don't like me?" I ask. I'm actually a little wounded.

"Well," Weston says. "*I* don't like you."

"You," I say, "only barely qualify as a person."

When he's safely shut back in my room, I head down the hall.

I open the door to reveal Mack waiting on the doorstep, still in the baggy sweatpants and faded graphic T-shirt she was wearing when she woke up last night. She smiles automatically when she sees me, though it turns into a grim look so fast I almost wonder if I imagined it.

"Morning," I say. From a fake enemy to a real one. Or an ex–real one, maybe. Honestly, I'm not sure what's going on with Mack and me anymore. Everything's topsy-turvy and inside out and I'm just doing my best to keep up with all the changes.

"You can't keep skipping school," Mack says as she pushes past me into the house.

I let out a short laugh. "You are *not* telling me you saw what you saw last night and your main concern is whether or not I have a perfect attendance."

"No, I'm not telling you that," Mack says patiently, her eyebrows raised. "What I am telling you is that if you take today off, my parents will start monitoring you *real* closely, and you're not gonna be able to hide this guy. We need to take shifts."

I blink. "We? *Who* we?"

"*Us* we. Me, you, and Henry."

I hesitate. "*Why?* I thought you didn't believe me."

"I'm not here because I believe you. I'm here because

something's going on, you obviously need help, and I'm nosy so I want to be involved."

Yeah, that tracks.

"And besides, let's say you're telling the truth, for argument's sake. It'll buy us some time while we figure out how to return him to his own dimension, or murder him, or whatever."

"Murder him?"

"'Murder him' is the wrong phrase. I mean, like . . . end his existence."

I gape, horrified, and Mack rolls her eyes. "What would *you* call it?"

"Um, I don't know, Mackenzie, *not that, though.* And why do you and Henry assume I don't want him here?"

It's Mack's turn to gape. "*Do* you? Why? He was awful to you last night."

I think back to the soul mate markings from yesterday. "I'm actually pretty sure he's just going through a phase. He'll be back to being nice tomorrow."

I think Mack's too exhausted to argue the point, because she just runs a hand down her face and sighs. "Look, we're getting sidetracked, and we don't have time. Can you message Henry and see if he can take tomorrow?"

I go into protective mode the moment Mack mentions Henry. I can't help it. "And when were *you* gonna take a shift, next week?"

"Uh, today, I was thinking, actually," Mack says, with an edge to her tone that I might sort of deserve. "I have practice tomorrow, and I need to be there. Today, I'm wide open. Maybe I got your cold and need to stay home to recover, you know? Plus, I'm literally right across the street."

"It won't be enough to watch from across the street," I say. "He can be sneaky."

"Give me your spare key, then. Zeke's got some sort of robotics thing after school anyway, so I don't need to get back until Dad comes home at five."

I narrow my eyes. Giving Mack full access to my house, without any preparation, could potentially end badly for me here.

"Don't go through my stuff."

"Why would I go through your stuff?"

"I don't know. To blackmail me?"

Mack gives me an incredulous look. "Last time I checked, the only thing you've got in your drawers is *H-MAD* merchandise and dirty clothes you can't be bothered taking to the hamper."

"It's been a year since you last checked."

"Has anything changed?" Mack asks.

I stare her down, then, finally bested, I scowl.

"I'll get you the keys."

"You're welcome," Mack calls after me as I retreat.

The thing is, I could stay at home myself without facing repercussions. After this morning, I'm pretty sure I'd be able to make the argument to Weston that we need Mack's parents to remain unsuspicious. But on the flip side, Mack is here of her own volition, and speaking to me, and neither of us are being nasty. At least, not super nasty. It's the first time I've had her around in a year, and I'd be lying if I didn't say a part of me kind of likes it, even if the other part of me insists otherwise. Besides, if she spends the day here, then she's in this just as much as Henry and I are, and there might be a time when we need to rely on her backup. So, fine. Great. She can take today's shift if she insists. It might even give us more to talk about at the end of the day than how much we can't stand each other.

I do my best to ignore the tumble of *very* unwelcome butterflies in my stomach.

.   .   .

When Zeke picks me up and lets me know Mack's staying at home sick, I do my best to act both surprised and sympathetic. If he notices how bad of a liar I am, he doesn't say anything.

He hands me the cord plugged into his car before he starts, and I look at it in touched surprise. Zeke got his license about a year before Mack and I stopped being friends, which made him our unofficial chauffeur when our parents either were unavailable or couldn't be bothered. We always fought over who got to put our playlist on, and Zeke lost more often than not. Mack and I split the other times at about a fifty-fifty rate.

"You're not even gonna fight me over it?" I ask as I plug my phone in.

"Nah. You get a free pass today. I'm not in a fighting mood."

He doesn't have to tell me twice. I pick a song that I know is at least kind of up his alley—I'm not in a fighting mood, either—and turn the volume up a touch. Almost immediately, he turns it back down. At first, I think he hates the song after all, but then he purses his lips.

"You and I have got to have a talk," he says.

"That sounds serious."

"Nah, nah, nothing like that. I just figured I'd take my opportunity while Mack's at home."

I nod and put my phone under my leg to pin it in place, giving him my full attention.

"Until this week, it's been forever since I've seen you, Ives. It's like you died."

"Nope," I say. "Full of life. I've been spreading it around, even."

Zeke, for obvious reasons, doesn't get the joke. I'm out here wasting my best material.

"Right. What happened to you two?"

"Me and Mack?"

"Mmm. Obviously something went down, but she won't tell us anything. She's my sister, so I have to take her side, but if she's been unreasonable and you need me to do some *Inception* shit to get her to see the error of her ways, tell me now. I can be subtle."

As tempting as that is—and honestly, it is; Zeke was always the kind of guy who did anything he could to minimize confrontation—I don't think spilling the details of a fight Mack clearly doesn't want her family to know about will help things in the long run.

"Nothing worth writing home about."

"Maybe it's time the two of you fixed it, then," he says. "I'm sure Mack's too stubborn to say it, but she misses you. I think you really meant a lot to her, you know?"

How much, I want to ask, but I don't.

"We'll see," I say instead, and I don't mean it in a dismissive way at all.

"I really hope you do see," Zeke says. "You're always welcome at Sunday dinner."

"I'm not sure Mack would agree."

"We can vote her off the island for a night. You're basically one of the family, anyway. You can sit in her seat."

I snort, and Zeke shrugs, like it's a perfectly reasonable suggestion and he can't think for the life of him why I wouldn't take him up on it.

I wish I could. I really, really wish I could.

Henry is shocked to see me at school. "What the hell is going on?" he asks the moment he's close enough to lower his voice. "Didn't you establish yesterday he can't be left home alone? Where is The Problem?"

"Don't call him that. And it's taken care of."

"'Taken care of'?" Henry echoes. "You killed him? Damn, Ivy."

"What?" I ask. "Why does everybody keep talking about killing him? No, he's *taken care of*. Emphasis on the 'care.'"

"Wait, what the hell does that mean?" Henry cries as we ascend the school steps. "Who's taking care of him?"

"Well . . . Mack is, actually."

Henry chokes and stops in his tracks. "Are you kidding me?" he hisses.

"She found out!" Before I go into detail, though, we need to get away from potential eavesdroppers. I gesture for Henry to follow me, and we pull over near a janitor's closet, in an unfrequented corner of the halls. Though the passing throng of students can still see us, there's no possible way for any of them to overhear or sneak up on us now. "Weston broke out this morning," I go on. "It's kind of hard to hide it, Henry, she lives right there."

"Okay, fine, I get that. But why is she involved now? It's none of her business."

"She offered to help."

"Since when do we fraternize with the enemy?"

"Since I needed someone to watch him while I went to school."

Henry looks wounded. "I would've watched him."

"Great news, because I was gonna ask if you can take to-morrow's shift."

Henry nods, then scowls. "And you can tell Mack I'm good to take as many as needed. We've got this without her."

"Don't you think it'd be nice to get some extra help?" I ask.

"In theory, absolutely, of course. If the mailman was free, I'd strongly consider it. But *Mack*—"

"I know. I get it. But she's actually been kind of cool about it."

Henry raises an eyebrow. "Is that so?"

"Yes, it's so."

"Has she apologized for anything?"

"Well, no—"

"Oh, good, so we're just gonna all act like nothing happened, then?"

"As long as she's our only option, then yeah, kind of."

"Ivy, she was *awful* to you."

"Yeah, she was. But, I don't know, I wasn't *completely* innocent, either. Maybe it's time to get over it."

Henry gasps and takes a dramatic step back. "It's like I don't even know you."

I give him a rueful smile. "Maybe I'm maturing."

"Parenthood will do that to you."

I choose to ignore that comment. "Anyway. Hopefully we'll figure out a way to get Weston independent soon. Like . . . soon," I say. Preferably before my parents get home. "Come over to my house after school?" I ask, before we split up to go to our lockers.

"*Duh*," says Henry, before narrowing his eyes. "But I am not being anything more than civil to Mackenzie. She's not my friend."

"Civil is acceptable," I say. We break away from our quiet corner and rejoin the halls, which have started to empty out as people pour into their respective classrooms. "See you in English."

The look Henry gives me tells me just how little faith my best friend has in me these days.

It's not, I think, entirely unjustified.

Like yesterday, I'm given updates about Weston's day in the form of written messages and photo evidence. Unlike yesterday, my stress levels lower as the day goes on, because it becomes abundantly clear that Mack's got the situation under control.

> He made me pancakes. I finished your honey. Consider that my payment.

Im sorry who the heck puts honey on pancakes???

> Me.

How have I known you for this long without knowing that fact?

> You never made me pancakes.

I guess its for the best. Our friendship would of been much shorter.

> Would've*

I'm going back to class.

> I'm disguising him.

What???

> Disguising, Ivy, I'm disguising him. You ever heard of disguises? Where you hide what you look like?

How

> I'll show you when you get home. You really should've done this earlier. He wants to go out.

Wait you're taking him out?

> No. I'll let you teach him that. Sounds exhausting. But at least now if he escapes in the night he won't be glowing everywhere.

Smart.

> Obvious. Can't believe you haven't done it yet.

I'm sorry if I've been a little bit DISTRACTED

> You should've involved me earlier. The whole thing's been mishandled since day one.
> No offense.

Offence taken.

Toughen up.

—

WHAT THE FUCK

What????

Mack?

What????

What happened

This motherfucker is magic

What? I know! I thought we established this

I didn't actually believe you though. I
thought you were just really gullible.

The shirt thing though

It was the middle of the night, I
figured I just saw it wrong.

Yeah no he's magic.

Yeah. I got that.

Ivy what the hell are we going to do?

You've got a magic teenager in your house

I'm working it out!

Not alone you're not.

"Why do you keep grinning at your phone?" Henry asks
when he approaches me at my locker.

I slam my finger on the lock button. "No reason."

"Has The Problem burned the house down yet?"

"No," I say, "but he's not a fire elemental. It's probably more
of a worry that he'll blow it away."

I mean it as a joke, but Henry looks alarmed.

"His elemental powers don't work, remember," I say.

"For now," Henry says darkly. "Let's not get complacent,
though."

I ignore him.

.   .   .

"Be nice," I say to Henry, half a second before Mack opens my front door. Henry's mom kindly offered to give us a lift to my house from school after we told her my ride was home sick.

"How was he?" I ask as Mack steps aside to let us in.

"Really good," Mack says. "Like I said, I fixed him up for you, too."

"You fi—what does that mean?" I ask.

"Well, gee, look who finally decided to come home." Weston saunters into the living room, and I double-take. He's still wearing this morning's outfit of a black leather jacket and slim-fitting pants—that's not optional, after all—but now he's wearing sunglasses and a beanie. Above his lip, a beauty mark has been drawn on in what looks like brown eyeliner, and he's got a thick, knitted scarf wrapped around his neck, covering his chin.

It's a choice, I'll give them that. I raise my eyebrows and turn to Mack, who's surveying Weston proudly. "Now it doesn't matter if he escapes. You're welcome."

"Did you buy an undercover celebrity costume online or something?" Henry asks. "Because that's what it looks like. It's somehow *more* obvious than the blue hair. Thank you, Mack."

Mack folds her arms and raises an eyebrow. "It's no more out of place than your costume," she says sweetly. "And no one's stopped you to ask why you're wearing that, have they?"

Henry touches the hem of his shirt—a button-up in a flamingo print that matches his shorts—with a wounded look. I jump in to change the subject back to Weston, feeling a little like a parent intervening in a sibling squabble.

"It was a really good idea to disguise him," I say, and Mack beams with pride.

Weston turns in a slow circle. "Mack said you'd think I look hot," he says, before striking a *very* subtle pose, one knee slightly bent. "I told her I don't give a damn what you think."

"You look good," I say pleasantly.

"Whatever," says Weston, primping himself.

"Thank you for staying with him today," I say to Mack. "Seriously. I really, *really* appreciate this. You didn't have to."

Mack hesitates, then gives me a small, almost shy smile. "It's no problem. I mean, I'm involved now, so . . ."

"Right."

"Yeah." She brightens, and the room brightens along with her. "Actually, I had a thought earlier today. There's something at my house that might be able to help him, but I didn't want to leave him while I went and got it. Should I go grab it?"

"Yeah, yes, please."

As soon as she leaves, Henry blows out his breath in a long whistle. "Can. Not. Stand. Her."

The room darkens again. "I know. But can you work with her?"

"For now. Maybe. But not if she keeps up with the jagged little comments."

"I'll talk to her." Even though Henry sort of started this one. I don't hate the idea of pulling Mack aside for a one-on-one chat. I won't accuse her of anything, of course. I'll just ask her to collaboratively work with me on a solution for her and Henry surviving the next couple of days. Like a coworker situation. It can't be that hard, right? After all, Mack and I seem to have figured out a ceasefire, and we have *way* more bad blood between us than those two.

Henry doesn't look especially mollified. "Maybe next time you could stand up for me? I know you don't want to go against your crush, but—"

"She is *not* my crush."

"Your ex-crush, then."

"I panicked," I said. "I hate conflict. But I'll have your back if she takes another dig, okay? I promise. But only if you promise not to start anything."

"Okay. Thank you."

"So, we're good, then?"

"No, we are not good, I want to strangle you. But if you think it's our best option—"

Before I can reply, Weston advances on Henry. Just as I have time to process the movement, he balls up his fist and pulls his arm back. Henry and I realize at the exact same moment what's about to happen. I shriek and grab Weston's shoulders while Henry dives on the floor, swearing at the top of his lungs.

"Weston!" I shout, holding on tight as Weston tries to shake me off. His scarf has come half-undone, and is dangling from his neck wildly as he twists in my grip. "*No!* No punching!"

"Holy fucking shit," Henry cries, scrambling to take cover behind the sofa. "What is *wrong* with him?"

"I will destroy you, vile scum!" Weston roars, still fighting against my grip.

I grip him tighter and struggle to hold him back while I crane my neck to check that Henry's okay.

"He doesn't know what he's doing, he's just following the story; oh my god, are you okay?"

"*The story?*" Henry hisses. He pokes his head over the top of the sofa to give me a bewildered look. "What *story?*"

"I'll explain soon." Weston finally gives up his struggle and, warily, I let go of him. When he doesn't move to pounce on Henry, I head over to help him to his feet, making sure to keep my body placed between him and Weston. "Are you okay?"

Henry straightens and shoots Weston a resentful glare. "Yes," he snaps. "But only because I have gamer reflexes."

Weston clears his throat, not taking his eyes off Henry. "Ivy, can I talk to you?"

"Oh, we're gonna talk," I say. "We are gonna have a long discussion about assault charges."

"That's true, I'll see you in court," Henry says, wheeling on Weston as the latter grabs my hand.

"You can't sue him, Henry, he's a fictional character," I remind him.

"Tell it to the judge."

"Be my guest," I say drily, tripping over my feet as Weston yanks me farther.

In the living room, which Weston apparently figures is private enough, he sits me down on the couch. He's softened his "hate" stance quite a bit. Does this mean we've transitioned into "love" as far as he's concerned? He did attempt to attack someone for me, I suppose. That's often how the whole "I've loved you all along" thing starts in your average hate-to-love tale. Love appearing in the passionate heat of danger and whatnot.

"Ivy," he says, "you have got to be more careful about who you invite into our space."

"Weston, this is *my* space. And actually, Henry is my guest, as are you. You don't get to go around punching my guests."

"I can't help it," Weston insists. "I hear you threatened, I see red. I'm very protective."

"Yeah, well, I'm gonna need you to take a second to evaluate the situation before acting," I say.

"If you hesitate, you die," Weston says, and I can't even be mad at him for the drama, because as far as he's concerned, it's kind of true.

"Sure, in a world where people have elemental powers. But Henry doesn't have those, and neither do I. Neither do you, remember? An unarmed person chatting with me is not an active threat."

"I'd rather overreact and attack the odd innocent than hesitate and lose you," Weston says. "I mean . . . not lose *you*. Just. Lose my nemesis. I enjoy our fights, okay?"

"Then we need ground rules. No punching Henry or Mack," I say. "Ever."

"I won't make any promises," Weston says. "Henry seems like an angry, angry boy, and he's never once addressed me personally. He only ever talks to you about me. Not to mention, Mack made multiple comments about me 'vanishing' today."

I cringe. "She did?"

Part of me had assumed Mack would come around to the idea of Weston after spending a day with him. On the other hand, this isn't exactly the best possible version of him, to say the least.

"Yes, she did," Weston says darkly. "I don't know what 'vanishing' is code for, but I can guess. I don't trust either of them, and, frankly, I don't think you should, either."

"Well, I know them a little better than you do, so, as long as you trust *me,* you should trust them."

I go to leave, but Weston grabs my arm to stop them. "Just tell me one thing," he says gravely. "Have either of them even *once* told you they see the way I look at you?"

"What?"

"You know, like . . . 'I see the way he looks at you, Ivy. He doesn't hate you. Not at all.'"

Well, if we need to find him a career in the real world, he's got some acting chops on him. If he didn't look quite so much like a certain existing actor, it could've been a real option for him. I gently remove his hand. "No, but—"

"*See?* How can you think they have your best interests at heart? It's like they don't even *want* you to find love."

Before I can reply, there's a knock at the front door.

"Now, Mack's back," I say. "Are you going to be nice to her?"

Weston looks pointedly at the ceiling and presses his lips together.

"She's not going to vanish you. I swear on my life. She just has a weird sense of humor. Okay?"

Weston takes a long, long time to reply. Finally, he scowls and follows me.

"Okay."

Chapter Eleven

PAST

Zeke answers the door when I arrive at Mack's house. He's swapped his usual contacts for glasses, and he's carrying his laptop under his arm. He steps aside to let me in, and then calls me back before I head upstairs.

"Ivy," he says, "you're into, like, fandom and nerdy shit, right?"

"You're one to talk," I say, slightly offended.

"I mean it as the highest compliment," he says hurriedly. "I'm working with my friend on a game idea, but we want it to appeal to girls, too. What kind of stuff do girls like in games?"

"Like, computer games?"

"Yeah, or phone ones."

I shrug. "I'm not really sure, sorry. I have one on my phone where you have to tip colored sand into different bottles, but other than that, I don't really game."

"Not even farming simulators?"

"What's a farming simulator?"

"Okay, I'm gonna send you some links tonight, and you

promise me you'll check them out, okay? It'll get you into gaming, I swear."

I give Zeke my word, and head upstairs to see Mack. She's on the bed pulling on her sneakers when I enter her room, and she straightens up as soon as she sees me.

"Hey," she says in a small, hopeful voice.

"Hey. How are you?"

"I'm . . . okay," she says. "How are you?"

"Okay. Kind of beat from yesterday still."

"Oh. How was it?"

"Good."

"That's really good." She finishes lacing her shoes, and then walks closer to me. Close enough that I can smell her perfume, a fruity sort of vanilla. "I'm sorry. I should've gone with you to the conference. At the very least I should've kept a better eye on my calendar so I didn't realize last minute."

It's all I wanted to hear. And I can tell from her face she means it, too. I wish I could go back to last week and redo the whole conversation.

"I'm sorry for yelling at you about it," I say. "And for saying it would've sucked with you. It wouldn't have."

"Did it suck with Henry?"

I grin. "Actually, no. It was a lot of fun with Henry."

"Okay, well, wanna go for a walk around the block? I want to hear all about it."

I point to my own sneakers. I learned a while ago not to visit Mack without dressing for exercise. "I figured we would. But tell me about the party first. How was Brianna?"

She waves a hand at Brianna's name, and a petty part of me *loves* that.

"She was fine. But, oh my god, there was *drama* between Avery and Danica."

We jog downstairs together as she launches into the story,

and even though I don't really care about Avery and Danica's fight, and even though my feet are still throbbing from all the walking at the conference yesterday, I can't wipe the smile off my face.

PRESENT

Mack has returned with a Ouija board.

Now, I have never used a Ouija board, because I am not sixty years old, but I know about them from movies. Enough to get the general gist, anyway.

"Are we having an exorcism?" I ask, stepping aside to let Mack in.

"You can't do exorcisms with Ouija boards," Mack sighs, as though *everyone knows* the ins and outs of Ouija boards and anyone who doesn't is grossly misinformed about the world at large.

"You're playing with Ouija boards?" Weston scoffs as he strolls in from the kitchen to see the commotion. He yawns, stretching his hands above his head. "Pathetic."

"Hush, you," I say mildly. After an afternoon of insults, they've begun to bounce right off me. They're still not, like, romantic, but at least they don't sting.

"You're a child," he says, taking several steps toward me.

"I'm rubber and you're glue," I say without looking up from

the box. That is, until Weston reaches my side and stares down at me until I reluctantly meet his gaze.

"Step on me," he says, his voice thick with desire.

Okay, that does it.

I call a meeting in the kitchen without Weston to discuss Mack's grand idea without bizarre propositions from my temporary enemy.

As we sit around the dining table nursing cans of soda I grabbed from the fridge, Mack lowers her voice to a whisper.

"I texted Zeke and asked him what he thinks about magic, and he was like 'Magic doesn't exist, everything can be explained by physics, take Ouija boards for example,' and I was all like 'Duh, Ouija boards!' If there's some sort of spiritual force out there, you can use this to ask them what the fuck is up. And my parents have one in the junk closet."

I consider it, and she studies my face before pouting.

"*What?* You can't at least try it?"

"But what difference does it make? However he got here, he's here, right?"

"If we know how he got here, we'll know how to send him back," Mack says.

I look at her blankly. "No. We're not sending him back."

"But—"

"*No.*"

She looks to Henry for support, but he just gives a tired shrug. "She likes him for some reason," he says.

Before Mack can tell me all sorts of things I don't want to hear about why I definitely should not like Weston—and I *know* she will, and it'll be convincing, because I know her down to her blood—I jump in with a topic change.

"What I *do* want to figure out is where to go from here," I say. "And unless the spirits have some really good connections in the rental market, I'd prefer to hear from you two. If you don't mind."

We decide to leave Weston behind with a video game and set up base at Mack's house for now, at least until everyone else comes home. It's too difficult to talk frankly with Weston in potential earshot, and, even aside from that, it feels a little rude.

We head to the yard, but not before Mack makes a pit stop at the refrigerator to grab us some lemonade and chocolate-dipped strawberries to take with us. This is one of the many things I miss about being Mack's friend. God-tier snacks.

We find a perfect patch of afternoon sunlight, in the middle of Mack's lawn, and sit in a small circle.

"So, last night, I figured something out," I say. "When Weston was yelling at me, he said something from one of my fanfics. Like, almost word for word. Then I realized, I wrote the exact same soul mate trope he used. And the sickbed trope, I used that in my latest fanfic."

"I'm not following," Mack says.

"I am," Henry says, a little too triumphantly. Mack shoots him an annoyed glance. "You're saying Weston's personalities are mimicking your fanfics. That's why he's acting differently every day."

"Yeah. And not only that . . . I think this version of Weston is, like, *my* version of Weston. That's why he seemed so off to you, but not so weird to me."

Henry's eyes are wide now. "Wait, is this why he tried to *punch me*? Why did you write an assault scene?"

"I'm sorry! It was part of my enemies-to-lovers fic. I was going through a thing, okay?"

"No, not okay. What does your therapist say about that?"

"It hasn't come up."

"Well, it *should*," Henry cries.

"Henry, enemies-to-lovers is a very well-liked trope. Plenty of people find it romantic. I'm not in the minority here."

"Oh yeah, the height of romance," Mack says. "That's exactly what I was thinking last night. This is so *romantic*, I'm so jealous."

"Jealous of Weston?" Henry asks slyly, and Mack's eyes widen. In horror? Or disgust?

"No," she says quickly. "Anyway, I was being sarcastic. *Obviously*."

"Don't 'obviously' me, I'm better at sarcasm than you," Henry snaps. "You can't school the teacher."

"Being prolific does not necessarily make you an expert."

"No, it doesn't. If it did, you'd be way better at—"

I don't dare risk letting Henry finish that sentence. "I think we can all agree insulting people isn't romantic in real life," I say loudly. "As I found out the hard way last night. Otherwise the tension between *you two* would be off the charts."

"The whole lesbian thing wouldn't have anything to do with it, then?" Henry asks. True. That, and the fact that Henry's aroace, but Mack doesn't know about that.

"Trust me." Mack smiles charmingly. "I could be the straightest girl alive and I wouldn't touch you with a ten-foot pole."

"But in books," I say, determined to keep us on track. "It's romantic. Hence, why I wrote it in the first place. *Hence,* why Weston inexplicably despises me today. Because he's following the script. He *is* the Weston I wrote in that fanfic. Today, at least."

Mack looks pensive. "So, how many fanfics have you got?"

"Four," I say. "And we've gone through three."

"Which would leave what being next?" Henry asks. "If your theory is correct."

"It is. And it'll be my coffee shop AU," I say.

"Which is?" Mack prompts.

"Coffee shop alternate universe. It's a sort of fic where you take characters and plop them in a coffee shop. In mine, Weston works in a coffee shop, and he meets the main character there when she goes in and orders her drink while he's working one morning."

Mack blinks. "Why?"

"Why not?"

". . . True. Then what?"

"Then . . . nothing. That was my last fic. I haven't written anything else, other than a few snippets for myself here and there."

Henry and Mack exchange a look I don't much like. It's a little too much like hope.

"What happens then, do you think?" Henry asks.

I can hear the unspoken implication loud and clear. Will Weston vanish when my material runs out? Do I only have one more full day left with him? Will I even get any warning, or will I just wake up to find him gone? The thought hits me like a kick to the gut.

"I don't know," I say. "We'll know the day after tomorrow, I guess. But until then, let's just assume he'll be here and that we need to figure out a solution. My parents get home tomorrow, so we need a plan either way."

Nodding, Henry pulls out his phone and navigates to the Notes app, while Mack sets about ripping grass out at the stem, piece by piece. A nervous habit I remember too well.

"To begin, let's list what we know," Henry says. "There was a storm. Ivy was home alone. She wished for Weston to be with her, she went to sleep—"

"You missed the part where the thunder replied," I say, and Henry writes it down dutifully.

"Strongly worded . . . discussion . . . with the weather . . ." he mutters as he does.

"The thunder didn't reply, Ivy," Mack says. "It was a coincidence."

"Oh, suddenly Miss I Was Wrong and Magic Does Exist doesn't buy that the thunder can hold a conversation?" I ask.

"Well, technically, thunder's just the sound of lightning," Henry points out, apparently reluctant to be taking Mack's side on this.

"Okay, fine, the lightning replied," I snap. Henry jots down the correction, then pauses.

"Could it have anything to do with climate change?" he asks.

"Henry, what the hell are you even talking about?" I sigh.

"There's a huge, unseasonal storm. Thunder, lightning, the works, then—bam, the lightning creates life."

"I'm not seeing the connection, either," Mack says.

"Okay, fine, gang up on me," Henry says. "But I'm making a note of this. If it turns out to be climate change after all, I'm never letting you live it down." When neither Mack nor I look particularly alarmed at the threat, Henry makes a show of finishing said note, and returning to the original bullet points. "Okay, what else do we know?" he asks.

"Weston's obsessed with Ivy," Mack says wryly.

"He changes every night," I say. "Every morning he has a different personality, and it lines up with a different fanfic."

"He has a magic reappearing outfit," Henry adds.

"He can conjure up items from thin air," I say.

"Wait, really?" Henry asks.

"I'm pretty sure. On the first day, he assembled a whole first-aid kit in, like, a second. I don't think we even had half the stuff in the house."

"We need to test this theory," Henry says. "See if Weston can summon, say, a vegetarian fried rice and black bean beef with sesame greens?"

"It's barely even five, Henry," I mutter. "And you just had *three* chocolate strawberries."

"Yeah, and I'm hungry again, okay? It's hard work fixing your life."

"He doesn't have any of those, like, air powers here," Mack cuts in. "Right? Doesn't he have powers in your show?"

"Yes," Henry says. "Well, specifically, it's a form of ancient elemental magic. Just calling them 'powers' makes them sound like superheroes. They're more, like, gifted experts in the art of—"

"Just write 'no powers' down," Mack says, and, looking annoyed, Henry does so.

"It *is* weird that he doesn't have control of the air element," he muses as he writes. "I can't think why. It'd be one thing if he were totally human, but he's obviously got some superhuman abilities."

That's true. He does.

But if I think about it, with everything I know, it isn't as weird as Henry says.

"It's because I don't write about his air powers in my fanfics," I say slowly. "At least, I'm pretty sure I don't. They're more focused on romance and stuff. Like, Weston as a *person*, not Weston as a magical being."

"But he does have magic here," Mack points out. "Outside of the air stuff. Is that something you wrote about in your fanfics?"

"No, not really." Weston's words from yesterday, when he tried to explain why he could keep me out of trouble but he couldn't make us fly, come back to me. "I think it's more, like, if something needs to happen so the fanfic can play out, then he can make it happen. He can conjure up first-aid stuff, and unlock locked doors, and get rid of obstacles that would keep us apart. All that sort of stuff. But if it doesn't follow the rules of the fanfic he's playing out, there's nothing he can do about it."

"Well, thank god you're more interested in romance than action scenes," Mack says. "Or the guy would be able to shoot tornadoes at people. Henry got lucky."

Henry turns purple. "*Lucky? Lucky* that I almost got *assaulted*?"

"No, lucky you didn't get your nose *blown off*."

Henry scowls, and turns to me. "You know," he says, "I am grateful for something. At least you never wrote an omegaverse AU."

"What's an omegaverse AU?" Mack asks, looking away from Weston.

"Long story short, Weston would be a werewolf or something," I explain.

Mack pauses for a long time. "People find that hot?"

"There's a lot to find hot about werewolves," I say primly. It's not even my preferred area of fanfic, but I'm not going to let them laugh at *any* fanfic tropes. These are my people they're talking about. Even if I don't have the time or knowledge to properly explain the ins and outs of omegaverse right now. "There's the protective aspect, the loyalty aspect—"

"Don't forget the bestiality aspect," Henry says.

"They're humans when stuff happens, Henry. Get your mind out of the gutter."

"So, is it, like, a danger fetish?" Mack presses. "Would Weston eat you?"

"*No*, Mack, that's not generally part of the fantasy," I say testily.

"Oh, but punching people is?" she shoots back, and Henry chokes on a laugh.

"Well, luckily for everyone involved, I did not make Weston

a werewolf," I say. "Anyway, back to the whole brainstorming thing. Anyone have any thoughts on our list?"

Henry holds out his Notes page and we lean in, scanning the words for a long while.

"Hear me out," Mack suddenly says into the silence. "Super-heroes."

"What about them?" I ask, looking up.

"Maybe you are one!"

I roll my eyes, but Henry holds up a hand. "No, no, let the girl speak."

Mack straightens and shoots Henry a grateful glance before continuing.

"What if you've been exposed to some sort of gene-mutating event, and you have the power to bring fictional things to life now? It's totally possible."

"Usually, I would argue that it's the opposite of possible," Henry says. "But now, truly, who knows? The laws of the universe are out the window and chaos is reigning, so, fuck it, maybe you're a superhero, Ivy."

"It's one theory," I say, feeling a little tired.

"And I know how we can test it," Mack says, jumping to her feet. "Let me grab my laptop. Be right back."

Moments later, Mack sets the laptop down before me and settles in next to me, close enough our legs are touching. She doesn't really need to sit this close to see the laptop, but I'm certainly not going to ask her to move. I hide my smile, and sit completely still, keeping the contact as it is.

"So, have you tried writing anything down since bringing Weston to life?" Mack asks, moving to type her password in. I look away while she does so, even though I probably already know it. Unless it's changed since last year, it's "cokenot-pepsi20." Still, it's not polite to stare, so.

"Nope," I say. "I've been a little distracted."

"The theory is untested, then. What if you can write him out of reality the same way?"

Henry rolls onto his knees, mouth open. "Holy shit, you could be on to something."

"For the thousandth time, I'm not sending him anywhere," I say. But as a jumping-off point, it's not such a bad one. Part of me thinks it's too good to be true, but maybe it's just that it seems too easy. In fairness, bringing Weston to life in the first place was easy. I barely broke a sweat. So why can't this be the solution? "But maybe that's how we solve Weston's whole living situation thing? We can just . . . write him a house, right?"

"Only one way to find out," Mack says. "Write that Weston gets a letter saying a long-lost uncle left him his house and fortune in his will or something. Boom, you're a trophy wife."

"'Wife' is a . . . strong word," I say, blushing. Mack cocks an eyebrow at me, obviously enjoying my discomfort.

"Wait," Henry says suddenly. "We aren't thinking big enough here."

"You want him murdered?" Mack asks. "I don't think it counts as self-defense when the threat's not active. Although maybe you'd get away with it if the victim doesn't technically exist?"

"That's not what I mean. You shouldn't just be focusing on Weston. What if you could bring people back to life, Ivy? You could resurrect the world's greatest minds! Albert Einstein, Marie Curie, Martin Luther King!"

I sit back, trying to process the idea. If it's true, does that mean I'm basically god? I don't feel like god. God would be way less of a hot mess.

"Let's try it out," Mack says excitedly. "Ivy, write something."

"What do I write first?" I ask as Mack hands me the laptop.

"Anything," Mack says.

"Write that a plesiosaur came to life," Henry says at the same time.

Mack shoots him a funny glance. "What? Why?"

"It's an impossible thing. If a plesiosaur appears, we'll *know* Ivy is magic."

"Don't you think an incredible disappearing shirt is proof enough?" Mack asks, as though it weren't only this morning that it wasn't proof enough for her.

Henry stares her down, then pouts. I lower the laptop lid so I can see him more clearly. "Did you just really want to see a plesiosaur, Hen?" I ask.

"Doesn't everyone?" Henry asks.

I shoot Mack a warning look before she can answer that. Mack shrugs back at me.

"Okay," I say with an air of determination. "Let's try to get you a plesiosaur."

Henry brightens considerably. "Thank you. *Oh,* oh my god, put in the original *H-MAD* cast auditions. Like, in a digital file or something."

"You're a genius," I say. "Good thinking."

"Why?" Mack asks. "Can't you just watch those online whenever you want?"

I shake my head absently. "Ugh, they keep saying they'll release them to the public to celebrate something or other, but they never do. It's a whole thing. And there's a rumor Chase bribed the producers during his, which is obviously bullshit, because Chase would *never,* and we want the proof so we can defend his honor and shut it down forever."

"It's so close I can taste it," Henry moans, sprawling back on his elbows on the grass.

"You could also consider writing in something about

Weston having a consistent personality," Mack says drily. "Just a thought."

"I *know that, Mack,*" I say, bumping my knee hard against hers. She does it back, harder. It feels like the sort of thing you do with someone you're close to, not someone you have a temporary cease-fire with.

Or, *or,* maybe I'm seeing things I want to see.

"I'm obviously going to include that," I go on. "But if we're going to do it, we might as well make the most of it, you know?"

"Like a cure for cancer?" Mack asks.

"Exactly. Like a plesiosaur and a cure for cancer, and maybe some spending money, or whatever."

Mack snickers. "You're literally a writer, and the best thing you can come up with to wish for is money?"

"Once you have money you can get most of the things you want anyway. It just buys me time to think of what I want later."

"Money can't solve world hunger," Henry says.

"No, it totally can." Mack frowns. "Any billionaire could afford to feed the world for a year, and think of how the world could look if hundreds of millions of people could work together on improving it instead of focusing all their efforts on surviving every day. Do you have any idea how many super-geniuses we have out there right now who can't reach their potential because they're trapped in poverty, when we *literally have* enough food in the world for everyone already? Like, you can't even measure how much the world has lost from that. Let alone the fact that it's just straight-up inhumane to let *anyone* go hungry when it's totally fixable."

Henry looks stumped, but not defensive. It's a good start. If he's going to be spending time with Mack, he'll have to get used to being wrong about stuff. A lot. The thing is, Mack's not the sort of person who starts arguments for the sake of it, or always has to be the devil's advocate. She's just naturally more competent than you, and isn't shy about letting you know exactly how wrong you are. Personally, I find it soothing. It's like, even if the answer seems impossible, when Mack's around, you know she either has the solution, or will figure it out.

"Okay, understood, we'll put 'solve world hunger' on the list," I say hurriedly.

"Thank you."

"And also money. Which, technically, I could've used to solve world hunger myself if you two gave me a second to sort it out," I add.

Mack covers her mouth with her hand, and it looks suspiciously like she's trying not to let me see that she's smiling. Her eyes give her away, though. They sparkle like hell whenever she finds something funny. I used to do everything I could to make her look like that.

"Okay, two things," she says, removing her hand. "One, why are you the only one who gets the money here? It's not like your magic's a limited resource, and Henry and I have spent a *lot* of time fixing *your* problem this week. We deserve a payday if they're being handed out."

"Okay, okay, we'll all be billionaires."

"Well, that's part of point two," Mack goes on. "I don't think we should be billionaires. It kind of seems like being that rich makes you want to hoard your money. I vote we add the big-ticket items into Ivy's story from the get-go, and limit ourselves to ten million each."

"Ten *million*?" I squawk. "That's *nothing*!"

"Okay, but I owed you five dollars last month and you came after me like a loan shark, so," Henry mutters.

"Yeah, Ivy, don't be greedy," Mack chides. "What do you need more than ten million for, anyway?"

"Um, I don't know? I'd need to give a couple to my parents; I'd need a mansion for them, a mansion for me; we'd all need new cars, and Dad's always wanted a boat, and yachts aren't cheap. And I'd want at least a couple mil to invest to provide us with a yearly income. . . ."

"Is magic money taxable?" Henry wonders out loud.

I throw my hands in the air. "*Is it?* Well, there's four million gone right there!"

"Not big on 'eat the rich,' are you, Ivy?" Mack asks.

"Mack, stop being judgy and let us have twenty million each," I say.

"Ugh, *fine*." Mack folds her arms, then looks sideways at me. "Joke's on you, I would've gone up to twenty-five if you'd pushed a bit harder."

I pull Mack's laptop closer to start typing, and Henry scrambles to stand behind me and observe the magic unfold.

Weston smiled happily. "Ivy, I have wonderful news. I have an uncle that I've never met, and he just died and left me everything. I now own a great big house only five minutes from here, and I have millions of dollars in my bank account. I'm going to go live there and I don't need a job because I will have money for life now."

Ivy clapped her hands. "Now we can be together without worrying about my parents or the world accepting you!"

"Oh, I almost forgot! He gave me this as well." Weston said. He pulls out a Tarddus–

"TARDIS," Henry says. "T-A-R-D-I-S. How are you this bad at spelling when you write this often?"

"Autocorrect usually catches it." I shrug.

"You sure about that?" Henry asks, leaning in to judge my

writing sample. I shuffle around so he can't see the screen, wounded.

"You do it, then," Mack snaps to him. Then she crawls around me to move to my other side, placing herself between me and Henry, blocking him out in the process. I do my best to hide how delighted I am at Mack's unexpected defense, but it's difficult.

~~Tarddus~~ Tardis and smiled at Ivy. "There's lots of gifts in it for you."

He pulls out a vial and a set of instructions. "Here is the cure for cancer. All the cancers with instructions on how to make it and it's really easy and cheap and anyone can do it with items they probably have in their pantry." He pulled out a bank card. "And here is my bank card so you can access my 60 million dollars, tax free. It all belongs to you now and the pin code is here." He passes her a four-letter code. Then he pulled out

I do some quick googling to check on the spelling, only pausing to give Henry a very brief side-eye.

Marie Curie, and Einstein, and Martin Luther King, and they are all shocked to be alive and in the future and they were also a bit sad that all their friends and loved ones were not there with them, and they were also eager to get to work inventing ways to make the world better!!

"Do you think I should resurrect their friends and family, too?" I ask, pausing. "It just seems like they'll be able to focus better if they're not grieving."

Mack sighs. "Fine. One family member each, though."

"Why?" I grumble. "It's not like we're rationing the magic." Mack stands firm, though, and I continue.

They were even more eager when Weston pulled out their favorite friend or family member to keep them company researching. Then Weston pulled out a plesiosaur

"No."

"Henry, I *just* checked it, it's right!"

He stabs a finger at the laptop like it's done him some great wrong. "What if something happens to it? If we only have one, the stakes are gonna be, just, so high. I don't know if you've brought any extinct creatures to life recently, but it's notoriously hard to keep them alive."

"Should I specify that it's immortal, then?" I ask.

"No," Mack says quickly.

"Do you have a death wish?" Henry cries at the same time. "If it's immortal, what do we do if shit hits the fan? Everyone knows when you bring extinct creatures back to life you have to—"

"Why do you keep talking about it like this is a common occurrence?" I ask, lowering the lid of the laptop. "No one knows what would happen, not even you."

"Um, yeah, they do. There's movies about it. A whole series, in fact."

"Just add in some more of them and call it a day," Mack says, with a heavy sort of resignation that tells me she doesn't think this a good idea, but that it's simultaneously not worth arguing with Henry over.

~~a plesiosaur~~ four plesiosaurs of breeding age, two male and two female, and gave them straight to SeaWorld for safekeeping. Then, Weston pulled out a lot of hair products and

*a new laptop and a golden retriever puppy, all the things Ivy
ever wanted and gave them to Ivy. Finally, Weston gave the
Tardis to Ivy.*

*"This has unlimited food in it," he said. "If anyone ever
wants food ever again, they can pull unlimited food out of
the Tardis. It will never spoil forever. There will be no more
world hunger now."*

"Ivy!" Henry protests. "You forgot—"

"Oh, right."

*"I forgot something," Weston says, putting his hand back in
and navigating around all the food. "Here is the raw audition
footage for H-MAD. Give this to Henry."*

*"Thank you, Weston," Ivy said ecstatically, and Ivy, and
Henry, and Mack, and Marie Curie, and Einstein, and Martin
Luther King and their friends and or family and the plesiosaurs, and the Seaworld staff, all cheer. After that, Weston
became a consistent predictable kind person, and the world
became a much better place to be.*

"It's perfect," Henry declares.

"How do you write that fast?" Mack asks. "You're superhuman."

I beam. "Practice."

Henry sits back and looks between Mack and me thoughtfully. "So, now what?"

"Now," says Mack. "We wait."

Chapter Twelve

PAST

"Señora Escalona has it out for me," I insist as Mack and I leave Spanish class.

"You think every teacher has it out for you." Mack laughs.

"Maybe they do," I say. "I'm starting to suspect there's a teachers' lounge conspiracy."

Mack snorts. "Stop."

"No, really. I think someone started a nasty rumor about me being a brat or something one day and they all made a pact to call on me for every hard question and catch me every time I ever even look at you."

"I think you're just a ball of anxiety who's terrified everyone hates her when, actually, no one hates you; we love you at best and are indifferent at worst."

"Okay," I say, making a beeline for my locker. "You could be on to something with the anxiety thing."

"Gee, could I?"

"It's just very important to me to be universally beloved," I say. "Is that so much to ask?"

"It could be a little much, yeah," Mack says, leaning against my neighbor's locker. "Hey, it's my turn to bring snacks to the team meeting tomorrow, and I want to make my banana bread. Mom offered to make it with me, but do you wanna come over and help instead?"

"When, tonight?"

"Yeah."

"Yeah, for sure," I say, grabbing my textbook. "But do you mind if we put *H-MAD* on? I missed yesterday's episode, and I was gonna watch it right after school."

I'm about to tell her I don't mind if she goes on her phone this time—I've thought about it, and really, I just want her company, and if she wants to do other stuff while I watch the episode, then I'm totally fine with it.

Mack lets out a deep sigh. "Do we have to?"

I close my locker and furrow my brow. "No. No, we don't. Um, I guess I can just watch it on my laptop later tonight."

"I'm sorry, ignore me. We can if you really want to."

Well, as convincing as that is. "Nope, the laptop is fine. I'm not gonna force you to watch it."

Mack smiles, and it's one of pure relief. "Okay, good. No offense, but it bored the hell out of me when you made me watch it last month."

So, I'm totally on my own for *H-MAD* stuff, then. It's an Ivy-only activity. That's . . . cool, I guess. It's not like I can't watch it alone, right?

So why does it feel like I just got slapped?

I hang behind Mack as we walk to her locker, dragging my feet. I'm being silly, I'm almost sure of it. Mack's rejection of *H-MAD* isn't a rejection of me. It doesn't mean that I'm boring, or that she doesn't want to be around me. She just invited me over to bake. We love baking together. And we go for walks, and we watch movies, and all sorts of things. So she doesn't love my favorite thing? I need to grow up and get over it. And I especially need to stop making her feel like she has to participate in *H-MAD* stuff.

Mack, who's digging through her own locker now, doesn't notice my sudden change in demeanor, which is also fine. I don't want to annoy her, or worse, make her feel guilty about not liking *H-MAD*. But at the same time, I wish she somehow magically knew I was feeling insecure, so she could hug me and tell me she definitely loves me, and I definitely don't bore her, and I don't have to feel weird about the possibility of my interests making my best friend not want to spend time with me.

That's when Henry passes us in the hall with a group of his friends. We haven't really spoken since the conference last week, though we've smiled at each other a couple of times. We're in that sort of friendship limbo zone, where we know we get along, but we don't have the foundation of months of shared experiences that makes conversation a given. Still, when we make eye contact now, he claps his friend on the shoulder to tell him to go ahead, and joins Mack and me at the lockers.

"Oh my god, the cliffhanger last night," he says.

"No, stop, stop, I haven't watched it yet!" I laugh.

"You what?"

"I procrastinated the Spanish paper and it took longer than I hoped."

"Oh, you wait, Ivy. You wait. It was crazy!"

Mack turns around slowly, one eyebrow raised. "Hi," she says to Henry uncertainly.

"Hey," he says. "Did you see last night's episode?"

She makes a strange face and shakes her head. "Nope. I don't watch it."

Right. I just decided not to make Mack sit through endless conversations about *H-MAD* not two minutes ago, and what am I already doing?

"You're in history with me, right?" I ask Henry.

"Yeah."

That works out well, because Mack has art class right now, on the other side of the school.

"If you promise no spoilers, wanna head with me?"

"Yeah, for sure."

Perfect. Now I get my *H-MAD* fix, and Mack doesn't have to stand awkwardly on the peripheries for it, bored out of her mind. It's a win-win.

"I'll see you at lunch, okay?" I say to Mack.

Her eyebrows shoot up in surprise. "Oh. Okay. Sure."

"Okay, bye!"

Henry and I head off together down the hall, while Henry hypes up last night's episode as vaguely as he can, as Mack watches us leave.

PRESENT

The next morning I wake up in my bed, and Weston isn't there. His nest is intact, though it's a mess of blankets and pillows all creased and crumpled. But the bird has flown.

I stare in confusion for a second, trying to figure out where he's gone. Could it have anything to do with our wish list yesterday? Has he gone to pick up his millions? Wait, does that mean the rest of the story came true as well? I'm suddenly wide awake. If so, where are the historical figures, and the cancer cure? My front yard? Or, like, the White House or something? I grab my phone, figuring if something like that went down while I slept it'd be national news, but before I can get that far, I note the many, many messages waiting for me from Mack.

> Ivy are you awake?
> Hey
> Hey
> Hi

Wake up

Now

Emergency

My heart sinks further and further with each message. Just as I get to the end, my phone begins to buzz.

"Hello?" I ask with dread.

"*Finally*." Mack's on the other end, and my stomach tumbles when I hear her voice. God, a couple of nice exchanges and, what, my brain thinks it's time to pick the crush back up where it left off? "He's here."

"Einstein?"

"What? No, *Weston*."

I see it coming right before the words leave Mack's mouth. So, I'm not a millionaire, then? "Where's 'here'?" I ask.

"Roast Me."

Well, if she insists. "You're way too judgmental for someone who used to have a crush on one of the Care Bears."

"It's the name of the *coffee shop, Ivy*," Mack snaps, and I fight the urge to snicker. "Also, I told you that in a moment of vulnerability, not so you could throw it in my face at the crack of dawn years later. Anyway, it's not a crime to be attracted to kindness."

"Do I want to know what he's doing at Roast Me?" I ask.

Mack's voice has a tinge of amusement to it, covered mostly by exasperation. "Apparently, Ivy, he is now somehow an employee at Roast Me."

I start digging through my closet for something, anything, to throw on. "I'll be there the second I can. I know you have practice this morning, but—"

"I'll babysit him until you get here," Mack agrees before I can even ask the question.

"Thank you, thank you, thank you."

.   .   .

As it turns out, Weston is indeed an employee of Roast Me. When I reach the coffee shop, I find him happily moving around behind the counter, operating the machines like he's been doing it for years. He's wearing an outfit I designed for him myself in my fanfic, a checkered shirt with the sleeves rolled up, loafers, and pants. He's also, thankfully, wearing his sunglasses and beanie, like I begged him to do from now on whenever he leaves the house. For some reason, this doesn't raise alarm bells with the staff.

Mack is dressed in bike shorts and a hoodie, and is watching Weston with an amazed expression.

"Hi," I say, and she swings around.

"Thank god," she says, grabbing my hand. I stare at it, forgetting about Weston momentarily. "Do you understand this?" she asks me. "I don't get how this is happening. Everyone's acting like this is *normal*."

Weston notices me at this, and he falls quiet. "Hi," he says in a soft voice. His eyes are locked intensely on mine, and when I meet his gaze he lets out a shaky breath. "You came."

I know what we're doing here. The original story follows Weston, a struggling but talented barista at a local coffee shop who recently left his previous career as an air elemental superhero. The barista's life is empty and lonely until a new original character in town, Yvette, starts coming in and ordering the same drink every morning. Luckily for me, barista Weston is someone I'm sure I'd actually want to know in real life. He's got life skills, cooking skills, and a great customer service attitude. Plus, he thinks Iv—*Yvette*—is wonderful.

After yesterday, I need that.

"How about we order a couple of drinks and sit together?"

I say to him. "You can take a minute away from the counter, can't you?"

The barista working alongside Weston gives me a pleasant, blank smile. There's nothing behind it. No light at all. "Of course he can," he says. "I'll hold down the fort in the meantime."

"I would've thought so," Mack mutters to me. "Given he was working alone when Weston showed up and asked for a job."

"Is that what happened?" I ask, baffled.

"Yup, right when I got here."

"And, what, the barista just said yes?"

"Yeah. He went all glazed over like he is now, too. It's really freaking me out, Ivy."

If I'm honest, I'm well past the point of being freaked out by any of this. I suppose I'm saturated.

"I'll be with you in a minute," Weston says with an honest-to-god wink. The customers around us don't even react to this. As far as their reactions betray, it's a perfectly normal activity for them to be served by a sunglasses-wearing stranger who's obviously flirting with the girl next to them.

They seem about as brainwashed as the barista does.

Wait, is this what he's done to my parents? To the school? When he made it so the school didn't report me for leaving early, or so Mom didn't call me five times a day, did their eyes glaze over just like this?

The thought makes my stomach pull and twist.

"Okay, we've got a vanilla latte," Weston says, and a tall woman steps forward. "It's not really a vanilla latte anymore, though. I added a hazelnut shot, a macadamia shot, and swapped the regular milk for oat. I'm actually really good at my job, and I can tell from looking at you that you're not great with dairy. It's time to get out of denial and get around plant milk."

The woman takes a sip of her coffee and gasps with an expression that's somehow both enthusiastically delighted and devoid of any real emotion, all at once. Like a toy doll. Her eyes are dead, even if her face is animated. "This is delicious," she says. "You're a coffee genius."

Weston laughs. "Yes, I am. Bye now."

The woman practically skips out of the shop. I stare after her in disbelief.

"Thank you so much for calling me," I say to Mack in a low voice as we step away from the crowd. "I don't think I would've put two and two together by myself. He would've been waiting here all day."

Mack moves past me to a pair of double-seater tables in the corner, as far away from prying eyes as possible.

"Aren't you gonna go to practice?" I ask as Mack takes a seat at the table closer to the rest of the coffee shop.

"Well, I've missed it now," Mack says wryly, and I groan.

"I'm *sorry*."

"You didn't do anything," Mack says. "Besides. It's a break in the monotony of normal life, right? I like being in on the joke."

"Some joke," I say, flopping down across from Mack. Mack shakes her head and points at the empty table next to us. Oh, right. It's not Mack I'm here on a date with.

"You know what?" Mack says, getting to her feet. "Hold my seat, would you? I'm gonna grab another drink, if we're doing this."

"Got it. Ask Weston to make it for you. You might as well get a free drink for all your trouble."

Weston and Mack return a few minutes later, Mack with an Americano, Weston with two iced coffees, both of which have a shot of hazelnut syrup and sugar. It's Yvette and Weston's whole thing in the story. They both like their coffee freezing, unbearably sweet, and not the least bit sophisticated.

Like me.

And every other queer person in America, in my defense.

"Thanks," I say to him when he gets comfortable. "So, early morning for you, huh?"

Weston nods. "I figured you need me to get a job, right? Why not follow my dreams and become a barista?"

Mack doesn't even pretend not to eavesdrop. She straight-up angles her chair around so she's basically the third person at the table, give or take a few feet of space.

"Were they even hiring, though?" she asks, with an amused expression that says she knows full well they were not.

Weston shoots her a confused look. "Why wouldn't they hire me?" he asks. "I make a much better coffee than the sewer water they were serving this morning. They're lucky to have me."

Actually, this could work. The way he went about this is slightly unhinged, but ultimately he has a point. I wrote him to be superhumanly good at making coffee, right? So, why shouldn't he be able to get a job doing it? And then, maybe he can rise through the coffee shop ranks. Open a franchise. Take over the caffeine world one sip at a time.

Most importantly, he could afford to rent his own place then.

Mind you, can he even earn a paycheck without any ID? Or a bank account?

And what would it mean for everyone around him? Is he going to brainwash the town so he can get a paycheck?

"It's probably best we go home for now," I say to him. "If you still want to work tomorrow, we can look into the logistics of it."

If he's still here at all tomorrow.

"So, Weston," Mack says. There's a sudden sting to her voice, and a stiffness to her spine. She folds her hands together and raises a single eyebrow at him. "You're all about Ivy, huh?"

Weston beams. "Absolutely. We're soul mates. Remember the tattoo?"

"I *do*," she says with false sweetness. "But it disappeared, didn't it?"

She crosses one leg over the other and leans back in her seat. It's like she's sized him up and found him lacking. I've never once seen her act like this—confident—cocky, even—yet cool. It's almost like she finds Weston threatening. Or maybe it's more accurate to say she wants Weston to know that *she's* a threat.

I say almost, because I can't think of any realistic reason that would be the case. The only reasons I *can* come up with I have to dismiss as pure fantasy before I even let myself latch on to them.

Weston runs his tongue over his teeth. "So? We found each other. It served its purpose."

"You sure it doesn't mean you're not actually soul mates?"

Weston appraises her coolly. "I'm quite sure, thank you," he says.

"What about Vanessa?" she asks. I look at her, surprised she remembers who Vanessa is.

"We broke up," Weston says.

Mack feigns sympathy. "I'm sorry to hear that."

Weston straightens in his seat, but lowers his head. "Thank you. It was hard. I used to think she was wonderful. Caring, selfless, rational. But then one day, I just realized she has absolutely no personality, no real goals, and the world wouldn't be a better or worse place if she'd never existed. She had absolutely no effect on the universe whatsoever."

I nod enthusiastically. "Totally. I totally get that. It sounds like you came to your senses."

"I did. It took me longer than it should've, but I did."

"Oh my god, Ivy," Mack says, shaking her head with a sudden giggle. "You and that poor girl."

I shoot Mack an irritated look. "Excuse me?"

"For someone who's a proclaimed feminist, you obviously can't stand her, and for no good reason, either."

I sniff. "I adore women, as you know. In all the ways they can be adored. But that doesn't mean I have to adore all of them."

"Yeah, but she's not, like, racist or abusive or anything. Right?"

"That you know of," I say darkly.

I know for a fact that Mack would agree with me on that point if she weren't so caught up in being right. But she is, so she doesn't.

"She just doesn't meet your lofty standards of what makes a person worthwhile."

"My *lofty standards*?" I ask.

"Yes, your lofty standards! You don't get to just write someone out of their own romance because you think you deserve their boyfriend more."

"You do when they're *fake*," I snap.

Weston looks completely baffled.

"She's got a fake . . . personality," I clarify, and he *ah*s.

"Admit it." Mack grins. "You're jealous of a *fake* person. You're jealous of her, so you pretend she sucks so you can justify it and you don't have to admit it."

"No, she sucks, so I'm jealous of her. You're mixing up the cause and effect here."

"Uh-huh, but you *are* jealous of her." Mack laughs.

I narrow my eyes. "And so what?"

"So, you would absolutely come for any other girl who talks about women like you talk about Vanessa!"

"I would never talk about a real woman like I talk about Vanessa. Have you ever heard me do that?"

"It's a slippery slope, Ivy."

"Oh, slippery slope, my ass," I cry, and Mack breaks out into laughter.

"Besides," I say. "I'm surprised you even know who Vanessa is. It's not like you ever listened to a word I said about any of it."

Suddenly, I can tell I've gone too far. Something akin to hurt flashes across Mack's face, and she stops giggling. I want to apologize right away, but I'm not really sure what I'd be apologizing for exactly.

"I listened," Mack says quietly. We lock eyes, and I'm suddenly aware of exactly where my heart sits in my chest. There's something about the way she says it that feels like a confession, a regret, and an unexpected intimacy, all at once.

"Hey, ladies?" Weston says somewhat awkwardly, and it's only then that I remember he's sitting across from me. "I thought I would be chatting with Ivy but, correct me if I'm wrong, this conversation seems difficult for me to join in on. Which is odd, considering it seems to be about *my* ex-girlfriend, but—"

My phone starts ringing at that moment, cutting Weston off. I give him an apologetic look before answering.

"Hey, where are you?" Henry asks. "I'm here."

In the confusion, I've completely forgotten it's Henry's shift to look after Weston today. Oops.

"We had a situation," I say. "We'll be home in about fifteen. Let yourself in."

"So, he's alive?"

"Yup."

"I figured none of it came true. If Martin Luther King came back to life, it'd probably be trending online by now."

I sigh. "Unfortunately. Middle class it is for the foreseeable future."

"I'm no worse off than I was yesterday morning," Henry says, "but somehow I *feel* like I am."

"I know. You can mourn the millions you just lost with a vacation day."

"Hmm. Some vacation. I think school is less stressful. Speaking of, did he do his whole hocus-pocus thing to get the school off my back for skipping today?"

"I asked him last night and he said he did, but I'll double-check. You told your mom you're coming to my house after school, right?"

"Yup. You sure it'll work?"

Well, I've yet to hear from own parents outside of the odd text to tell me they're safe and way too busy to bother me with a phone call, so. "I'm pretty confident, yeah."

"Good. How is our new friend today?"

I'm pretty sure he's not referring to Weston's emotions. "He's . . . really lovely today, actually. We're at the coffee shop."

"Of *course*."

Mack has a sour look on her face again. All traces of humor have suddenly vanished in the span of that phone call.

For the life of me, I can't figure out what I said.

"Mack's here, too," I say. "She found him."

"Really? And how's *Mack* doing?"

He says it in a bizarre, singsong sort of way. Very different to his usual tone when we discuss Mack. I lean backward, hoping Mack can't hear Henry's voice through the phone.

"Hey," I say to Mack and Weston, remembering something. "Can you two excuse me for a second?"

They nod, and I head out the front of the coffee shop for some privacy.

"She's fine," I say. "Why?"

"Oh, nothing. Just . . . she was very helpful yesterday, wasn't she?"

"So?"

"So . . . she doesn't like Weston much, does she?"

"Neither do you."

"Right. But she seemed—come on, Ivy, you had to have noticed?"

"Noticed what?"

He takes a while to answer. "She seemed . . . sort of . . . she never had a crush on you, did she?"

"What? No, why?"

"Just wondering."

I want to press him for clarification, but I also don't want to leave Mack stranded with Weston for too long. I make a mental note to ask him what he means later. For now, I have a more pressing thing to talk about before I head back in.

"Hey, Henry?"

"Yeah?"

"Weston's . . . yesterday, he said he feels sort of uncomfortable around you. He said you've never spoken to him directly."

"Oh."

"I'm sure you weren't doing it on purpose or anything."

"I was. He creeps me out. He gives off seriously weird vibes. It's, like, Weston Razorbrook but not. Human, but also not. I'm not into the uncanny valley."

"The what?"

"The uncanny valley. It's when things look human but something's just a little off. It sets off our evolutionary alarm bells. Some people think that at one stage in our evolution, there were creatures that might have looked a little bit too much like us, but weren't human, so we've still got the freaked-out reaction built into us."

My mouth falls open. "Oh. Cool. That's a horrifying factoid to get first thing in the morning."

"You've had your first cup of coffee already, haven't you? You should be able to take it."

"Ha-ha," I say bluntly. "Look, I'm only bringing it up because if you're gonna babysit Weston all day, you're gonna have to be able to talk to him. Even if he reminds you of the alien species that used to hunt your ancestors or whatever. Are you okay with that, or do I need to stay home today?"

"No, fine, I'll talk to him," Henry says. "But I'm *gonna* be freaked out by him. I can't help it."

"You'll get used to him," I promise. "He grows on you."

"Doubt it."

"Love you."

"Yeah, yeah. Just bring him around so I can get this over with."

I hang up, and take a deep breath. It bothers me that Henry doesn't like Weston. Not because I expect him to or anything. It's just that Henry likes everyone, barring Mack, and he had a good reason for that. If Henry thinks something's off about Weston, should I be wary? Or is Henry just weirded out about the whole magic-is-real thing?

No. Weston's odd, but he's good. I wrote him to be good. He's just an acquired taste. Henry will get there, sooner or later.

And maybe a day alone with him is just what he needs to get there.

Chapter Thirteen

PAST

"Around the corner, around the corner," Henry cries, and I shift my analog stick hard to the left. "GET HIM," Henry screams, and I shriek and send a laser beam in the direction of the movement. A cloud of orange fire and smoke billows up from the area where my beam landed, just by the side of the abandoned building I was sneaking through. "Yes, Ivy, yes," Henry crows, and I pump my fist in the air in victory.

"Okay, meet me at the base," I direct Henry, steering my character in that direction. We fall silent, side by side on my couch, concentrating.

While our characters run, Henry clears his throat. "Um, Ivy, you're bi, right?" he asks.

"Yeah."

"I thought so. You came out a couple of months ago, right?"

"Mm-hmm."

"So, what does that mean? In a practical sense?"

I slow my character to a walk—I've reached a forest area

where there aren't too many enemies—and glance sideways at Henry. "It means I can like more than one gender, I guess."

"Sure, but how does that play out? Like, are you attracted to Weston and Vanessa?"

I snort. "Weston? Yeah. Vanessa? Hell no. Just because I *can* be attracted to a certain gender doesn't mean I'm into every single person in it. Like, you don't get a crush on everyone you ever meet, do you?"

"Nope."

"Exactly. Even if they're the gender you're attracted to, right?"

Henry is quiet for a long time. I sense, suddenly, that something's coming. Before he can even speak, my mind flies back to months ago when I came out to Mack. She handled it so well—better, I think, than I did when she came out, because I was too busy going into a bi panic about the fact that my crush was a lesbian, and I wasn't even dreaming. She made me feel so good about confessing. What did she do? Can I replicate that for Henry, if he says what I think he might be about to say?

"I'm actually not attracted to any gender," he says casually.

What was it Mack said? "Congratulations"? Yeah, that would feel weird coming from me right now. Better play it by ear.

"Oh?" I ask. Oh, well done, Ivy, very celebratory.

"Yeah. I mean, like, not sexually or romantically or whatever. No crushes. I don't want to kiss anyone."

"Cool," I say. I'm trying to be casual, because he's trying to be casual, but I think it came out as too casual. Damn it, Mack did this much better than me. "So, do you mean asexual? Aromantic?"

"All of the above."

"Nice."

A grin touches Henry's mouth, and he breaks out into a chortle. "Nice," he mocks.

"Shut up, it is! It's awesome."

He doesn't take his eyes away from the screen, but the smile stays on his face. "Yeah?" he asks eventually.

My character resumes her journey through the forest. "I always heard queer kids have a way of finding each other. I guess it's true."

Henry jumps onto a rooftop—the safest place in the game—and finally looks at me. "It wasn't really an accident, though," he says. "It's partly why I asked you if you were going to the conference. I wanted to meet another one."

"Another one?" I ask in disbelief, and he buries his head in his arms.

"You know what I mean!"

"You make us sound like we're infiltrating the allocishets."

"Yeah, I figured, now that I know someone who was walking among us, I should go walk with her," he deadpans.

"It's a good little army we're building." I smile.

"That was the plan from the start. You were a perfect first recruit." He jumps down from the roof, which I guess means we're back to serious talk. The sort of conversation that's easier to hold without making eye contact. "Um, I don't really want to tell anyone else yet. I just thought I'd say it out loud, to see how it felt."

"How did it feel?"

"Okay. Weird."

His character and mine finally meet at the base, and our figures stop in front of each other.

"But it feels like the truth," he says.

I get that. When I first noticed I was getting crushes on girls, it took me longer than I'd like to admit to accept that they were actually crushes. Maybe it's because girls are always talking about how gorgeous other women are—which is fair and correct—but I figured that's probably all it was for me. An appreciation. An intense, all-consuming, passionate *appreciation,* often of one very specific girl at a time, all day, and most nights, as well. How are you supposed to catch on that the way *you* think women are breathtaking is different to the way all the other girls seem to think women are breathtaking? It's very confusing.

Then, when I finally figured out that I *did* mean breathtaking in a different way, a part of me was afraid, because it meant I'd have to do all sorts of things I wouldn't if I were straight. I'd have to figure out how to come out, and how to talk about it, and how to tell if someone is a safe person to discuss my sexuality with. I'd have to deal with homophobia, and biphobia, and unrequited crushes on straight girls, all while simultaneously trying to navigate the other parts of teenage crushes, which are humiliating enough to begin with, let's be real.

But through all that, another part of me was relieved and felt lighter, because I'd figured out an important truth about myself. And I love that truth, because it's *me.*

Sometimes, you really just need to say scary truths out loud to someone you trust.

I take a deep breath. "I can tell you a secret, too, if you want?"

"For mutual blackmail material?"

"No." I laugh. "For bonding."

"Is that what we're doing?"

"Yes."

Henry's character starts dumping all his loot in the storage chests on-screen. "Well, stop stalling, what's the secret?"

I roll my eyes and pull up next to him to wait for the chests to become free. "I like Mack. Romantically."

He lets out his breath in a loud *woosh*. "Huh. What's that like?"

I think about it. "Unrequited love sucks. It hurts, man. I keep reading into things, and thinking maybe she likes me, but then I figure I'm probably imagining stuff and projecting onto her, and it's a mess all the time. Plus, I feel like I let her down over and over again, and it's like being gutted whenever I think about it. And, like, the worst part is, I was prepared to get unrequited crushes on straight girls who couldn't like me. But I guess I forgot that I can also get rejected by queer people who like girls just fine, they just don't like *me* in that way, which is, you know, amazing for my self-esteem."

Henry laughs at this. "Honestly, it sounds like shit. You're not selling me on the whole 'unrequited romance' thing."

"I stand by what I said. You'd hate it, trust me."

Henry's smiling again, the comfortable, slightly awestruck sort of smile of someone who can finally say exactly what they mean, because everyone in the room knows the context behind it. I remember that feeling—like, when I could tell Mack I thought a girl was pretty, knowing she knew, for the first time, that I probably didn't mean it the way straight girls mean it. It's satisfying, the way slotting in the final jigsaw piece of a thousand-piece puzzle is satisfying, to know people are taking your words the way you mean them. We play in a comfortable silence for a little while, and then he purses his lips.

"I don't like that she hurts you."

"Mack?" I ask. "She doesn't."

"She did before the conference."

"That was just an argument," I say. "We're past that."

Henry's character finds a group of enemies and promptly starts murdering them, blood spraying across the screen. My character hurries in his direction to back him up.

"Yeah, well," he says, "she better not ever hurt you, or she'll have to answer to me. No one messes with my friends."

"That's very chivalrous of you," I say as my character reaches his side. It's too late for me to help. He's already wiped the area clear of enemies.

My phone buzzes, letting me know the delivery person has arrived. "The pizza's here!" I say, jumping to my feet.

"Already?" Henry asks, stretching.

We pause the game, and Henry follows me outside to collect the pizza, which is when I notice Mack across the road. She's in the middle of taking the trash to the curb, and she pauses when she sees me, something that looks an awful lot like betrayal flashing across her features.

"Hey!" I call out to her, but she just lifts a hand weakly, and then turns back inside. Frowning, I greet the delivery person and stand there for a few seconds, just in case Mack pokes her head back out. She doesn't.

"You did invite her, right?" Henry asks.

"No, I didn't think she'd want to come," I say.

"Hmm," he says. "Maybe give her the option next time?"

And put her in the position where she has to tell me how boring she'd find it? Gee. That sounds fun.

The worst part is, this is all amplified by my feelings for her. Would I even be this stressed about whether or not she finds me boring if I didn't secretly want her to tell me she wants to spend every waking moment of the day with me? Probably not.

This really shouldn't be this hard, should it? I shouldn't be this worried that I'm going to make her hate me. She might stop liking me if I keep bringing up *H-MAD*; she might stop liking me if I try too hard not to bring up *H-MAD*; she might stop liking me if I keep asking her to watch it; she might stop liking me if I don't invite her when I watch *H-MAD*. I don't want to lose her—desperately, I don't want to lose her—but if I was meant to have her, would it be this hard? Or would we be designed for each other?

It feels like that's it. Which means my crush is even more pathetic. I should wait until I meet someone who matches me. Someone who it's easy with. Someone who the universe throws me together with. Not someone I have to carefully thread the needle with, getting everything just right, all the time.

If only it were as easy as switching off my feelings.

Sighing, I head back inside with Henry.

PRESENT

It's my first lunchtime without Henry in the longest time.

I stand at the entrance to the cafeteria, steeling myself. I can do this. I'm sure I can do this. I can sit alone. No one's going to be judging me. No one's going to even notice me. Everyone is the main character of their own lives, and to them, I'm background scenery at most.

I've survived a lot of curveballs this week. If I can do that, I can eat lunch alone.

So, gritting my teeth and steadying my breathing, I take my place in line, grab a tray, and pick out my food. There's a long table near the cafeteria wall with half its seats still empty, so I make a beeline for it, sitting at the far end of it. Fixing my eyes on my food, I count to ten and look up. Not a single person is whispering about me, because of course they aren't. My fear of doing things alone is irrational. I know this. But it still makes my heart race.

Look at me doing it, though.

My moment of pride is surprisingly cut short, however,

when Mack slides in across from me like it's totally normal. Like we do this every day.

Just like she used to.

"Hey," she says, and I play along, totally casual.

"Hey." I hope she can't tell how excited and shocked I am from my tone.

Mack stabs at her salad, then her eyes flick up to me and lock on. "I read a couple of your books last night."

At first, I think she means the books on my bookshelf, which strikes me as unlikely, given I'm not missing any. Then, I realize she means my fanfics.

"You did?"

"Yeah. They're good."

Coming from someone like Henry, Mr. "I love people and making them feel good and also everything to do with *H-MAD*," this wouldn't be much of a compliment. But coming from Mack, it leaves me briefly speechless. Even setting aside her general disinterest in *H-MAD*, she's not really the gushing type. In fact, I'd assume she's lying, if not for the fact that I've never known Mack to give someone a fake compliment in her life. The real ones are hard enough to pry out of her. And I should know. I've tried plenty of times in the past.

"Thank you," I say. My cheeks are turning red, which is horrendous of them.

Mack swallows a mouthful of romaine, then nods. "I noticed they're not heavy on the fantasy, though. Like you said, Weston doesn't do that air control shit once in the two I read, but I think that's why I enjoyed it, because I'm not really big on fantasy books. Yours are more like romances, though. In a really good way, I promise. Where do you get all those ideas?"

In all the time we've known each other—in all the time I've been *writing*—Mack's never once asked me anything about the process. Hearing those words come out of her mouth makes me warm right down to my fingertips.

"Oh. I don't know. Sometimes I'll be going through something really emotional, and I'll think of how I wish it went, and it just feels amazing to write it down. Like, I can pretend real life went that way, I guess."

"And then you can just sit down and . . . write. For hours?"

"Yeah. Everything else stops existing when I do. It feels like I'm safe from everything, you know?"

Mack smiles. "Actually, yeah, I do. That's how I feel during volleyball. It's like tunnel vision, and it doesn't matter if I've got too much homework, or if the girl I like doesn't like me back, or anything like that."

She glances at me, and I meet her gaze, and it feels like being transported back in time.

"How is volleyball going?" I ask.

"Pretty good," she says. "I hurt my wrist a month or two ago and I had to do my captain duties on the sidelines for a while, and I'm getting back into things, but I feel like I've fallen behind the other girls now. I'm sure I'll get the hang of it again, but it's wild how quickly you lose fitness when you take a break."

"I'm sorry," I say. "I didn't know that happened."

"It wasn't broken or anything. Just, you know, it's not advised to do a sport where you have to hit a ball as hard as you can when you've got an injury already."

"Generally not the best idea," I agree with a grin, and she giggles.

"No."

"That sounds tough."

"Yeah. And, you know, it's hard for me to feel like I'm falling behind the other girls," she says, and then she looks suddenly pensive. "Or maybe you don't know, really."

"What?"

She watches me carefully as she speaks. "You know, the day I told you I couldn't go to the conference? I don't know if you remember, but I was in the running for captain then. When I realized I'd double-booked, the first thing that went through my head was, well, I can't go, I've committed to Ivy, and she needs me. The second thing is that those girls were going to go out together, and form bonds, and take photos without me, and I might lose this opportunity I'd been working so hard for. You have to be a team player to be the captain."

Huh. I mean, I'd known that she was in the running. Now she puts it like this, it *does* make sense that the party had that extra layer of importance to her. I don't remember cutting her any slack as a result, though. Had I gotten too zeroed in on the fact that it was Brianna's birthday—too jealous, and sure that Mack was just waiting for any excuse to ditch me—to even consider that she might be choosing the party out of obligation more than anything?

"I didn't even think of that," I admit. "I think I was so, like, primed to take anything about *H-MAD* personally back then that I overreacted. I'm sorry."

Mack nods, but it's in a distracted sort of way, as though she's considering whether to go on. I guess she decides to, because she snaps back to me and clasps her hands together.

"You know, I don't regret becoming captain, but it can be a *lot* sometimes. Like, I don't know if you noticed, but volleyball is a super-white sport. That changes things. It makes me feel like I have to prove I belong there, and I'm committed enough, and talented enough, over and over again. The pressure is on, just, *all* the time. It sucks to have to feel like I have something to prove, and it is *tiring*. I mean, imagine what would've happened if I'd skipped an event the whole team was going to *right* before they assigned the role. I couldn't give them an easy excuse not to pick me when I was the one who'd earned it."

She's always been the hardest worker on the team, hands down. The first one there, last one to leave. The first one to encourage the girls struggling, and to congratulate the girls killing it. It hadn't surprised me at all when she got captain. But somehow, I'd missed that she was under that much pressure. That she was feeling trapped into sacrificing things like a day at a conference she'd already paid for, with her best friend, simply to stay in the running for an opportunity she'd already earned a hundred times over.

Maybe if I hadn't been so jealous, and defensive, and self-involved, I *wouldn't* have missed it.

"That sounds exhausting," I say.

"It is, honestly. I'm exhausted all the time. But I'm also proud."

The words make me feel a rush of affection toward her. "You should be," I say. "I'm proud of you, too."

Her eyebrows shoot up and drop, like it's not what she expected to hear. "That—huh." She laughs. "That means a lot, actually."

I'm blushing now. I can feel my cheeks heating with it, and there's no way she can't see that. How embarrassing. "So," I say quickly. "You wanted to go to the conference with me?"

"I told you that to begin with."

"Right. But I didn't believe you. I'm really sorry. The whole captain thing—the timing of it—it didn't even occur to me."

"I wish I'd just told you."

So do I. But she didn't, and how much of that is because I didn't create a space where she *could*? I'd been so ready for her to let me down around *H-MAD*—so caught up in whether or not she enjoyed it, and what that meant about her feelings toward me—that I'd completely missed how she was feeling, and what was going on in her life. It hadn't even occurred to me to ask *why* she cared about that party so much. I'd just assigned her a narrative in my own head—one where I was the main character, and everything other people did was directly related to me and how they thought of me—and rolled with it. I thought I was in love with her, but I hadn't even tried to see things from her perspective, or thought about how things are harder for her, or even bothered to *ask*. The bare freaking minimum, and she didn't get that from me.

How self-absorbed *am* I?

"I'm sorry you didn't feel like you could," I say, shame sitting like a clump in my windpipe.

Mack takes a sip of her drink and looks thoughtful. "You know, it was really important to me back then that you thought I was invincible."

I smile. "What?"

"Yeah. Like, I wanted you to think I was doing really well, and I had all these friends, and I had it all together, and everything was easy. Maybe it was just that I liked that you always said I was the competent one, that I could solve any problem, and handle any challenge. I don't know. All I know is I didn't want to let you know I was struggling. Just as much as I wanted you to figure it out on your own and help me."

Well. As right as she is that I haven't gone through anything like that myself, I sure do understand the feeling of wanting someone to just *know* something is wrong, when it seems like the most obvious thing in the world. If only they'd pay more attention. If only they cared enough to.

"I wish I did," I say simply, and Mack gives me a funny smile.

"Anyway," she says, straightening. "Obviously, it worked. Here I am. Captain."

I smile. "I'm really proud of you."

"It feels good to tell you that," she says. "It feels good to talk at all, honestly."

The words make me feel warm right down to my fingertips. "I'm glad you found out about Weston," I say.

"Me too," Mack says without hesitating. "I honestly thought we'd never talk again, before that. But now it feels like nothing ever changed."

I'm not sure about that. To me, it feels like a whole hell of a lot has changed. But I'm not sure that's a bad thing.

"Why did it?" Mack asks when I don't reply.

"You know why."

"I know we had about a thousand arguments, but I don't know why they meant we had to stop being friends. I thought we resolved them."

I bark a laugh. "We didn't resolve them. We'd just push past them every time and pretend the fight didn't matter, and I don't know about you, but I did it because I didn't want to lose you. Then, eventually, I realized losing you was an inevitability."

Mack frowns and shifts in place. "What does that mean?"

"It means we had nothing in common. I didn't like volleyball anymore, and you hated *H-MAD,* and you hated conferences, and you hated Henry."

"I didn't hate Henry."

"You called him a 'huge freaking loser.'"

"I did not!"

"That's a direct quote, Mack."

"I did *not* call Henry a loser," Mack insists, and I decide to let it go, even though Mack one thousand percent called Henry a loser. I'm starting to suspect I was much more in the wrong than I used to think I was in everything that went down, so this is not the hill I'm going to die on.

"Well, you definitely weren't his biggest fan," I allow.

"Yeah, because—" Mack cuts herself off and falls into a strained silence.

I don't push her to reply. And, like I expected, she eventually collects her thoughts and continues.

"Because you *were* his biggest fan, and you weren't mine anymore, and you hadn't been for ages, and I didn't know how to fix that. Then he waltzed on in and he didn't even have to try. He was just already the kind of person you wanted to be around. Plus, you were always saying how pretty he was. I figured you'd found someone, and the first thing you were doing was choosing them over me."

I furrow my brow. "I wanted to be around you. How many times did I beg you to come to conferences with me, or watch an episode with me?"

"I did."

"You didn't."

"I *did*," Mack says firmly. "At first. But you didn't want me to just chill with you. You wanted me to be as into it as you were, and you knew I wasn't, and it upset you. I knew it did. And it always made things really uncomfortable and weird, so I stopped trying. I couldn't make myself enjoy stuff I just didn't. Even if it was the only way to spend time with you."

Obviously, Mack has a point. It *did* upset me that she didn't get into my hobbies. But it wasn't exactly because I expected her to like whatever I liked. It was more that I felt guilty for dragging her along to stuff she was obviously not enjoying.

Then, I started talking to Henry, and we realized we were basically the same person. It'd seemed like the perfect solution. It didn't have to be Mack and me. It could be Henry, Mack, and me. Or Mack and me, and Henry and me, and Mack and her teammates. Henry and I could do fandom things together, and Mack and I could find new things to bond over. Reinvent our friendship. Find out who we were together now that we'd started growing into different people. Because different people could still love each other, right?

But Mack hadn't seen it like that.

You were his biggest fan, and you weren't mine anymore.

"Mack," I say. "I wasn't trying to replace you with Henry."

"You didn't have to try," Mack says. "It happened pretty easily from where I was standing."

"I didn't care that you didn't like the same stuff as me. I just cared that I had no one who did."

"Same difference."

"I promise, it's not." I wanted her, too. I'd always wanted her.

Mack's staring into space with a pained look, like she's remembering a feeling she doesn't especially want to revisit.

"You cared, Ivy. You called me a boring jock, remember?"

"I did not!"

"You definitely did."

"I would never."

"Apparently you would."

We lock eyes, and I break away first. "Well, I don't think that," I murmur.

Mack sighs, long and heavy. "And I don't think Henry's a loser."

"Thank you."

"And I don't think you're an obsessive nerd with no life."

I wince. "I forgot you said that, actually."

"Oh. Damn it."

"Could've gotten away with that."

"So close."

Everything seems so straightforward right now. Why did it all feel impossible to fix last year? Maybe we weren't growing apart like I feared we were at the time. Maybe we were just growing, and instead of allowing ourselves and our friendship to evolve, we both railed against those changes, trying to keep things as they were.

If that's the case, what does that mean for us now? Can I accept that Mack and I have different interests without projecting my fear of abandonment on her over it? Can I show her that there's plenty of space for both her and Henry in my life? Can we create new traditions together, where we're both getting what we want? Or do we leave us in the past?

I don't want to leave us in the past.

I take a sip of water and, steeling myself, I voice the question I'm terrified to hear the answer to.

"Can you be friends with people you don't have a couple of big things in common with?"

Mack doesn't even hesitate. "I think so. You might just need different friends for different parts of your life."

I raise my eyebrows in a "well, duh" sort of way. "Uh-huh. And what do you think I was doing with Henry, exactly?"

Mack's face goes through an interesting array of emotions at this. Surprise, understanding, and then something akin to embarrassment.

"Well, when you put it like that, it makes perfect sense."

Is it true? Did I never simply sit Mack down and explain to her what Henry meant to me, and that it didn't mean I loved her any less? Why didn't I? Could we have avoided all this if I'd just toughened up and gotten vulnerable?

"It felt like you liked him more than me. I kept trying to tell myself I was being stupid, though. Then you told me you didn't want to be friends at all anymore, and you went off with him instead, and it felt like proof I was right the first time. You just . . . left me for him."

As soon as the words leave her mouth, she looks like she wants to take them back. They hit me with full force.

The day that I finally ended our friendship, I'd felt . . . weirdly relieved. Like I finally had control. Like I was making a call that'd end both of our misery, when neither of us were brave enough to. Somehow, I'd thought she was relieved, too. At least she was no longer on the hook for babysitting me whenever I had to be around people. Aka, all the freaking time.

But she wasn't relieved, was she?

I hurt her, didn't I?

The realization makes me want to throw up.

"The stupid thing is I never saw it coming," Mack admits. "I guess, even though I knew you were getting upset, I thought we'd figure it out sooner or later. I thought you were someone I couldn't lose. Until, suddenly, I did."

Oh.

My lunch is completely forgotten at this point.

"You know," I say, "the irony is you didn't even lose me, exactly. Not in a, like, 'I don't like you anymore' sort of way. I liked you too much, I think, and I could feel you pulling away, and I didn't want you to leave me. I guess I figured if I left you, I wouldn't have to go through the whole . . . being-devastated thing."

I can't believe I'm admitting this. My airway feels tighter and tighter, like I've got a boa constrictor wrapped around my neck. Maybe this is how I die. Suffocating from extreme embarrassment and vulnerability around the girl I'm pretty sure I never stopped liking, no matter what I tell myself.

Mack's giving me an unreadable look. "You liked me too much, huh?" she asks in a funny voice, so funny I wonder if she knows. Like, *knows*. But it's impossible to tell, and I've more than exceeded my upper limit for embarrassing, vulnerable confessions without reciprocation to recharge me. So, I shrug noncommittally.

"Yeah. But I wish things went differently. I mean, you and Henry actually seem to get along okay these days," I say. The subject change feels much safer.

Mack grins. "I regret my old fantasies now."

"Fantasies?" I echo.

"Yeah. I used to lie in bed at night and just think of all the ways he might vanish. You know, like, his parents deciding to move away, or he goes for a hike and is never heard from again. Not, like, murder fantasies."

"Just ones where you're chilling out, totally innocent, and the universe conspires to make things work out perfectly for you," I fill in.

"*Exactly.*"

"So, what you're saying is . . ." I clear my throat. "You used to be really into fanfiction about our lives."

Mack, looking both horrified and amused, blinks. "Yeah. I guess so."

"Well," I say lightly, "we're finding out more things we've got in common by the minute. At this rate, we might even end up friends again."

"We won't have a choice if we keep it up," Mack agrees.

"Weston won't be happy at all," I say.

"Oh, don't stress too much about that. Isn't he vanishing tomorrow, anyway?"

I glare at her, and she holds her hands up. "I'm kidding, I'm kidding. Kind of."

"I don't know," I say. "I hope not."

Mack studies me. "And have you got a plan for him yet? Given your parents are returning . . . when?"

"Around eight."

"Eight."

Refusing to meet her eyes, I shrug again.

"Okay. Does that mean it's up to me to figure out a solution again?"

She doesn't sound even a little mad about it.

"If you'd be so inclined, a solution would be much appreciated, yes."

She rolls her eyes, and I'm almost sure the amusement in them is real.

"Got it. Well, when should I come by and try to save the day? Right after school, or . . . ?"

"Yeah, I'm not busy," I say. "Come by whenever."

"I will." She pauses, then lowers her voice. "I think you need to tell him, by the way. Weston."

"Tell him what?"

"Everything, Ivy. That he's from your fanfics. That you don't know how he got here, or how long he'll be here. That he has no history, no ID, no connections. That he basically doesn't exist."

I gape at her. "Oh, I'll just drop it into conversation over dinner, should I?"

"No, Ivy, you sit him down, you take a deep breath, and you tell him."

"*You* tell him."

"I didn't bring him into the world. Besides, I think he needs to hear it from you. And he needs to hear it tonight. Otherwise, how's he gonna understand why he's hiding from your parents, or how to get a job, or apply for a house? If he doesn't vanish, we need to think realistically and make a *plan*. And he's gotta be involved."

As much as I hate it—as much as the thought of dropping a bomb like this on Weston makes me feel ill, and as much as I wish I could keep living in denial—I know she's right. As usual.

Keeping Weston in the dark isn't going to help me in the slightest, and it definitely won't help him.

"Fine," I say. "I'll tell him tonight. With you and Henry."

"Done." When I give her a faint smile, she reaches across the table and squeezes my hand, and my mind goes temporarily on strike. "You'll be okay," she says. "It'll be okay. We'll figure it out."

Swallowing, I squeeze back, and hold on until she eventually lets go.

The bell rings, and for a moment, we stay sitting. I don't want to break the moment, because right now, in it, I feel like I never lost her. But it's not the truth, which makes it fragile.

"By the way," she says, standing up. The moment shatters, and I don't think she even notices. I fight to keep the disappointment off my face as she continues. "I found a typo in one of them."

I scrunch up my nose. "That's all I ever hear. I'm not good at spelling, okay? You have to look past the rules and find the vibes."

Her face is funny. "I don't mean you spelled something wrong. I mean, you did. Lots of things. But that's not what I'm referring to."

I pause halfway through packing up my tray. "Oh?"

"Yeah. You, uh, called Weston 'Mack' in one of the scenes. Yvette and Mack."

I stare at her. I understand her words, but my brain isn't quite ready to accept the utter humiliation of their implication. It's simply not possible that I did that, and Mack herself saw it. Nope. The universe can't hate me that much, it's a step too far.

When I don't reply, Mack shrugs and turns on her heel.

"Anyway. See you tonight," she says.

She's too far away to hear me by the time I finally work up the courage to open my mouth and answer her.

Chapter Fourteen

PAST

"Do you wanna come by for a walk after school?" Mack asks.

It's the start of lunch, and we're sitting in the cafeteria, in our usual spot near the windows. Henry is with his usual group of friends a few tables over. He has a standing invite to sit with us, and sometimes he does take us up on it, but more often than not it's just Mack and me. I scrunch up my napkin in my fist and give her a sheepish look.

"I can't, I'm sorry. I'm watching the new episode with Henry, and then we're gonna play some video games and stuff."

It's obviously the wrong answer. Mack's grip on her soda can tightens.

"When are you ever not?" she says icily.

"What?" I ask, wary at once. "It's just Mondays. It's our routine."

"Just Mondays? You were with him on Saturday, too."

Okay, that's not fair. "Yeah, and I invited you."

"To watch a cast interview."

I shrug at her, getting annoyed. It feels like she's picking a fight on purpose. "So? That's what Henry and I do. You're welcome to join if you want, or not."

"Oh, no, I get it," she says. "Henry and you have your own little thing, and I can come and third-wheel if I want, but I shouldn't expect to do anything I'd wanna do."

"Maybe you should invite us to do something with you, then," I say. "Then you can pick the activity."

"I just asked you."

"And I wasn't free. Ask me on a night I'm free."

Mack glares at me. "Uh-huh. And when are you free next, Ivy?"

"I don't know. Whenever."

"Tomorrow?"

"You know my parents don't like me having people over two nights in a row." She throws her hands up, and I drop my palms on the table in frustration. "Mack, you know that's one of my rules. You just said tomorrow to make me look bad."

Like I said. She's trying to pick a fight.

"No, I'm just not used to having to work around your incredibly busy schedule with your new boyfriend," Mack says. "I guess I have to book you weeks in advance now."

"He's not my boyfriend," I snap. "And you're not my only friend anymore, so you might have to get used to it."

"Sorry, I forgot you're so in demand now. I'll make sure to get my ticket."

"Mack," I say, "you have always had more friends. Don't forget, I literally met Henry when you ditched me for them."

"Oh my god, are you going to bring up that stupid conference every single time we have a fight about anything?"

"It's relevant! I've always had to be the one who knows I won't always come first with you, because you have other priorities. Now I do, too."

And I should be allowed to have a life outside of her, shouldn't I?

"Don't worry, you've made it very clear I'm not a priority."

"Not my only one, no."

"Not one at all."

Now I'm just plain mad. She wants a fight? She can have a fight. "Maybe you would be if I didn't feel like I had to tiptoe around you all the time," I say. "'Don't talk about *H-MAD*.' 'Don't invite me to *H-MAD* stuff.' 'Don't leave me out of *H-MAD* stuff.' 'Don't watch *H-MAD* with Henry because I want you to be free to exercise with.'"

"Wow," Mack says, and her tone is cutting. The derision in it makes me angrier, and even though I know I'm being a little unfair, it feels good.

"I know I'm not good enough for you as I am," I go on. "You've made that clear. I'm only allowed to be friends with you if I do the things you like, or talk about the things you like."

"Do you hear yourself right now? You know you're describing yourself, right?"

"You literally called me boring!" I cry.

"I did not call you boring. I would never."

"You did. You said you were bored out of your mind watching *H-MAD* with me. But it never occurred to you that maybe I'd get bored hanging out with the volleyball girls while they ignore me, or going outside to walk around and around, or talking endlessly about the girls even after I quit the team, huh?"

"Right," Mack seethes. "So what you're saying is I'm a boring jock."

"I'm saying volleyball is boring to me, and I haven't liked it in forever, but I talk about it because that's what you do when you're friends with someone. You pretend to care about their interests."

Mack lets out a bark of a laugh. "Wow. Well, please, Ivy, don't feel like you ever have to pretend to care about my interests. You already don't even pretend to care about me, so why bother?"

"Totally, Mack, because me daring to have another friend in my life means I don't care about you at all, you got me."

"All I'm saying is, it seems like when you're given the choice to hang with the boring jock you've been friends with your whole life and the huge freaking loser you met, what, last month? You pick option B every. Single. Time. Admit it, you've replaced me with a boyfriend."

"Henry is not a loser!"

"'Oh, I'm Henry, let's watch a director's cut of a show we've watched a million times and shoot fake people with fake guns while we make sarcastic comments.'"

"Yeah, very accurate impression there, Mack, well done."

"See, you've even picked up his sarcasm. You're morphing into him."

"Am I?" I ask. "Well, if I'm a huge freaking loser, and so is Henry, and you can't possibly pretend to care about anything we care about, then that's all we need to know, isn't it?"

Mack opens her mouth to reply, then hesitates. "What do you mean?"

"I mean there's no point in hanging out at all," I snap.

Mack locks eyes with me, and I get the distinct impression that if she could throw her tray at the window without getting detention for it, she would.

"Doesn't sound like it'll be any different from how it is right now," she says.

"Perfect," I say, before I can stop myself. Before I can realize the implications, and that this is the last thing in the entire world I'd ever want. That if I close this door, it won't lead to us passionately admitting our true feelings for each other, terrified at the loss we almost faced—it'll just lead to loss. I'm coasting on rage, not logic. "It won't be a loss for either of us, then."

Mack gives me a tight smile. "Sounds good to me."

PRESENT

"So, I've been thinking," Henry says, clutching his coffee mug with trembling hands.

The three of us—Henry, Mack, and I—are seated at my kitchen table. Mack and I found Henry and Weston safe and sound after school today with no major incidents to report. However, although both of them are safe, it's a stretch to say they're both exactly how we left them this morning.

"Wh—" I start, but Henry barrels on at top speed. He seems to be vibrating. I'm not sure exactly how many drinks Weston served Henry today, but I don't get the impression that many of them were caffeine-free.

"What was I thinking? I've been doing a lot of thinking. I've had a whole ton of thoughts, and some of them are useful thoughts. I thought I should tell you some of the useful thoughts. The both of you. You and Mack. Weston isn't really a great conversationalist, but it's not his fault, it's mostly that he doesn't have any of the context he needs to understand anything

I have to say, so he's just been making drinks for me while I think."

"Hazelnut macchiato, lightly salted, with three pumps of syrup," Weston says at my side, placing the drink in front of me with a flirtatious wink. Let the record show that I did not order a drink. It does sound interesting, though, so I accept it graciously. Weston returns to my kitchen bench, which is littered with coffee pods, syrups, and milks, and promptly gets started on another drink. Henry insists none of it was bought; one moment the bench was empty, the next, it was like this. Given the speed at which Weston assembled a first-aid tray the day he was born, I'm inclined to believe Henry's version of events, even if it just makes me more annoyed that our world-peace-and-bucketloads-of-cash idea didn't work. Why couldn't I have written a fanfic where Weston was a secret billionaire before all this went down? *Why?*

Henry has stopped talking and is gazing at the wall behind me. Mack shoots me a worried look.

"What, specifically, were you thinking?" I prompt, and Henry startles, as though he forgot he was speaking.

"Right. Um. I was thinking a lot, and I thought, like, Weston needs a job, right?"

"Ri—" starts Mack.

"And who does he look like?"

"Myself," Weston pipes up from the counter.

Henry points a finger at him so excitedly he almost leaves his seat.

"Exactly, exactly. He looks like himself. Who looks like Chase Mancini. So, I thought, hmm, maybe cosplay, but I don't know if cosplay is all that lucrative, unless you do, like, viral videos and stuff, but that seems like more of a long shot to me; correct me if I'm wrong. But, um, then I thought, like . . . like, impersonation, right? He could totally be a Chase Mancini impersonator. He could go to parties, and, like, galas and stuff as Weston for a hundred dollars an hour, or fifty an hour, or whatever the rate is, I don't know. Comic-Con! They do that stuff, right?"

When he sees my skeptical face, Henry waves a hand at me.

"No, no, they totally would, don't get all down on the idea. Then he wouldn't even need to do the whole hat and glasses thing. He could just say he's a method actor. It's perfect, you can't tell me it's not perfect."

"It'd be a flawless plan," Mack says, "if he lived in the city. Or LA or something. I don't know if there's enough impersonator roles in, like . . . the whole of Philadelphia to pull it off as a career."

Henry twitches visibly. "Part of the plan is him moving to New York. I thought that was implied."

"*Oh,*" Mack says, brightening. "Okay, now I'm on board with Henry's plan, actually."

Weston arrives with a drink for Mack.

"Iced vanilla espresso, no foam, with cream," he informs her, and Mack holds out a hand to accept it with a nod.

"Anyway," Henry says, before taking a sip of his own coffee (short ristretto three-pump pumpkin spice). "I figured we can make him a website or something, maybe look up some casting agents?"

"Casting agents?" I repeat.

Henry hesitates. "Maybe? I don't know how you get a job as an impersonator, I'm spitballing here."

"Well I like the barista idea," I say, gesturing at our drinks. "It's his passion, he's good at it. . . ."

"As long as the skill set doesn't disappear tomorrow like the tattoos did," Mack says.

Or like he *might,* mouths Henry, and I shoot daggers at him.

Henry, bouncing his leg and drumming his fingers on his knees, takes another sip of coffee. With a stern look, Mack grabs the mug and slides it over to her side of the table.

"Killjoy," he mutters.

"You'll thank me later," she says.

"Okay, so, maybe the job thing waits until tomorrow, then," I say. "At least until we know all the variables."

"Which leaves tonight," Mack says.

Tonight will be . . . interesting, to say the least. Of course, it's occurred to me to simply ask Weston to alter reality so my parents are happy for me to have over a teenage boy they've never met—one who just so happens to look exactly like Weston Razorbrook, who they definitely would recognize—but I really, *really* don't want to. Seeing the empty faces of the barista and customers in Roast Me was creepy enough. I don't want to inflict that on my own parents. Not even for a night. Not even if it makes our lives easier. We have to hide him the old-fashioned way: with deceit and manipulation.

"Tonight will be fine, I think," I say. "Weston, you're fine with hiding in my walk-in whenever my parents knock, right?"

"I will meet your parents when *you're* ready for that, Ivy," Weston says.

God, I love the sensitive-barista version of him. I really got it right with this story, huh? And I wrote it before my enemies-to-lovers fic, too. Maybe the more you try to understand love, the further from it you get.

Or maybe reading dozens of fanfics a week just corrupted me over time.

Almost unconsciously, Henry gets to his feet and starts slowly pacing around the room.

"We need to figure out logistics for tonight. Where's he

gonna stay when Ivy's parents come home?" he asks. "What if they start walking around checking if there's any damage to the house? That's what my mom does. She acts like she's not, but she totally is."

"He can hang with me," Mack says. "Weston, how do you feel about helping me practice my volleyball serves?"

He considers it, and shrugs apathetically. "I guess?"

"Sorted," she says decisively. "And if you still need a place for him tomorrow, I can sneak him into my basement and do a shift after my parents are in bed. He can sleep on the couch."

"And I'll take him the next night," Henry says. "I have the biggest bed, so it'll be fine, as long as he keeps his voice down."

"I would prefer to stay with Ivy," Weston says, sounding slightly put out.

"I know," I say. "But we're just trying to keep you safe until we can get you in a place of your own."

"Which surely shouldn't take more than a couple of days," Henry says drily. "I mean, how hard can it be to save up a deposit, figure out a fake ID, and secure a rental?"

"Henry," Mack chides. "One thing at a time. Ivy knows it doesn't make any sense, but we don't have any better options."

Actually, I hadn't thought about it in that level of detail, because every time I try to think logistics I feel anxious and overwhelmed and my brain starts making a static sound until someone distracts me with something. When they put it like that, this is a really bad situation. There's no way we can keep this up for long enough for Weston to leave the nest. And that's if everything goes smoothly. How the heck do we find Weston a fake ID?

Mack sees my terrified expression and softens. "Ivy, we'll figure it out," she says. "There are options. If he can get a cash-in-hand job somewhere, it'll be a great start. We'll ask around at school, see if Zeke knows anyone. Worse comes to worst, he can just hypnotize some coffee shop employees again, right?" I open my mouth to protest, but she plows on quickly before I can. "And if we can find a cheap shared house full of people who aren't too picky about background checks, he won't even need anything too official. We can *totally* get him a fake driver's license that's good enough to fool a bunch of college kids. If Zeke doesn't know *anyone* with a fake ID, I'll be *very* surprised."

"Zeke doesn't seem like the partying type," I say, trying to cling on to her words nevertheless. It's fine, because she said it all confidently, and if Mack's confident then I need to trust that. We will figure this *out*.

"By the way," Henry says. "Mack, I spent a lot of time thinking about us today."

"Us?"

"Yeah, us. Because I hated you a bit before, but now I don't hate you at all. I think, now we've gone through trauma and stuff, we should try and form a trauma bond."

"Trauma bonds aren't good things, Henry," Mack says.

"Oh. Well what about a regular bond, born of trauma?"

"I think that's still called a trauma bond," I muse.

Henry tips his head back and groans. "So, we can't bond at all?"

Mack clears her throat. "I know what you mean," she says. "You'd like to be friends."

"Isn't that what I said?" Henry asks.

Mack considers it. "We can. But I should probably apologize first, if we're going to do that. I don't think I ever did, did I?"

"Apologize?" Henry asks, before blowing a raspberry. "For what? I didn't even know you called me a loser."

"Except, clearly, you did know," Mack says. "Given that it's information you have."

Henry gives her an innocent look, and I refuse to meet Mack's eyes.

"Well, I'm sorry," she says. "I was jealous, and I took it out on you, and you didn't deserve that."

"Thank you," Henry says. "And I'm sorry for all the millions of way more insulting things I said behind your back in response over the past year."

"What?" asks Mack.

"What?" asks Henry.

"Fresh start," I say quickly. "That sounds great for everyone."

"Besides," Henry says, "there was nothing to be jealous about. I wasn't into Ivy, and she wasn't into me. I'm both ace," he says, holding up one finger, "and aro," he says, holding up his second finger so he's making a peace sign. I'm not sure it's intentional, because he's trembling quite a bit from the caffeine still.

Henry looks over at me, full of pride. "And now two people know," he says.

"Look at you go." I grin. "You're killing it."

"*Thank* you."

"Who said I was romantically jealous, though?" Mack asks, and my stomach swoops at the question.

Henry shrugs. "Because it's way more common to have multiple friends than multiple lovers?" he asks.

"Don't use the word 'lovers,'" I moan.

"Why not?" Henry demands. "What's wrong with 'lovers'?"

But before I can reply, Weston joins us with his own drink. At once, we fall quiet, and the other two look at me. Okay. This is it, I suppose. I promised them I would tell Weston about his origins before my parents came home. That leaves now or, alternatively, never.

"So, Weston," I say. "Whatcha drinking there?"

"Christ on a bike, Ivy, rip the Band-Aid off," Henry mutters.

"*Ivy,*" Mack groans.

"*Okay, fine.*" I sigh, and face Weston again. "We have something to tell you."

Weston, who was happily stirring his drink, pauses. "Okay?"

"Now, it's a little strange. It might be shocking to hear. But you just need to let me explain, because we—I—think it's important you know."

Weston nods, the picture of seriousness, and, taking a deep breath, I dive in.

"There's a TV show we all love"—I glance at Mack—"Henry and I love, called *H-MAD*. It's about a group of teenage models who get elemental powers after a portal to another dimension opens near their photo shoot."

Weston's mouth drops open. "Wait, what?"

"Yeah. I know. Do you see where I'm going with this yet?" I ask.

"He's magic, Ivy, not psychic," Henry mutters.

Weston, still gaping, shakes his head. "*Wow.* I've never heard of it. How can they do that without consulting us?"

I open my mouth to reply, then process his words again. "Hmm?"

"You can't think it's a coincidence that they made a TV show that *happens* to follow my life story, can you?" Weston asks reasonably. "It sounds to me like they heard about us and ran with the idea. That must be illegal. Isn't it?"

I look helplessly at Mack, and she gestures at me to go on.

"Well," I say. "The thing is . . . the main characters of *H-MAD* are Weston Razorbrook and Vanessa Sweetfierce."

"They used our *names*?" Weston cries.

"Ivy, you're gonna have to get to the point," Mack urges.

Okay, okay. "No, you don't understand," I say. "You were

in the show. Kind of. I wrote fanfiction about the show—stories about the characters—and I sort of . . . created you, accidentally, I think?"

Weston's expression is unreadable. I take that as a sign to keep going. "I don't really know how it happened. There was a storm, which may or may not have been relevant, and I wished for you to be with me, and then I woke up, and you . . . were. Are. That's why you're here."

Weston shakes his head slowly. "That makes no sense."

"That's what we thought, too," Henry says. "And yet, here we are."

"Think about it, Weston," I say. "How did you get here?"

"Like, this morning? You brought me here with Mack. We were at the coffee shop—"

"No, before that. How did you end up at my house? A few days ago, you were here. How? How did you find me? Did you look me up? Take a car? A bus? What were you doing right before you came to my house? How did you get inside?"

He opens his mouth, then closes it. Something a little like panic flashes in his eyes.

There it is.

"I . . ." He swallows, then looks between the three of us for help. "Hold on, hold on. Do you think I could have amnesia?"

"That depends," Henry says wryly. "Ivy, did you write an amnesia fic by any chance?"

"No, Henry, I did not."

"Then, no, you don't have amnesia. You just didn't exist before Ivy wished you into existence. Or wrote you in. Or whatever went down."

Weston slowly gets to his feet and starts to pace around the room. The three of us watch him warily, but we don't speak. It's fair enough that he should take some space to process things.

I'm sure I'd feel similarly scrambled if I realized I had no business being alive.

"But . . . but I feel real," he says. "If I wasn't real, wouldn't I know?"

"You are real," I say hurriedly, and he gives me such a hopeful, heart-wrenching look that I almost regret telling him at all. "You've just been real for a little . . . less time than the rest of us."

"But it puts us in a hard position," Mack says. "None of our parents will let you move in in a million years, but you don't have anywhere else to stay, you have no record of existing at all, you have no money. . . ."

Weston paces faster and faster.

"We did come up with a great plan that involves you moving far away," Henry adds. "If that helps."

Weston snaps his head around to give him a startled look. "How far?"

"We can talk details later."

"It might not come to that anyway," Mack says. "You might vanish tomorrow, you see."

Weston stops pacing altogether, distress clear on his face, and I whirl around. "*Um.* Can the two of you possibly *not*? For, like, a few minutes, at least?"

Henry and Mack have the grace to look chastened. Weston, however, looks like he might pass out.

"Why would I disappear? What do they mean, Ivy?"

I jump up and take his hand in mine. "You aren't going to disappear. I promise. It's just, I have four fanfics, and it's been four days, and . . . I mean, I wrote a story about someone who takes care of someone, a story about soul mates, and a story about someone who falls for a guy who works *in a coffee shop.* Is that ringing any bells?"

Weston squeezes my hand so tightly I lose circulation.

"Huh," he says shakily. "I guess it *was* a bit weird when the tattoos disappeared."

"Yeah, *that* was the part of this week that really shook me to my core," Henry mutters. "Disappearing ink. You're so right."

"And now we're not sure what to expect for tomorrow."

"It's *wide* open," Mack says, and Weston's eyes wander over to her like he'd forgotten she was there.

"I don't want to vanish," Weston says quietly.

"Oh," Henry says, shuffling in closer to Mack. "Oh, no, I actually feel kinda bad for him now."

"Hmm," Mack says, but she sounds decidedly unmoved.

I wrangle my arm from his death grip and put it around his shoulders instead. Mack's lip curls as I do it, but she doesn't say anything, so I pretend I don't notice.

"You won't vanish," I say to Weston. "I brought you here because I wanted you here, right? So, if I still want you here, you'll totally still be here tomorrow. And I do."

Weston takes a deep breath and steels himself, leaning into me as he does. "Okay. I trust you."

"Good."

Mack folds her arms and starts tapping her foot. I ignore her even harder than before.

Weston draws a shaky breath and looks up at me. "But, um . . . can you show me some of it? This show, these . . . fics. Please?"

I light up, and lead him directly to my room. With audible sighs, Mack and Henry follow at our heels.

Chapter Fifteen

PAST

"I'm sure it wasn't as bad as you think," Henry says, taking a corn chip from the plate of nachos Dad fixed us for dinner.

"It was bad," I say. I crunch down on a chip of my own for emphasis. "I think it's been boiling over for a while."

"Yeah, but that can happen to anyone," Henry says. "Cool off, take a sec, go back and apologize."

"And demand an apology," Mom says from the kitchen. Eavesdropping again, apparently.

"Yikes," Henry says. "Was it that bad?"

I shrug and focus on the nachos. Mom pokes her head out of the kitchen.

"Yes, it was," she says. "Mackenzie said some very uncalled-for things about the two of you."

"Me?" Henry yelps. "What did she say about me?"

"She called you a geek, Henry," Mom says, all outrage.

"Mom!" I cry. "She did not. No one even uses the word 'geek' anymore, it isn't the seventies."

"Well, what word did she use?" Mom asks, frowning.

"It doesn't matter." I try widening my eyes at her to silently plead for her to drop it and leave. She does neither.

"Loser," Mom says, snapping her fingers. "She called you both losers. And, I'm sorry, but whatever the disagreement is, that's just crossing a line."

"She called me a loser?" Henry asks, aghast.

"MOM!" I screech. "I wasn't going to tell Henry that."

"Well, he deserves to know," Mom says. "I know you want to defend Mackenzie, but you can't go through life covering for everyone all the time."

"Mom, please," I beg. "Let us have a private conversation."

She sighs like I'm making the most extraordinary request she's ever heard. "I'm sorry, but I can hear everything, and I'm mad. No one calls my baby girl names, not even Mackenzie."

"What did I ever do to Mack?" Henry asks, wounded. The plate of nachos is momentarily forgotten, so I *know* he's upset.

"Nothing," I say. "She's just jealous of you."

"Of me?"

"She thinks I replaced her with you." I try to say it casually, but my voice cracks, betraying me. I want to be fine, but I'm just not. There was something different about our fight today. It felt huge, and final, and unforgivable.

I grit my teeth and force the tears to stay inside my head. So what if it was? We're better off apart anyway. That much should be obvious by now.

Henry takes one look at my expression, then stabs at the melted, soggy part of the nachos with a fork. A corn chip tears in half under the assault.

"Screw her," he says. "Your mom's not wrong. She's dead to us, as far as I'm concerned."

Yeah. Screw Mack. If she feels that way about Henry and me,

I'm glad it's come out, finally. She can go hang with the volley-ball girls, and I'll spend time with someone who actually likes hanging out with me.

The thought is vicious. Maybe that's why it feels so good.

PRESENT

Weston sits on my bed looking equal parts forlorn and bewildered, surrounded by *H-MAD* merchandise. He's gripping my Weston Razorbrook pencil case in two hands on his lap, and he has a blanket with a blown-up image of his own face draped around his shoulders for warmth. On my desk we've set up my laptop, and Henry is currently in the process of queuing up compilation videos of the most riveting *H-MAD* scenes he can find.

We've already shown Weston the scene of his near drowning from last week, along with the scene of them getting their elemental powers, the scene where they're first betrayed to the shadow demons, and Weston and Vanessa's first kiss. That one was at Mack's very insistent request, and she seemed quite disappointed when Weston simply watched it with glazed-over eyes. I'm not sure what she was expecting exactly.

"I kind of remember all of this," Weston says. "But it's a blur. Like something that happened a lifetime ago. It's like . . . nothing was all that important until I met Ivy."

"Mm," Henry says. "That sounds like a really healthy way to think about a teenage crush."

"Do you count as a teenager if you're four days old?" Mack muses aloud.

Weston's brow furrows deeper still.

Just as Henry clicks on a clip of Weston discovering his first air powerup, I hear the sound of a key turning in the lock. I freeze, not even daring to breathe. That couldn't be what I think it is, right? It's not possible. We have time still.

We *had* time.

Mack, Henry, and I look at each other in a panic as my parents call out "hello" from across the house. They weren't supposed to be home for another forty-five minutes at least.

We're screwed.

"Hi!" I call out automatically. "I'm coming! One sec!" Then I turn to Weston urgently and hiss at him. "They can't know you're here."

"Got it," he says. "Should I take care of it?"

By wiping their free will? Not unless it's an absolute last resort. "*No*," I say firmly before turning to Mack, panic tingeing my voice. "What do we do?"

Mack hesitates, then straightens. "Henry, stay in here with Weston. Ivy and I will distract her parents and find a way to get them in the backyard. I'll text you when we're there, and you run him down the street."

Thank god for Mack.

We close the door behind us, pause for a breath, then head into the living room where I throw myself into my parents' arms.

"I missed you two," I cry, and it's mostly true. At least, outside of the fact that my life was a little too chaotic to miss them quite as much as I assumed I would.

"Oh, you too," Mom says, pulling away first to fix her rumpled coat. She has her hair scraped up into a claw clip and bags under her eyes. She seems beat from the flight, which is promising. A tired mom is a mom who's less likely to notice my friends breaking out of my room a few feet away. "Our flight was pushed earlier, so we thought we'd surprise you!"

"And see if we could catch you in the act of throwing a house party," Dad says, sticking the tip of his tongue out at me like he's twelve.

"But instead we find you here with Mack!" Mom exclaims, splaying her fingers at Mack, like she's a game-show host showing off the grand prize. "It's so lovely to see you. You've been missed in this household."

"And not just by us," Dad adds, gesturing between himself and Mom, as though that wasn't clear enough.

Mack shoots me a sly grin and my face heats up. I look away instantly in an effort to hide it, but it's too late. My dark secret has been exposed. I *haven't* been totally, completely chill with having Mack as my enemy. I haven't even been fine with her being my ex–best friend, if I'm brutally honest with myself. And now she knows that for a fact, if she hadn't already figured it out.

Why is there nothing more embarrassing than for someone to find out you like having them in your life before you're good and ready to tell them so yourself?

"Do you need a hand bringing your stuff in?" Mack asks, perfect-child mode activated.

"No, we've only got a few things," Dad says, waving a hand.

"Oh, great," Mack says brightly. She catches my gaze and widens her eyes just the smallest bit. It's enough for me to notice it, though. I assume this means she has a plan to distract them while Weston and Henry escape, which is awesome news, because I've got nothing. "Actually, we had a question. We found something super weird in the garden, and we were a bit freaked out about it, but you were flying at the time, so we figured we'd just leave it and hope it didn't do too much damage in the meantime."

"Damage?" Mom and Dad repeat as one, before turning directly to the kitchen.

Mack's a genius.

At that moment, though, a crash rings out from my bedroom, and Mom and Dad suddenly have a more pressing danger to worry about.

My parents fling around to look at me. "What was that?" Mom demands.

"I left my backpack on the bed," Mack says, before I've even come up with an answer. "It probably toppled off."

The thing is, it's a great excuse. But Mack spoke just a little too quickly and smoothly. I can see the suspicion in Mom's eyes immediately.

"It didn't sound like a backpack," Dad says. They're already heading in the direction of my bedroom. Christ, I hope Henry and Weston have the good sense to hide in the closet. If we're lucky, my parents won't think to check. If we're unlucky, I hope Mack has more luck with her third attempt at improv.

"It did to me," I say. Like that's going to do anything but make them more suspicious.

"I'm sure it was," Mom says, in a voice that tells me she's sure of nothing of the sort. "Let's just double-check, though."

"Mom, if I was throwing a house party, don't you think it'd be a bit hard to cram everyone into my room?" I say, following it up with a laugh that's way too loud for the hilarity of the joke.

Mack shoots me an alarmed look, and I cut my laugh in half.

We reach my bedroom, and I have to fight the sudden urge to reach out and grab Mack's hand. Mom flings open the door and . . .

Nothing. They've hidden. I hold my breath as we enter, and that's when I notice the closet door is wide open.

But they're not inside.

They're not in here at all.

I don't have time to dwell on the "how," because I'm too busy being thanking the universe for the "what."

"Huh, her backpack *didn't* fall," I say, like it's mostly uninteresting to me. "Weird. House noises maybe?"

Mom shoots me a sideways glance. "Maybe."

"Anyway," Mack says, darting forward to grab her backpack. "I'd better get home. But it was nice to see you both again."

"*Great* to see you, too."

"Come back around anytime."

As soon as Mack leaves the house, they turn to look at me as one with suggestive, curious looks. I sense an inquisition fast approaching.

"We've worked some things out," I pre-empt.

Mom claps her hands. "That's wonderful, honey. I'm so proud of you. Tell us *everything*. Hold on, let me make a coffee, then we can go over it. Hold that thought."

My phone buzzes, and I check it surreptitiously to find a message from Mack.

> They escaped out the window.
> Everything's under control.

The tension leaves my body in a rush, and I basically ragdoll where I stand, my head tipping backward.

"So," Dad says while Mom rushes to the kitchen. "How did everything go this week?"

Well, isn't that the million-dollar question?

"Fine," I squeak.

"Get all your homework done?"

"Yup." Are Mack and Henry okay with Weston? I really should check on them.

"Did that teacher give you any trouble?"

"Uh, nope, no problems."

"Did you finish the bananas?" Mom calls from the kitchen.

I cringe. "I . . . not all of them."

They're actually sort of black now.

Dad gives me a disappointed look. For a wild moment, I consider telling them what I really got up to this week, if only to demonstrate to them how good they had it when uneaten fruit was the height of their daughter's bad behavior. But I have more important things to worry about. Namely, checking in on Mack and Henry, and making sure they're okay with Weston. I didn't mean to dump him on them with no warning like this. What if they've lost him? Or he's fighting to come back to me? Or Mack's parents spot them?

"Hey, can I go over to the Gleasons' real quick?" I ask. "I forgot to ask Mack something."

"No, Ivy, it's almost dinner time," Mom says. "You'll be bothering them. Just text her."

She says it in her usual "end of story" tone, so I don't even bother pushing back. I *can* just text Mack and Henry, I guess. If worse comes to worst and there *is* an emergency, they'll let me know.

Good thing my parents will be in bed in a few hours. And now I know how easy it is to escape out of my bedroom window, I might just have to try that out myself. After all, how else am I going to smuggle a guy into my room? The front door?

It turns out that sneaking through the window is harder than Weston and Henry made it seem. Although, maybe that's only because I wasn't there to witness it. In fact, now that I think about it, it might explain the crash we heard earlier, because it takes just about every last ounce of my balance and dexterity to twist my body in a way that gets me through the gap, and I almost fall twice. But, somehow, I do make it through, and across the road Mack and Weston are already waiting for me in the dark. We all move toward each other and meet in the middle of the road.

"Weston, can you give us a second?" I ask.

"Of course." He wanders down the street until he's nothing but a pair of bobbing, glowing blue orbs in the darkness.

"What's up?" Mack whispers.

"I just wanted to ask . . . this afternoon, you were weird about Weston potentially staying forever. Like, more than usual."

Mack waits. "That's not a question," she says finally.

"Pretend it was, then."

"Uh, okay. I am fine, but I don't really want him around, for reasons I think I've made clear. Does that answer your not-a-question?"

Not really. I shift my weight, and lower my voice. "I don't . . . *like* him or anything, you know."

"Didn't say you did," Mack says, but the corners of her mouth quirk upward.

"I know. But I don't."

"Okay. Well, why *do* you want him around so badly, then?"

"I . . ." I falter, trying to figure out an answer that feels true, but is also satisfying. Because the only *true* answer is *I like having someone who won't ever leave me,* and I'd rather eat a whole bowl of rocks than admit that to Mack. Mostly because she would hear the implication hovering right beneath that. "I think he's nice. And he likes me a lot, obviously, so do you blame me for liking his company? And I'm sort of attached to him. I hoped maybe you and Henry would be by now, too."

Mack's face is not the face of someone who's attached to the guy who might be disappearing in the morning.

"You sure it's got nothing to do with the fact that he's your perfect person?"

It's the last thing I expected her to say. "What do you mean?"

"Well, he's *your* fanfiction character, right? You wrote him to be your idea of the ideal love interest. I'm not judging you," she says when she sees my expression. "I'd probably want my dream person to stay, too, if they were standing in front of me saying how much they adore me and all that shit."

I shake my head. "He's not my dream person," I say, and Mack sticks her bottom lip out. She looks surprised to hear it.

"I prefer someone who challenges me," I add, and if she looked surprised before, it's nothing compared to how she looks right now.

"Right," she says. "Do you, um . . . mean someone in particular? Or is that just a general sort of . . ."

I panic. My mouth answers before my brain can even weigh up the pros and cons of telling the truth, and, as usual, that results in a lie. "Just in a general sort of way."

"Of course," she says. "I was just curious. Nosy, I guess."

I wonder if it's what she was expecting to hear. If it's possible there was something she wanted to hear. But surely not, right? If Mack wanted me to like her, there would've been signs. I know her to her core. I know when she's lying, and I know when she's secretly afraid, and I know when she's bored but pretending not to be. I would know if she'd started looking at me differently. It would be silly to hope otherwise.

"Anyway," I say, drawing a deep breath to slow my suddenly thudding heart down. "Thanks for looking after him."

Mack's eyes flicker from mine, to my chin, and back up again. "No problem. Good night."

"Night."

I gesture at Weston and he silently makes his way over to me. I don't look back, but I have the strangest sense that Mack watches us leave, all the way until we reach my window. By that point, however, she's gone.

I wonder what happens tomorrow if I *do* wake up to find Weston has vanished. Will Mack vanish along with him?

He *is* the only reason she's back in my life, after all. Without him, will I be enough?

I want the answer to be yes—I want to believe these past few days have reminded Mack how much we *do* like each other, just as they've reminded me—but deep down, I'm not sure if I *am* enough as I am.

What do I mean to her? If anything?

Back in my room, I change into my pajamas and climb into bed. Weston hovers by the wall, watching me with a heavy silence. I want to fill the quiet with something, but I really don't know what to say. Does he want comfort? Is he able to grasp the concept of mortality? Is he even technically mortal?

Is he afraid?

"Aren't you tired?" I whisper when he continues to stand.

He looks at me with a sad sort of smile. "Not really."

"Oh. Do you wanna talk?"

"You have school in the morning. You should get to sleep."

I hesitate. It's true, but on the other hand, this might be our goodbye. Shouldn't I take every second with him I can?

"Actually," he says, suddenly brightening. "Do you think . . . would you mind if I read your fanfics?"

It's the last thing I was expecting him to ask. I blink, and he goes on.

"It's just . . . I'm nervous about this whole 'disappearing' thing. And if I only get a little longer here, I'd like to see what you wrote about us. The kind of person you think I am."

Well, when he puts it like that. I tiptoe to my desk, grab my laptop, and open my fanfic website, where I'm still logged in. I bring up my author page and give him a quick tutorial on how to navigate to each story and read them. He clicks eagerly on the coffee shop AU fic, and settles into the blankets with a look of satisfaction.

"Hey," he says, right before I leave. "Thank you. For imagining me to life. I had a good one, thanks to you."

I study his face, committing it to memory. If it's the last I see of him, I'm glad it was a moment like this.

Although I hope it's not the last I see of him.

Chapter Sixteen

PAST

"Okay, we need to talk about Mack," Mom says. "Let's make a plan."

I respond by curling up into a tighter ball on my bed, but the body language means nothing to Mom. "I don't feel like it," I say, but even that doesn't get me anywhere.

"I know, but we don't always feel like doing the things we need to do," she says. "Now, let's figure out a way to talk to Mack. I think it's important for you to apologize for some things, Ivy, but there's also some things Mack could've done differently. If we communicate that clearly . . ."

I zone out as Mom goes on. The thing is, she means well. She always means well. But "do you want to talk about it" isn't part of her vocabulary. She thinks that if I'm left to my own devices, I'll mess everything up. And she doesn't want me to lose something so important to me.

But the thing is, I'm not ready to apologize to Mack. And I'm really not ready for an action plan. All I want to do is cry on someone's shoulder, and tell my side of the story—a heavily edited version that makes me sound totally innocent—and be comforted. I want to sit there and participate sparingly, while someone who cares about me makes it all go away.

I want that person to be Mack. I want her to knock on my window, and climb inside, and apologize for everything. I want her to say she loves me. Romantically, platonically, I don't care. I just wish I hadn't lost her love.

But that's not going to happen.

"Mom," I say again, and she stops, giving me a wounded look. Telling her I don't want to talk about this is only going to make her dig her heels in. Time for a new tactic. "I'm getting a migraine," I say. "I think I might need to go to bed."

She kicks into action immediately. Suddenly, she has a problem she can easily fix. A few minutes later, I'm lying in the dark with a cold, wet towel, a packet of painkillers, a sick bucket (*just in case*), and a thermometer (*If you feel hot or cold, use it. I'll come and check it for you in half an hour*).

At last, I'm left alone.

Whatever works, right?

Once my door's closed, I pull out my phone and scroll in silence. I stalk Mack's profiles. There haven't been any updates or new photos, so I look at the old stuff and bask in the sadness and hurt of it all.

If I concentrate really hard, maybe I can convince myself it was Mack who heard I was sick. Mack who rushed over to make sure I was okay. And she'd apologize for everything while she took care of me, feeding me soup and giving me everything I needed. Then, when I was finally better, she'd admit her deepest feelings and tell me how scared she was of losing me.

Hey. It's actually not that bad an idea for a story.

Not that it's anything new. It's been done a million times, by a million authors, in a million ways.

But as I'm picturing it, the words appear in my head. They're practically begging me to write them down. It feels, somehow, like if I do, they'll offer me some form of release. One that no amount of conversations with my parents, or Henry, could ever give me.

I've read fanfic before. Last year, it tided me over between seasons of *H-MAD*. Some of them are fantastic. Like, could-be-published level. But plenty of them are filled with spelling mistakes, or left unfinished, or way too short. In other words, it's open to anyone who's willing to give it a shot.

I could do that, couldn't I?

I pull up the Notes app on my phone and stare at it for a long time. You never have to show anyone, I remind myself. It's just for you.

So, I start typing.

When Weston heard Iris was sick, he felt like he'd stepped off a cliff without a parachute.

PRESENT

I wake up the next morning with a sinking feeling, and, drawing a deep breath, I tiptoe across to the closet and push open the door. We left it open a crack last night, enough for Weston to get some fresh air, but not so much that my parents would notice him if they came to check on me for any reason.

His makeshift bed is still there. Weston, however, is not.

My stomach sinks, and I rest my back against the closet doorframe while I take the fact in. I was braced for this, I think, but it's still a punch to the gut. He's really gone, huh?

Even after knowing him such a short time, I feel the loss of him. I think, if I'm honest, I didn't expect him to vanish. Maybe a part of me thought—or, rather, hoped—that he would never leave me. I mean, you bring someone to life from the ether, it's reasonable enough to think they might stick around, isn't it? Like, if they don't, can you really expect anyone to?

Speaking of the ether, is that where Weston is now? Or is

he somewhere else, in a parallel universe, maybe? Is he happy? Does he remember me?

I hope so.

I text Mack and Henry the news right away, but neither reply. It's still early, I guess. With a sigh, I rub the sleep from my eyes and head to the kitchen to make myself some cereal. I can already hear Mom and Dad speaking down the hall. Life's really back to normal, then. The last few days suddenly feel like a bizarre dream.

That is, until I enter the kitchen and find Mom and Dad sitting at the table, eating toast with Weston.

As I freeze in the doorway, the three of them turn to greet me, like nothing at all is odd or unusual about this.

"Morning, Ivy," Mom says, somewhat distracted. Dad takes a bite of toast and doesn't even look up from his phone. Weston, placed between them, is beaming. And glowing, for that matter. He hasn't even put on his disguise—not that I think it would've made much of a difference here, but still.

I'm thrilled to see him.

I'm bewildered to see him.

I stare at the scene before me, uncomprehending. "Uh . . ."

Weston seems to read my mind, because he gives me a toothy grin and leans his elbows on the table. "I met your parents this morning. They're as great as you told me, Ivy."

Mom raises her eyebrows, apparently mildly interested in the compliment, but doesn't speak. Oh, sure. This is perfectly normal. It's definitely no big deal that they've just caught me sneaking a glowing blue guy into the house while they slept. Just another Friday morning in the Winslow house.

The only explanation here is that it wasn't the last few days that were a dream: I'm dreaming *now*. Though it doesn't feel much like a dream.

"I . . . what?"

"Oh," Weston says. "I know you said not to come down, but I knew they'd be fine with everything. And they are! See? There was never anything to worry about."

A part of me is pretty sure I know exactly what he means, but a bigger part of me doesn't want to go there. It is too early for me to process the fact that my fake soul mate has not only stayed in this realm of existence, but he appears to have taken it upon himself to mind-wipe my parents. Just like I quite specifically chose *not* to ask him to do.

I haven't even had my *cereal* yet.

"You know," Dad says, the first indication he's noticed anyone else is even in the room with him, "I'm not sure why that was in question. Who cares if you have a boyfriend? It's not hurting anyone."

Mom gives an absentminded nod of agreement. She has that same glazed-over look as the barista in Roast Me. She's here, but she's not. Is there a part of her in there who's watching everything, railing to get out so she can ground me until I'm fifty? Am I going to find out the hard way when I get Weston to remove whatever weird spell he's placed on them?

It's that potential, hidden version of her that I address now. "I'm . . . really sorry. I shouldn't have . . . it's only, I . . ."

"They said they're happy for me to stay as long as I want," Weston says, to my disbelief. "Forever, even. Isn't that great? It solves all our problems."

Now, this is too far. "Forever?" I repeat to him.

"Mmm," says Mom.

Dad says nothing.

And what, exactly, is that meant to entail? Zombified smiles from Mom and Dad for eternity? Weston can't be serious. And how did he even manage to pull this off? I thought he could only change reality to allow for my fanfics to play out? Which fanfic is this? Did I write one I've forgotten about? Entitled "Child Bride," perhaps?

"You don't even know who he is, do you?" I ask Mom. She gives me an annoyed look, like she can't understand why we're still talking about this.

"He's Weston. Your boyfriend."

I fight to keep my voice steady. Maybe if I try, I can wake her up. If she's in there somewhere, it shouldn't be that hard to get her attention. "Uh-huh. And what else? Do you know his last name? Where he's from? Why he's here? He could be here to kill me, for all you know."

Dad puts his phone on the table with a pointed thump, and looks at Weston.

"Are you here to kill Ivy?" he asks.

Weston shakes his head pleasantly, and Dad gestures to him like I have my answer. And that's it. No questions, no pressing for more details. No freaking out that he's been staying here, or that he spent the night in my room. No planning the next steps, or asking to speak to his parents.

If my parents *are* in there somewhere, they're locked in tight.

I turn to Weston, and my stomach clenches with a sick sort of fear.

"What did you do?" I ask him.

Weston places a hand on my shoulder and squeezes it. It's an almost paternal gesture. I guess it's meant to be comforting. It's anything but.

"You'd better get ready for school, Ivy," he says. "I'm driving."

Usually, my parents drop me off at school on their way to work. And even if they don't have work for any reason—like today, which they both booked off to recover from the trip—they don't let me take the car. They'd just make the trip themselves. But, of course, neither of them argues with Weston.

In all fairness, now that he's effectively given them both lobotomies, it probably isn't the best idea to get in a car with them at the wheel anyway.

Great. He's my chauffeur this morning, then.

Maybe, if he gets me to school in one piece, I'll ask him to chauffeur Mom and Dad if they need to leave the house at all today. At least until he snaps them out of whatever state he's put them in.

I message Mack and Henry multiple times on the drive to school, but neither of them answer me. Of course. I'm in a full-on crisis here, and they both choose today to have better things to do than help me with my problems. What kind of friendship is this anyway?

When Weston pulls into the school parking lot, I grab my backpack, ready to quickly duck out. But then he unbuckles his seat belt.

"You're coming in?" I ask blankly.

"Of course," he says. "I'll just need to go enroll, then I'll see you in class."

Wait. "Enroll . . ." I repeat, but I know. Of course I already know.

"Yeah," Weston says. "Now I don't need a job, where else would I go?"

I want to say he can't go to school here—not least of all because he looks exactly like Chase Mancini—let alone the fact that he glows—but I know the answer to that before I even say it out loud. He'll simply make it so it's not a problem, won't he? Just like he did with my parents.

Now he has something to do with his days, and he doesn't have to hide. We won't need to stash him in a closet or basement at night, or figure out a plan for him moving forward. It's all fixed.

But at what price?

"Weston," I say when he climbs out of the driver's seat. "You did something to my parents, right?"

He nods calmly and locks the car. "Now they aren't mad at you for hiding me. You're welcome."

I take a deep breath. "Right, but you changed everything about them. It's not just that they don't mind you being here. It's like they don't care about anything. They looked half asleep."

"Oh. That was for you." Weston smiles. "I know you found them much too involved in your life before, so I got you some space."

I process this, biting my lip, and his face falls somewhat.

"Don't you like it?" he asks.

"Weston, I . . . appreciate it, but they didn't feel like my parents. Can you change them back, please?"

He gives me a long, searching look. Then, finally, he starts walking toward the school. "Anything you want, Ivy," he says. "I'm doing it for you. It's your world."

I breathe a sigh of relief as I follow him. That was way easier than I'd feared. I guess it makes sense that Weston's having some growing pains figuring out how to fit into the world. Or, rather, how to make the world fit around him. Surely he can find a happy medium, though. One where my parents are their normal selves 99 percent of the day, except for the part where they don't have a problem with Weston crashing here until he finds a job? Which is another thing we have to discuss. Even real kids usually leave the nest to support themselves eventually, so Weston's belief that he's going to simply stay at my house for the rest of his life is going to need a reality check. Fast.

No one even looks twice at us as we walk through the front

doors of the school. Somehow, Weston might as well be any other new student. Just as unremarkable as I am. I feel more and more unsettled. How has he brainwashed everyone around us into thinking this is normal? What are they seeing? Does he not look like Chase Mancini to them? Or has he erased the knowledge of Chase Mancini from their minds altogether? And how far does this spread? Will he still go unnoticed if we leave school? What if we leave town?

Apparently oblivious to my growing alarm, Weston squeezes my hand and tells me he'll be back, before making his way to the admin office to get enrolled.

Enrolled. In my school. As a junior, with me, I guess.

My mind racing, I turn on my heel in the hallway and crash right into Mack.

"Oh, hey," she says, catching and steadying me with a giggle. "Good morning."

"*Mack*," I say, going limp in her arms. "Thank god. You didn't reply to my texts! This morning has been insane. Weston went out and told Mom and Dad everything, and they were all, 'Oh, no problem, we're so happy to have you here, how about you *sleep in the guest room moving forward*,' and he's gone to the office to enroll, apparently, because that's a normal thing to do, and now I'm wondering if it's maybe a trick, I don't know, what do you think?"

Mack, who was listening calmly the whole time, now gives me a serene smile.

"That's such great news. I'm so glad for you, Ivy."

"What?" I ask. "It's not great. It's confusing at best, and at worst, something bad might be happening. Don't you think it's weird?"

"Oh." She considers this. "If you do, I guess."

"Well . . . I'm not sure," I say.

"I'm not sure, either."

"I was hoping to get your opinion."

"I think you're right."

"That something bad could be happening?" I ask.

"If that's what you think."

Did we just go in a full circle? I pull back and study her face closely.

"Are you okay?"

"Of course I am," she says with a small laugh, and she sounds genuine.

We're standing somewhat in the middle of the hallway, but the students are moving around us seamlessly, parting right down the center. I glance at them, puzzled, before turning back to Mack.

"Okay, so, do you think we should go check on Weston?"

"If you want to, then let's go."

"I . . . okay . . ." I say. It's not a "no," but somehow that's a thousand times more frustrating than a "no" would've been. Why is Mack so passive about all of this suddenly? Was it something I said last night? "Okay, then."

Before we've even taken our first step, though, I spot Henry moving through the crowd in a shocking pink sweater. Oh, thank god.

"Henry!" I call, and he comes over to us.

"Good morning," he says, shifting his backpack's weight. "How are you two?"

"Um, been better," I say. "Listen, long story short, Mom and Dad found out about Weston and it was really strange. They said they're gonna enroll him here—"

"Fantastic news," Henry says. "Now we'll get to see him every day."

"And we don't need to worry about hiding him anymore,"

Mack adds, and then she claps her hands. She honest-to-god claps her hands. And that's when I know something is very, very wrong.

"Mack," I say urgently, stopping in my tracks.

She looks at me, and that's when I finally see it. Her usually perfect brown eyes are now totally empty.

"Yes?"

All the blood in my body feels like it's sinking to the ground, pooling in my feet and fingertips. The world starts to blur as I speak. "What happened to you?" I ask, even though I know the answer, because what else do I do?

"Nothing happened to me."

It's strange. Even though I know there's no one there, and there's no point, I can't help but reply. Just in case, somehow, this is different. Because Mack is meant to be different.

"You're acting weird."

"Oh, I am? I'm sorry, I'll stop."

"Okay."

She stands still, like she's waiting for me to say something else. Finally, she smiles.

"Have I stopped enough for you?"

I blow out all the air in my lungs until I'm completely de-flated, and then I curl over into myself, clutching my hands to my stomach.

"What the fuck?" I whisper to myself.

"I'm sorry, I don't understand the question."

"What has he *done*?"

"What do you think he's done?"

Henry bends over and touches me on the upper arm, causing a chill to run up my spine. "Please don't be upset, Ivy. Whatever the problem is, we can fix it together. We'll never abandon you."

"You can count on us," Mack agrees.

At that moment, the bell rings, and I'm out of time to check on Weston. Instead, I get tugged down the hall to class by Mack and Henry. As we walk, I notice something odd, which is far from a first for today. Everyone we pass seems to notice us. No, I realize. They notice *me*. Everywhere I look, students are smiling at me, and nodding at me, and making space for me to walk through like I'm the queen of this school.

Or some sort of celebrity.

I want to ask Henry and Mack what's happening, but somehow I already know what their answers are going to be. Nothing of any value, that's for sure.

We take our seats and Mrs. Rutherford enters.

By her side is Weston.

He lights up and waves as soon as he sees me. All I can do is stare at him.

"Class, we have a new student joining us," Mrs. Rutherford says. "Everyone say hello to Weston Razorbrook."

The class chirps "hello" in a scattered round, and I look around to scan everyone's faces. They're all sitting perfectly still, smiling at the front of the classroom, with the same vacant eyes Mack and Henry have. Nothing about their reactions indicates even one of them finds anything out of the ordinary about this.

The thing is, there's no way in hell other kids here don't watch *H-MAD*. Henry and I might be the most enthusiastic fans I know, but *H-MAD* isn't some indie property with a tiny cult following. It's huge. Chase Mancini has tens of millions of followers. The fact that no one in the whole classroom recognizes Weston's appearance or name isn't just unlikely, it's got to be impossible.

Whatever this is, it isn't just my parents, or even Mack and Henry. He's done it to everyone, hasn't he?

"Hey everyone," Weston says. "I just transferred here so I

could be around my beautiful girlfriend, Ivy, all day every day. You all know Ivy," he says.

As one, the class turns around to look at me, chairs and table legs squeaking against the floor. While I sit, dumbfounded, the class breaks into applause for me. One of the most popular guys in school, Ben, honest-to-god whistles with his fingers. At the back of the room, Lily and Nevaeh, two of the volleyball girls, wave to me like we're the best of friends.

I'm fairly certain I enter a dissociative state.

"Thank you, Weston," Mrs. Rutherford says. "Rian, how about you move to the back of the class so Weston can sit next to Ivy?"

Rian, the nonbinary student who's sat at the desk to my left all year, starts collecting their stuff without even a moment's hesitation. When they've moved, Weston saunters in and takes their seat.

"Weston, what is going on?" I hiss.

He beams at me. "I fixed some things here, too."

"I can *see that. Why,* though?"

"I'll explain after class. But do you like it?"

My high-pitched laugh is much louder than I meant it to be.

"No, Weston, I don't. Put it back. *Now.*"

Weston deflates and looks at the desk briefly, his forehead creased. Then he nods to himself, like he's giving himself a silent pep talk. "It's an adjustment. But when you get used to it, you'll love it."

"No, Weston—"

"All right," Mrs. Rutherford says in a firm voice. "Now, did everyone do the reading I assigned you all? Ivy, this doesn't apply to you, of course. You're perfectly capable of keeping up without homework preparation cutting into your downtime."

I sit motionless as the class pulls out the material from last lesson. So, it's not like everyone has total amnesia or anything, then. Just complete personality transplants. Cool, amazing, rad.

My phone dings in my pocket, and I clap my hand to my thigh. I forgot I put it on loud so I wouldn't miss Henry's or Mack's replies to the Weston situation this morning. Replies I never got, of course. God, how is it possible that was only this morning? It feels like I've lived the most stressful year of my life in the last hour.

"Ivy, you can get that, you know," Mrs. Rutherford says. "I know you can multitask."

Weston turns to me with a proud look. "I added that in specifically," he says.

Added it in to *what*? His freakish spell?

I pull out my phone. It's an email notifying me of a new comment on my fanfic story, "Ivy and Weston's Happily Ever After."

I've definitely never written a fic called "Ivy and Weston's Happily Ever After."

It's one of my most loyal readers, Razorsharpsmile. They're my first commenter on basically everything, and they've even beta-read for me a couple of times. They're a life saver when it comes to spelling and grammar, which isn't my strong suit, to say the least.

> Love love LOVE!!!!! It's a bit different from your usual style but as always so heartwarming and butterfly-inducing. Is it a one-shot or are we getting updates? (I'm greedy!)

With a growing sense of dread and trembling hands, I open my profile. Sure enough, I posted a new story last night. Apparently.

"After Ivy accidentally brings Weston Razorbrook to life, she discovers that the perfect person for her was in her head the whole time," reads the story summary.

Weston.

He had access to my profile last night. He must have written this and uploaded it. I don't even have to read it, because I'm suddenly sure what it says.

Weston has to follow the rules of the fic he's in. So, we were on to something when we tried changing reality with another fic. But it's not me who has that ability. At least, not since the night of the thunderstorm.

It's Weston.

Weston, who was born of magic. Weston, who's had that magic somewhere inside of him since the day I met him.

Without hesitation, I slam the delete button on the fic while Weston watches, before he can try to talk me out of it, or stop me in any other manner. But he doesn't even try. He just sits there calmly, while Mrs. Rutherford drones on at the front of the class.

"That won't work," he says simply as I press the confirm button.

I freeze, and glance at him.

"You didn't upload the story that brought me here," he points out. "It's not about the website. It's about the words, and what they mean."

"And what do they mean?" I ask. My voice is thin and raspy.

Weston locks eyes with me and smiles slowly. "You tell me."

Chapter Seventeen

PAST

"So, it's an open-world RPG set on an abandoned island, but it also has a survival element so you get to grow a little farm and stuff in between missions."

I'm nodding before Henry even finishes his description. "Done," I say as we approach Roast Me. We decided to grab iced chocolates before heading home to download this new game Henry's fixated on me trying. "You had me at open world, but farm stuff. You know I'm a sucker for farm stuff."

"And you know I couldn't give less of a crap about farm stuff if I tried."

"It's okay, I'll stay at the base and tend to the farm while you go on your murder spree. We'll be a perfect team."

Henry gives me the side-eye. "This feels very gender role-y."

I push open the heavy glass door and laugh. "If any kids come to watch for some reason, we can switch roles real quick so we don't set a bad example."

We enter the coffee shop, and stop smiling as one when we see her. Mack's standing at the counter, picking up a drink.

Henry grabs my wrist and yanks me swiftly into the shop behind Mack's back, and we press ourselves against the wall. At first, I think we make it without her seeing me, but then I notice her turning her head to look at us in her peripherals. Just far enough to see us, but not far enough that she doesn't have plausible deniability if she doesn't acknowledge us.

Which she doesn't.

God, seeing her makes every inch of my skin prickle, even after all this time. Maybe Mackenzie Gleason isn't the kind of person you can get over. Maybe she digs in like a splinter and stays there. You can almost forget about her—almost—until you bump into her and the wound is rubbed and suddenly the pain is hot and bright all over again.

I'm hit by the sudden urge to run up to her and ask her to stay. To drag her to the nearest table to drink iced chocolates with Henry and me, and involve her in our conversations. To see if we can interest her in a farming game, or coming to the movies with us, or going on a group hike somewhere. To do something she wants to do, because I want to be around her, not hammer in a life-ruining point I made months ago.

But before I can even try to gather up the bravery to do it, she leaves, and all I can do is stare after her.

"Gee, that was awkward," Henry says.

"She definitely saw us, didn't she?" I ask him.

"Yep."

"Yeah. I thought so." I breathe out through my nose in a huff, and approach the counter. "Whatever. Screw her."

"You would if you could."

"Henry! *Shh!*"

"Sorry, sorry. I told you not to tell me things in confidence. I'm the worst at secrets." He smirks, and then sobers. "So . . . do you still like her?" he asks.

"Like her?" I ask. "She's selfish, and flaky, and so freaking boring. All she wants to do is go outside, run around, talk with bland people about bland, small-talky things. And she called you a loser! She thinks she's better than us, because we're nerds, and she's all sporty and social."

"True. I'm not social at all," Henry deadpans, and I huff, because he is purposely missing the point.

"Not only do I not like her," I declare. "I can't freaking stand her."

And, just like with Alice Kennedy, it becomes true, because I say it enough times to make it so to anyone who cares enough to listen.

I can't stand her, I can't stand her, I can't stand her.

So if she doesn't want me, it can't hurt.

It's safe. I'm safe.

PRESENT

This isn't real.

None of it's real. Or, rather, it is real, but no one has any self-control, aside from Weston and me. They're brainwashed puppets, only allowed to do or say things for my benefit. Are they conscious beneath all of this? Do they know they don't have free will? Or have they drifted off somewhere else while their bodies go on autopilot?

I steal a glance at Henry beside me. He's listening intently to Mrs. Rutherford—so intently he doesn't even notice me looking. Is he in there? Is Mack, sitting in the row ahead of us, so close I could touch her shoulder if I stood up and stretched out, in there?

Either way, I have to help them. And sitting here and playing along isn't going to achieve that.

It feels like only seconds later that the bell rings. Is Weston controlling time as well? I don't know if I can put that past him at this point.

Weston takes me by the arm and steers me out of the class-room with the sea of students, firmly but not forcefully. I wrench my arm back to myself, and he tips his head to one side in al-lowance.

"I want you to see some things I think will soothe your soul," he says, beckoning me down the hallway.

Mack and Henry are walking behind us, side by side. I glance at them desperately, but neither of them react other than to give me matching vacant smiles.

As we pass students, they turn around one after the other in a domino effect to wave and smile at me. Students I know, stu-dents I don't, students I've barely spoken a word to in my life.

Hi, Ivy! Ivy! Ivy!

On a nearby wall, two students I know by face from the grade below us are affixing a life-size poster of my face to the wall, with the words "Ivy for Prom Queen" written across it in glitter print. Where did Weston get that from? When have I ever said I wanted to be Prom Queen? I'm happy enough in the background, and I always have been. I don't want to be adored. I just wanted people to sort of like me.

"I know prom isn't until next year," Weston says, "but I thought we'd get the campaign started early. Oh, and here's something else I put in for you."

He grabs my arm again and swivels me around to a new vending machine that's never stood here before.

"Look. It's stocked just for you. There's a few of them around the school now. Reese's, cookies, Lay's chips, pretzel sticks, Kit Kats . . . I haven't missed any of your favorites, have I?"

I stare, gobsmacked, at the selection. It could've been hand-picked by me.

I suppose, in a roundabout way, it was.

"If I did forget some," Weston goes on, "just let me know.

I'll fix it right away. Oh, you don't have to pay, either. Just scan your fingerprint." He gestures to the scanner next to the coin slot. "Everyone else pays, of course."

Even though he lost me again at the last part, he must see in my face that I'm briefly interested in what he's offering for the first time today, because he brightens considerably.

"Not only that," he says, "but I changed your grade records. Straight As all around. Ivy, you pick a college, and it's yours. The world's your oyster. My job is just to make it the way you want it."

My head's swimming, and everything is moving too quickly. Can he really offer that? A world designed for me? Where I can follow any dream, any whim? Where money stops being an object? "If I can have whatever I want," I say, "start by giving Henry and Mack their own minds back."

Weston places a gentle hand on my shoulder. "Ivy. Just because you *think* you want something doesn't mean it's what you *really* want."

With that, the momentary spell is broken.

Once or twice, Henry and I played a game with all the cheat codes activated, just out of boredom and curiosity. And here's the thing about that. It's fun, at first, while the novelty is still there. But before long, you realize there's nothing left to do. There's a vast emptiness to a game where every challenge is erased, every reward handed over without question. There's a good reason why we've only done it once or twice.

And in the world Weston's proposing, I wouldn't even have a friend to play with. No one to commiserate with when the treasures lose their shine, and no one to go back to the start with.

Just Weston. My perfect guy, here to help me live a perfect life.

Good joke.

I break into a jog, clenching my fists at my sides, as Weston hurries after me.

"What are you doing?" he demands as I storm through the halls.

"I," I say, "am going to delete the original story off my laptop."

Weston sighs. "That won't work, Ivy."

"Yeah, well, no offense," I say, "but that's exactly what you'd say if it would work, so forgive me if I try my luck anyway."

Weston gives me a look that's equal parts amusement and exasperation. It's strange to see. In every incarnation of Weston I've seen, the one thing he's always had is a certain innocence. He was never especially in control, and he was definitely not one step ahead of me. But this version of Weston is an entirely new person. Is it because this is the real him—whatever that means? Or is this the him he wanted to be?

Or, the him he thinks I want him to be?

The options make my head hurt.

"It doesn't work like that, Ivy," he says, picking up speed to reach my side. "It's got nothing to do with where the words are written."

"I don't believe you."

"You can choose not to believe me all you want, but it's true. What do you think made this all happen in the first place? Stories. You willed your fantasy into reality. You wanted me here, badly enough to create me. You can't think pixels on a computer screen have that draw, Ivy. It was never about that."

I ignore him and sprint down the school steps. Mack's and Henry's shoes clack against the steps right behind me, and I turn to look at the two of them. They give me mindless smiles in unison. The effect is mildly terrifying.

"You guys can stay here," I say to them. "I'm good."

"Of course we're coming with you," Mack says.

"We wouldn't make you do something like this alone," Henry adds.

"Right," I mutter.

Weston raises his eyebrows at me, like I should be falling over myself to thank him for this. I scowl and continue on.

"How is this even working, anyway?" I ask him eventually. "We *tried* to write our own new story, and nothing happened. How come you got to?"

Weston gives me a patronizing look, like it's the most obvious answer in the world. It truly isn't.

"You willed me into reality," he says. "You created me with all of your passion and dreams, and hope. All of your desire for *more*. I'm made of your longing. Of course I can employ it to continue bringing your deepest dreams to fruition."

"So, what, I just didn't *want* the other things enough?" I ask flatly.

He simply looks back at me without answering.

"That's bullshit," I mutter. "Of course I wanted millions of dollars."

He just shrugs, even more patronizing than before, and I decide to stop engaging. Less talk, more vanishing.

When we reach my house, I ask Mack and Henry to wait inside Mack's house and, luckily, they do. I'm relieved to be rid of them and their creepy blank smiles, even though I feel a stab of guilt for basically ordering them around, because I'm pretty sure they don't have the ability to say no to me if I'm forceful enough about it.

Weston, however, follows me inside. My parents are standing in the kitchen. I have the eerie feeling that they've been standing there, immobile, all day.

"Hi," I say, barreling past them before they have a chance to react to my coming home early. What are they gonna do, ground me? Not in the perfect world Weston's made for me.

"Ivy, come on," Weston says. "If you just slow down, we can talk about this. We'll figure it out."

Nope. I fly to my room, grab my laptop, take it to the bathroom, and lock myself inside, slamming the door in Weston's face. Then, I pull up the story he wrote about us last night.

Ivy and Weston's Happily Ever After

Ivy and Weston met when Ivy brought him to life. Before she brought him to life, he was nothing but a fanfiction character. After she brought him to life, he became her world.

Having Weston in her life solved all of Ivy's problems. Her overbearing parents stopped trying to dictate every moment of her life, now happy to give Ivy the freedom to experiment and do the things that would make her happiest. Ivy's parents were happy for Weston to stay in their house forever, so he could be near Ivy while she finished school. He also enrolled in her school and got proper identification, so he could get a job and a house and everything.

Not only at home was Ivy's life improved. At school, she became the most popular, beloved girl there, and everyone was always happy to see her. Her teachers loved her and never told her what to do, because she was too special for rules, and Weston knew that. Also, Ivy's best friends, Mack and Henry, were always by her side. Ivy didn't like going places alone, or doing her favorite things alone, and now she never had to again. Ivy had everything she ever wanted.

After Ivy and Weston graduated together, they bought their first house with a generous financial gift given to them by Ivy's parents. There, they lived together for one year, until

Weston proposed, and Ivy happily said yes. They married in a park, with Mack by Ivy's side as her maid of honor, and Henry as the best man. They bought two golden retrievers, and had three children, all boys.

But how did they get to this point? It all started when Ivy wrote a fateful fanfiction, on a fateful night, and made a fateful wish, a wish that came from her soul, a wish she barely understood the true meaning of. . . .

Yeah, I have the gist. I smash the delete button, then clear the autosave folder. Then, for good measure, I clear the trash folder, too, and double-check the story isn't saved as a draft in my fanfiction account. Then, when I'm satisfied, I close the computer and peek outside the bathroom door.

Weston's leaning against the wall with his arms folded, looking bored. When he sees me, he gives me a mischievous grin. "Hi."

"Weston, please," I say. "Can you please undo it? I don't like this."

"Like I said. You're adjusting."

"I'm not *adjusting.*"

"If you didn't want this, it wouldn't be happening."

With a groan of frustration, I push past him and head back to the kitchen. Mom and Dad are both in the living room, Mom on her laptop catching up with some work, Dad, once again, on his phone. Neither of them look up when I enter.

"Mom, Dad," I say, not because I think it will help, but because I don't know what else to *do*. "I don't want Weston to stay here."

Mom glances up. "Why, honey?"

"I just don't. He doesn't live with us."

"Yes, he does."

"I don't want him to."

Mom looks over at Dad for help. When he doesn't assist her, she sighs. "Ivy, you're a smart girl. If you've got a problem, you can figure it out. We support whatever decision you make."

Dad grunts in agreement.

Weston stands by the hallway entrance, waiting for me to realize this is hopeless. If he won't listen to me, and my parents won't get involved, then . . . what?

I turn to him and lock eyes with him. He looks delighted at the challenge.

"I don't want you here," I say, with as much conviction as I can possibly muster.

"You'll come around," he says pleasantly.

"I mean it," I say. "You're not welcome here."

Mom doesn't even look up from her laptop when she chimes in this time. "That's not true, honey. Your father and I are very happy for Weston to be here."

Weston gestures toward them like this is somehow a pass for him. Like he isn't literally deciding what they do and don't say.

"Well, I'm not," I insist, mostly to him now, because he's the only truly sentient person here anyway. As strange as that is to say. "And I'm not going to come around. Even if you were my boyfriend, I wouldn't want you living here. I'm *sixteen*. I'm meant to text you a few times a day, and maybe go out to the movies on Saturday, or hug you between classes."

Weston looks distinctly uninspired by this. "That's not very epic. What happened to that vivid imagination I love?"

"Oh, it's here," I say, turning on my heel. "I can *vividly* imagine you fucking off."

"And yet," Weston calls after me. "Here I still am."

Yeah, sure. For now. Okay, clearly my imagination isn't going to solve things here, vivid or not. But there will be a solution, somewhere. If I can just stop panicking, I'll be able to figure it out, I'm sure of it. Although this would be a hell of a lot easier if it weren't versus a world of Weston's creation.

Where is Mack and her problem-solving mind when I need it most?

Well, Mack is across the street.

As for her problem-solving mind, that's another story.

There has to be a way to bring her back, though. There has to be.

This time, when I run, Weston doesn't follow me. I dart across the road before even thinking to check for cars—are cars allowed to hit me in Weston's version of the universe? Or does Weston only control the people I know?—and knock on Mack's door.

Mack and Henry answer together with their calm, terrifying smiles. A part of me knows just from looking at them that this is hopeless, but I have to talk to Mack anyway.

Leaving Henry where he's standing, I grab Mack's hand and pull her to a corner of her front yard. Trying to ignore the knowledge that Henry is watching us with empty eyes a few feet away, I take both her hands in mine and speak to her in a low, urgent voice.

"Mack. I need you to wake up."

"I am awake."

I squeeze her hands, hard. "No. The real you. The real you is in there, I know you are, and I need you to snap out of it. I can't fix this without you."

She gives me a confused look, but doesn't reply.

"I can't fix it without you," I repeat. "I don't want to live in a world without you. I just got you back."

"I'm right here." She squeezes my hands back, and for a second, it feels real. "I'm not ever leaving you."

"You *did leave me*," I cry, wrenching my hands away. I know I'm not talking to Mack—that, really, no one's listening to me—but I don't care. I need to say this. "You left me last year, and now you're gone again, and you weren't *supposed to*. You're supposed to be here, really here. I want to listen to your volleyball stories and go to your games. I want to go on walks, and I want you to roll your eyes when I talk about *H-MAD*, because it doesn't matter if you don't like everything I like, because I like *you*, and you like me, and everything else just isn't that deep. It's just not. We can grow. But I can't grow alone."

Mack takes a step back. "But I do like everything you like," she says, and I give up. She's not here at all, so why am I even trying? No one's here. It's just me, and Weston, the guy that came from my own mind, and the fake reality he made for me. Which isn't really all that different to being completely alone, if I think about it.

"Ivy."

Weston speaks somewhere close behind me. I didn't even hear him approach. I whirl around and scramble backward, putting enough space between us that I can react if he moves. He gives me a surprised look.

"I did this for you, you know," he says. There's a real tinge of hurt in his tone, too. "I fixed your life *for you*. We aren't enemies."

I bark out a laugh. "*Who said I wanted my life fixed?*"

"You were miserable! You only had one friend, and you were constantly terrified he was going to leave you any minute, just like Mack did, right? And speaking of Mack, she couldn't stand you. She had no interest in being around you until I came along, did she?" He continues advancing toward me, slow and smooth. He has all the time in the world. Who's going to interrupt him, after all? Certainly not Henry or Mack. "Admit it," he says

THE PERFECT GUY DOESN'T EXIST   275

softly. "Didn't it cross your mind last night that if I were to disappear, so would your reason for being around her? The *one* thing you had in common? Or were you too in denial about it?"

I lock my jaw and stay silent. He doesn't look angry or aggressive. But he does look *knowing,* and that's worse somehow. I want to wipe the look off his face.

I don't want to be seen this clearly.

But I suppose it makes sense that, if he came from my mind, he should know parts of it even I don't want to acknowledge.

"The thing is," Weston goes on, "you never need to worry about that again. I'm not going anywhere, so neither is she. She is never going to leave you again, Ivy. I promise. I can give you everything you ever wanted, you know. I will never abandon you. I will watch the shows you want to watch. I'll never let you face a crowd alone. I can give you Henry and Mack, and make sure they *never* leave you. I can give you that level of safety and security for the rest of your life. I can calm your parents down, I can make the teachers stop bullying you, I can make your classmates adore you."

"But it's not *real,*" I cry, and he laughs in my face.

"Since when have you ever cared about reality? Come on, Ivy, you would've been perfectly happy for Mack to pretend she enjoyed being around you, as long as you never had to know it was a lie. Is that what you want? Should I change your memory so you never question any of this? Because I can do that, too."

I shake my head vigorously, my chest tightening, and he tips his head in acknowledgment. Whether that's an agreement to leave my memory alone or not, I'm not sure.

He goes on. "You spend half your life escaping into fantasy worlds. Your entire friendship with Henry is based on TV and gaming. You *like* the fantasy. Now I'm letting you live in it."

"I don't want it," I say. "Please."

"What do you want, then? Anything at all, you name it, and I'll change it. I can edit this however we want. If you want me to move next door, I will. If you want us to be millionaires, you've got it. If you want to move to the Bahamas, we'll have tickets tomorrow." He takes a step toward me, and I take one back. He pauses, looking wounded. "I can and will give you the world, Ivy. But I can't send you back to the hell you were living in."

I lift my chin and keep my voice as steady as I can. "It wasn't hell."

"Then why did you spend so much of your free time escaping into our love stories?"

"It was never our love story!" I snap automatically. "It was me and Mack's."

The words come out of my mouth before I've even thought them. I start, shocked to hear them. Something flashes in Weston's eyes, not anger, but something else.

"You wrote about me," he insists.

"You were a stand-in," I say, realizing the truth as I speak it. "That's what I do. I write stand-ins. I wasn't writing fanfiction about *H-MAD*. I was writing fanfiction about *me*."

Weston's eyes narrow, but he doesn't say a word. I continue on, half to myself.

"You never even had any elemental powers in them, like Mack said," I say. "I wasn't writing fantasy. I was writing the romance I wished I was living. I wanted our fights to be meaningless. I wanted us to love each other so much that we couldn't keep away from each other even if we argued all the time. I wanted to walk up to her in Roast Me and ask her for a drink instead of pretending I didn't see her last semester. I wanted us to be soul mates, because it'd mean we could take anything the world threw at us and make it, because it was just fate. I wanted her to look at me and know that I was hurt, and how to fix it. I wanted her to fix it. I didn't want to have to be the one to take the first step."

Weston studies me, and then shakes his head. "No. You wrote about *me*."

But I didn't. Not really. Weston was only ever a vessel. An idea. Not something I ever truly wanted. Or even grasped.

Almost as though he can read my thoughts, Weston crosses his arms and breaks eye contact. "So, it's always been Mack? Only Mack?"

I turn to look at her. She's standing where I left her, on the front lawn, motionless. Her vibrant eyes are empty, and her usually upturned mouth is still.

All I want is for her to be back inside that shell. I want to run to it, and wrap my arms around her, and stay just like that for as long as she'll let me. I want to share my life with her. All of it. The bits that sometimes make her eyes glaze over, and the parts that make us both happy, and the new things we might be introduced to together, now that we finally understand where we went wrong. I want her as she is. Not as my soul mate. Not as someone who psychically knows my every wound, and how to fix them. And definitely not as my enemy.

I just want her.

"Yes, Weston," I say softly. "It's always been Mack. I'm so sorry."

Weston nods, and turns away from me. It looks like he's considering something carefully. When he turns back, he looks resigned, but calm.

"Then I'll give you Mack."

I hesitate. That seems too easy. "What?"

"I want you to be happy. If being with Mack will make you happy, I can do that. I can make her all of those things. She can be your soul mate, she can comfort you, she can make you coffee, whatever you need." His eyes are suddenly bright.

"No," I say. "I don't want Mack to play a part."

"You don't even have to know it's a part. She'll be as close to her old self as you want her to be. We can write your romance however you want it. Whatever needs to be done, we'll do it. I'm your scribe, Ivy." He holds his hands out, palms up. "What do you say?"

I look back to where Mack stands. What would that world be like? A world where Mack is everything I ever imagined her to be? With the sparkle back in her eyes, and her own personality back, just . . . with the added feature of being wildly in love with me? A world where I don't even know it's not real?

What if I helped Weston create the world I *really* want?

What if? It's an enormous question, with a million answers.

But only one answer matters. No matter what that world looks like—no matter how fine-tuned we could get it—it wouldn't be real.

And that's the thing, isn't it?

I give him a sad smile. "I say no."

Weston, who watched me closely the entire time I pondered his proposal, looks shocked at my decision. "No?"

I guess I can understand his disbelief. After all, only days ago, the thought of shaping my own reality was intoxicating.

"No," I repeat. "It doesn't matter what you do to Mack, it still won't be real, so I don't want it."

"But it's your words," Weston says in frustration. "It's what you wanted so badly, remember? You created this, and now that you have it, you're rejecting it. Help me understand why."

"Because," I say, "I'd rather have Mack like she is. Even if we don't have very many things in common anymore, and even if we argue, and even if she never speaks to me again. I'd rather never see her again than have her in my life every day because I forced her to be there. I want her to be happy, and to have her life the way she wants it. Even if that means it's not with me. And the same goes for Henry, and my parents, and everyone. It's not always *about* me, and I'm okay with that. I need you to be okay with it, too."

Weston shakes his head slowly. "Don't answer hastily."

"There isn't any other answer."

"If you change your mind, it'll be too late."

"I know."

Weston looks around. At Henry, at Mack. At our eerily quiet street. My house, with its empty driveway. Then, finally, back at me.

"But you'll be right back where you started."

I meet his eyes and hold his gaze. "I really don't think I will be."

That's when I notice the strangest thing. Around us, the world seems to be losing its opacity. Houses, trees, cars—even Weston. It's all desaturating.

Weston, blurry at the edges, comes closer to me. When he speaks, even his voice is distant, like he's growing further from me instead. "You don't want me?" he says.

"No."

"You never wanted me."

It's a statement, not a question.

"That's right."

"Arc you sure? If you didn't want me as badly as all that, how did you bring me to life?"

"I don't know," I say truthfully. "But I do know it was never about you. I just wanted to be happy, I think. Only I didn't know how to get there."

"But you do now?"

"I do."

Weston raises a hand, then drops it. Then, he stares, lost in thought. Slowly, his bewildered frown fades into a smile, which becomes a laugh. "Oh," he says, shaking his head in wonderment. "That makes perfect sense, then."

He's more than half gone at this point. When I look down at my arms, I realize I'm fading, too. It's funny. I don't feel like I'm going anywhere.

"It does?"

"Of course." Finally, he smiles back at me. "If you didn't bring me here, how would you have realized how to get there?"

I'm not sure I immediately understand his words, but it's a riddle he leaves with me, because in a moment, he's altogether gone.

And then so am I.

Chapter Eighteen

PRESENT

I wake up slowly, and then I stare at the ceiling, attempting to get my bearings. I'm back in my bed, I know that much, and my phone says it's 6:30, but is that A.M. or P.M.? Is it tonight? Tomorrow morning? And how did I get here?

When my mind's clear enough to think of it, I google the date and time and find out that it's apparently 6:30 in the morning . . . this morning. As in, the morning I just lived.

Blurry-eyed, I stumble out of bed and check the closet. Weston's pile of blankets is still in the closet like it was this morning . . . well, the last time it was this morning. Does that mean he's in the kitchen with my parents again?

I count to five to steady myself, then walk briskly into the kitchen, where I find Mom nursing a cup of coffee at the table. The room smells familiar, like burnt toast and Mom's moisturizer. It feels just like any regular morning before my parents left the state.

There doesn't seem to be anyone else here. But is it a trap?

"Morning, baby," she says to me, brightening as soon as she sees me. "How'd you sleep? Have your cramps let up yet? I can get some more bananas today if you need them."

"That's okay. I'm good," I say carefully. "Where's Dad?"

"Bathroom. Do you need something? I can help."

"No," I say, sliding into the seat across from her. "Just wondering."

The smile she gives me is tired, but warm and genuine. No dead eyes. No strange energy.

Does that mean no Weston, then?

I send a text to both Mack and Henry, to be sure.

> Weston's not here. Is he with you?

Both respond "no" within the minute. I can't believe it. He's gone.

He's gone.

Still, just to be doubly certain . . .

"Hey, Mom? Can I go to the mall with Mack for a few hours after school?"

All traces of tiredness are suddenly gone from her face. "What exactly happened while I was away? Have the two of you figured things out?"

"I—"

"Because, Ivy, I really think you need to. You haven't been yourself since the two of you fell out. Of course, Henry is wonderful, my god, this has nothing to do with that beautiful soul. But you and Mack, you have history."

"Right."

"Of course you can go," she concludes. "What are you going to do, though? Have you thought about what you might say? If you want to run through an apology now, I can go grab my laptop and we can get brainstorming, because I find if you script these things ahead of time—"

Okay, so she is one thousand percent back to normal. Which is fine, and good, and exactly what I wanted to hear.

Except it also kind of isn't. And maybe I don't have to accept that.

"I don't know. I think I'll just . . . see how it goes when I'm with her."

She's halfway out of her seat at this point, and I can *see* her deflate.

"Oh. I'm not sure that's such a good idea, Ivy. You know how you can get emotional, and if you just prepare beforehand—"

"Thanks," I cut her off quickly. "Thank you. Really. I'll think about things today."

Mom studies my face, and something akin to understanding crosses her features. "No notes?" she asks, but it's not in a hurt or frustrated way at all.

"No, thank you." I grin.

"All right. Well, good luck. You can tell me all about it when you get home."

I give her a gentle smile. "Sure. I'll let you know how it goes."

The gist of it, anyway. But I think I'll keep it briefer than I usually would. I might not want them to be completely uninterested in my life, but that doesn't mean I have to give them a play-by-play of every second of it, either. There's got to be a balance between being independent and being alone. And I think I'm starting to grasp where that line lies.

Mom squeezes my hand across the table. "You've got this, honey. Good luck. I know how badly you wanted this."

I'm not sure if she knows exactly how badly I wanted this. I'm not even sure if I knew until this week.

But now that I do, I'm going to do everything in my power to fix us.

Mack sits across from me in the food court sipping her juice, her large eyes growing wider and wider as I recount my last day with Weston. Well, an abridged recount. I leave out the parts involving my intense, undying feelings for her. Which does make the story a little difficult for her to follow, I think, but she does her best to keep up.

"So, you just told him you didn't mean to bring him here and, poof, he vanished?" she asks.

"Sort of."

"Wow," she says. "If we realized it was that easy, Henry and I would've made you do it sooner."

Well, it's kinder than Henry's reaction was when I explained it to him this morning at school. His was more along the lines of *I told you so, but would you listen to me?* No. *And will you listen to me in the future? Don't give me that look, Ivy, you know I'm right. I'm always right.*

Honestly, I think he was still on a caffeine high at that point. Apparently he didn't sleep a wink last night, because every time he drifted off, he hallucinated his bedroom door slamming. He did manage to get a nap in during history class, though, so all's well that ends well.

I grin, and then it fades. "You know, if I'm honest, I think part of the reason I wanted to keep Weston around so badly is because it was bonding us. Like, it gave us something in common. We were hanging out again."

"You and me?"

"Yeah. I don't know, I guess I've been a little worried you wouldn't wanna do that anymore now he's gone. I wasn't even sure if you'd say yes to coming here."

Mack looks thoughtful. "I actually think this week was one of the best ones I've had in a long time," she says finally. "Stressful, but the best. And most of that is down to the fact that I had you back for it."

There's something about the way she says those words. *Had you back*. It doesn't feel like she means it casually. Maybe it's in her tone or the look in her eyes, or maybe it's my brain picking up on some other micro-cue I couldn't put into words if I tried. Regardless, it gives me the push to say what I say next.

"The typo wasn't an accident, you know," I say. "I mean, it was, but it wasn't meaningless."

She doesn't ask what typo, which tells me she's been thinking about it at least a little since finding it. The typo where I wrote "Mack" instead of "Weston." A little Freudian slip that should've told me from the start what my stories were really about.

"I couldn't have accidentally written anyone else's name," I clarify, my cheeks heating as I do so. I'm not technically admitting anything, but at the same time I'm admitting everything. I couldn't feel more exposed if I stood on this table and announced to the food court that I was crazy about the girl sitting across from me.

Mack stares at me, her juice all but forgotten. "I hoped that was the case," she admits. "I just didn't know if I *should* hope."

"You . . . hoped it was?"

"Of course." She smiles sheepishly. "I thought you knew. I thought I was obvious. Especially when we were starting to break up."

"You . . . are you saying back then, you . . ."

"Liked you? Oh yeah. Huge crush."

"And now?"

She answers to the table, not me. "Oh yeah. Huge crush."

Her words hit me like a hurricane. I feel like if I weren't sitting, the force of them would have knocked me backward.

Why didn't she tell me sooner?

Is this real? Did she truly just say that to me?

Do I say it back?

"I wasn't being reasonable last year," I say, changing the topic like a coward while I process and wait for my chest to loosen enough for me to properly breathe. "You don't have to be interested in my hobbies, or do them with me."

"But I shouldn't have made you feel like you couldn't ever talk about them, either," Mack says quickly.

"You shouldn't have to be bored every time you hang out with me," I protest.

"It's not boring to hear you talk about *H-MAD*," Mack says. "I promise. I want to hear your opinions, and your little rants. But I shouldn't have been a hypocrite about Henry. You found someone you could share *H-MAD* stuff with, and instead of letting Henry step in and do the stuff I didn't really want to do with you, I got all possessive. You didn't belong to me, and I wasn't fair."

"Well, if I'd tried harder to introduce you two instead of rubbing him in your face, you might not have felt jealous in the first place," I say.

"Maybe we were both being idiots, then."

"Oh, we definitely were," I say, and we both laugh weakly. She stares at me, and I think I know exactly what she wants to hear. After all this time hiding it, and refusing to say the words—even to myself, half the time—it's enormous. So huge, I could drown in it.

But somehow, I say them anyway. "So, um . . . I like you too. Just so you know."

The silence that follows lasts a lifetime. This, I think, is one of those moments. The rare ones where, somehow, you get everything you've ever wanted, and it's so warm, so vivid, the world explodes into a Technicolor version of itself, and none of it feels real. Because real life is never this perfectly wonderful.

Mack's smile is small, and alight, and hopeful. "You do?" she asks.

"Oh yeah," I say. "Huge crush."

I really think that I could've offered her ten million dollars, and a cure for cancer, and world peace—the whole lot—and she couldn't have looked more amazed than she does right now.

It's not until I speak again that I realize how big my own smile is: wide enough to hurt my cheeks. "I would really like to have you in my life again, please. And I'd especially like it in a nonplatonic way, if that's an option. Um . . . is it? An option?"

In response, Mack leans forward, reaches out, and takes my hand.

And suddenly, I wouldn't change a single thing about the last week for the world.

Epilogue

Chase Mancini's signing line is about three miles long. Seriously. Halfway through, I have to send Henry off for refreshments so we can replenish our strength while I guard our spot in line. But, bit by bit, we start to inch closer. I can even make out Chase's facial expressions now. He's jovial, chatting pleasantly with everyone who dumps their pile of merch on the table to get signed. We weren't told until we got here that we were limited to only two signatures each, so people have been bringing literal carts full of merch with them. Disappointment all around.

Above us are promotional posters for *Hot, Magical & and Deadly: The Movie,* which is what the actors are all in NYC to promote. It's still far away enough that we don't have any official images or stills for the movie—just a logo on a black background— but even that's enough to give me chills of excitement.

The movie was announced on Chase's social media the day after Weston left forever. It turns out that Henry had been right at the start—that *was* the secret news Chase was teasing the morning Weston appeared in my house. When the announcement went live, Henry had burst out laughing and suggested maybe that's why Weston left when he did, so he could go and star in the movie. I hadn't found that quite as funny as he did.

My phone vibrates with an email from my beta reader, Razorsharpsmile. After everything, I've decided to go in a different direction for a little while, so I'm trying my hand at original fiction. Just to see how it goes. A sapphic story, actually. But not at all a self-insert. At least, mostly not a self-insert. All writers draw from life, anyway, so if the love interest happens to be a high schooler with a keen interest in track, then that's just because I know how to realistically write a girlfriend who loves sports. It's called writing what you know, right?

"Here we go," Henry crows, and I shove my phone in my pocket halfway through reading the email. We're next in line.

My skin prickles as I look at Chase, and my heart speeds up just a little. It's like looking at Weston again, but it also isn't. Chase has dark brown hair, and brown eyes, and a completely different demeanor from Weston. My Weston, at least. But still, it's close enough that, for just a second, my body goes into fight or flight. In the end, Henry has to give me a little shove to prompt me to walk up to Chase with him.

"Hi," Henry gushes, thrusting a poster and the official series guide at Chase to sign. "Henry Paramar. Huge fan."

"I'm Ivy," I say, suddenly shy. I pass over my pencil case and favorite poster.

"Thank you so much for coming by," Chase says with a glittering smile. "You two going to see the movie when it comes out?"

The Australian accent makes him even less like Weston. My skin gradually stops prickling. "Of course," I say.

"Definitely, at the premiere if we can," Henry says. "Can you give out guest tickets?"

Chase laughs and starts signing.

"No, I'm serious," says Henry. "I can give you my number, you can text me, we can make this happen if you want to."

"Why would he want to, Henry?" I hiss.

"Um, because we're literally his biggest fans? I think you've proven that."

"Yes, Henry, but he doesn't know about that."

"Know about what?" Chase asks, glancing up from his signing with a look of mild alarm.

"Fan site," I say, at the same moment that Henry says, "She's got a shrine in her wardrobe."

Chase gives us a tight smile and ducks his head back down to keep signing as I shoot Henry a venomous glare.

Henry accepts his newly signed merch with a "thank you," and just as Chase turns to me, Henry jumps back in. "We have to know," he says. "In your audition—"

"Ah."

"There have been rumors—"

"I know all about the rumors," Chase says.

"So . . . ?"

Chase beckons us to lean in, and we do as one. He lowers his voice to a whisper. "I've signed an NDA. I can't tell you what happened in the audition, guys."

Henry looks crestfallen.

He's still crestfallen as we reach the nearby coffee shop we've agreed to meet Mack at. "I can't believe we didn't find out from Weston when we had the chance," he groans, flopping into a free seat.

"I made him up, Henry," I remind him. "He wouldn't have known."

"Um, sure, but counterpoint, you said on the last day he had free rein to conjure up anything that would make you happy.

You could've at *least* asked him to produce the tapes so you could watch them before you vanished him for good."

I choke. "Okay, wow, sorry I was a little too distracted by the fact that you and Mack and everyone I know were trapped inside your own minds with no way out to take advantage of the situation."

"Apology not accepted." Henry sniffs.

Through the crowd, I catch sight of Mack approaching, laden with shopping bags. I spring to my feet and rush over to her to relieve her of some of the bags.

"*Hey,*" she says, giving me a quick kiss. I return it, and then go back in for another, deeper one, looping my hands around the back of Mack's neck. The skin there is down-soft, and I scrape the tips of my fingernails across it, causing Mack to make a surprised, happy noise in the back of her throat.

"I missed you," she whispers against my lips.

"It's only been a few hours," I say, and Mack tips her head in acknowledgment.

"Yeah. I still missed you, though."

We head back over to Henry and sit at the table. "How'd you do?" I ask her, gesturing toward her haul.

"*Great.* I got a new pair of sneakers on mega-sale, and some cute new tights, and a couple of hoodies. The shopping here is so much better. We should really make the effort to come here more often."

"Don't they have Lululemon in Philly?" Henry asks.

"It's not the same," Mack says sagely, and I nod to back her up.

"Have your parents messaged much?" Mack asks, and I pull out my phone to check.

"Nope," I say. "Not since I first got here."

They wanted to make sure the bus didn't crash on the drive up. Baby steps.

"Wild," Mack says. "They're finally letting you grow up."

"Something like tha—" I break off as a nearby commotion catches my attention. At the entrance to the coffee shop, a group of girls have started jumping in place, waving and calling out. Mack and Henry look over with me just as Chase Mancini comes into view, flanked by security.

"It's not Weston, it's not Weston," Mack chants under her breath. I know how she feels.

Chase goes to the counter and orders something we can't quite make out. Then, amazingly, he sits at the empty table closest to us. Henry steals glances at him like he wants to try his luck around the audition secrets again. Mack sits with her back rod-straight, fists clenched.

"He's *definitely* Chase," I tell her, taking one of her hands in mine. "Listen to his accent."

She nods, and squeezes my hand with a smile.

A waitress brings Chase's coffee over, and he thanks her, then takes a sip. As soon as her back's turned, he makes a face at one of his security guards.

"God, the coffee's *so* bad in the US," he says to them. "Tastes like bloody sewer water."

I gasp, and Mack chokes. We make eye contact and, together, we burst into giggles, while Henry, who wasn't there that morning, looks between us in pure confusion.

"Okay, coffee, then home?" Mack asks when we catch our breath.

"Yeah," I say. Then, I glance at my phone. The bus doesn't come for another hour. "We could probably fit in a walk first, though. What do you think?"

Mack rests her chin on her hand and grins at me. The exact kind of grin that makes her eyes sparkle the way I love. "Sounds perfect," she says.

Acknowledgments

A book doesn't appear from thin air, and that's never been truer than for this one. To Eileen Rothschild and Lisa Bonvissuto, thank you for the huge amount of work you both put into getting this book here, through multiple huge edits and one entire rewrite. I quite literally could not have done this without you two.

Thank you to my agent, Jess Mileo, and to the team at Wednesday Books for continuing to be such an amazing and supportive group. Special thanks to Rivka Holler, Alexis Neuville, Dana Aprigliano, Meghan Harrington, Sara Goodman, Melanie Sanders, Jen Edwards, Gail Friedman, Katy Robitzski, and Sara Thwaite!

Thank you to Kerri Resnick for an incredible cover design, as always, and to Venessa Kelley for the beautiful artwork! I knew from the first time I saw your illustrations that you would be an incredible fit for the cover, and you blew my expectations out of the water.

To the UK and Commonwealth team at Hachette, with special thanks to my editor, Nazima Abdillahi, and my publicist, Emily Lighezzolo: thank you for continuing to bring my stories abroad, and to my home of Australia.

Huge thanks to Becky Albertalli, who helped me completely overhaul the plot of this book one very emotional night, and Cale Dietrich for always being there to workshop ideas and check in on how my deadline is tracking. To Jacob, thank you so much for helping me with the aroace rep! And to Mackenzi, thank you so very much for your incredible brainstorming skills. To my authenticity readers, thank you for your time and wisdom. To my early readers and those who provided advance praise, thank you so much for your support!

To my day-in, day-out friends, Becky, Claire, Jenn, Cale, Diana, Stella, Jono, Paige, Ryan, Steph, Chelsea, Sarah, Mum, Dad, and Cameron: thank you for my ongoing stability. It was hard won this year.